BOY IN THE SAND

BOY IN THE SAND

CASEY DONOVAN
ALL-AMERICAN SEX STAR

BY

R O G E R   E D M O N S O N

alyson books

LOS ANGELES • NEW YORK

MANUFACTURED IN THE UNITED STATES OF AMERICA.

THIS TRADE PAPERBACK ORIGINAL IS PUBLISHED BY ALYSON PUBLICATIONS INC.,
P.O. BOX 4371, LOS ANGELES, CALIFORNIA 90078-4371.
DISTRIBUTION IN THE UNITED KINGDOM BY TURNAROUND PUBLISHER SERVICES LTD.,
UNIT 3 OLYMPIA TRADING ESTATE, COBURG ROAD, WOOD GREEN, LONDON N22 6TZ ENGLAND.

FIRST EDITION: OCTOBER 1998

02 01 00 99 98   10 9 8 7 6 5 4 3 2 1

ISBN 1-55583-457-4

LIBRARY OF CONGRESS CATALOGING-IN-PUBLICATION DATA
   EDMONSON, ROGER.
    BOY IN THE SAND: CASEY DONOVAN, ALL-AMERICAN SEX STAR / BY ROGER EDMONSON.
    ISBN 1-55583-457-4
     1. DONOVAN, CASEY. 2. MOTION PICTURE ACTORS AND ACTRESSES—UNITED
STATES—BIOGRAPHY. 3. GAY ACTORS—UNITED STATES—BIOGRAPHY.
   4. EROTIC FILMS. I. TITLE.
   PN2287.D524E34 1998
   791.43'028'092—DC21   98-22310 CIP
   [B]

CREDITS
FOREWORD BY JERRY DOUGLAS IS EXCERPTED FROM HIS HOMAGE, "THE LEGEND OF
   CASEY DONOVAN," WHICH APPEARED IN THE APRIL 1992 ISSUE OF *MANSHOTS*.
FRONT COVER PHOTOGRAPH BY ROY BLAKEY.
BACK COVER PHOTOGRAPH COURTESY CAL'S BROTHER.

CONTENTS

FOREWORD

In this day and age, when anyone who has made more than two adult films is a star, and anyone who has been making films for more than a couple of years is a superstar, how does one classify a performer who helped to create a genre, who starred in half a dozen features still widely considered classics today, whose career spanned nearly two decades, and whose presence in gay adult films set standards and created conventions that prevail today? One word might do: legend.

I had the good fortune to work with Casey Donovan on four different projects, two onstage (*Circle in the Water* [1969] and *Tubstrip* [1974]) and two on-screen (*The Back Row* [1972] and *Score* [1972]). In addition he wrote a monthly column, "Letters to Casey," for *Stallion* magazine for five years (1982-1987) while I was its editor. I worked with him creatively on more projects than any other director, and when he died of AIDS-related complications on August 10, 1987, I was asked by several publications to write an obituary or homage, the implicit reasoning being that I no doubt knew him better than most, perhaps better than anyone. And that was not the case. I hardly knew him at all.

One reason for this may have been that he was a chameleon, that he could be all things to all people, that his public self and his private self were diametrically different, though each reverberated with echoes of the other. Although he delighted in being Casey Donovan—"my greatest role," he'd often say—he was also John Calvin Culver, "Cal" to his friends. The facade of both men seemed much the same: a fair-haired, open-faced, well-built, medium-sized American male who wore the phrase "boy next door" as if it had been coined just for him.

That, I am convinced, was the single greatest secret of his success. He looked so damned conventional that the acts he performed on-screen came as a jolting surprise each time a viewer witnessed them. As a result, gay men all over the world took heart. If a boy-next-door–type like Casey could actually be a homosexual—and a happy, uninhibited homosexual at that—then there was hope for gay men everywhere that other boy-next-door–types could be had too. He was, in short, the wet dream come true.

Cal was as sexually driven as any individual I've ever known. He would appear at my *Stallion* office to drop off his column, usually about noon, and with a giggle try to determine how he could go to the baths, service at least one client (and usually more), attend the theater, and hit the Central Park rambles before retiring for the night. He liked to joke that, like Dorian Gray, he would hate to see the portrait in his attic. But his column was always in on time, he was unfailingly responsible, and he always, somehow, looked sensational whenever the camera was about to roll or an audience about to assemble.

Over the years many people have asked me what it was like to work with Casey Donovan, and I have never thought of our creative collaborations as being vastly different from my work with dozens of other talented actors and actresses, both onstage and on-screen. He approached stage and film work in much the same way. He began by creating the character—on film usually, but not always, it was Casey Donovan—and by studying the script, even on porn films. Rehearsals and shoots were always filled with his laughter, easy and laid-back, even in the middle of an intense sex scene. But performing or filming was always a *job* to him—and a job he took very seriously.

On the set of an explicit film, he remained involved in every aspect of the production. The day before we shot the lengthy three-way at the end of *The Back Row*—an all-night session in a now-demolished theater that was even sleazier than it appeared in film—he came to me and inquired if we had remembered to purchase douches for everyone in the scene. When I assured him we had, he personally delivered one to each of his costars, thus ensuring that the scene could proceed without any unnecessary problems.

Cal was rarely given to self-doubt—at least in public—but after that scene was shot, he pulled me aside, as dawn appeared, to express his concern that maybe the scene—indeed, the entire film—was too strong. He was worried that "Casey's fans" might not buy the golden boy as sleaze pig. He was quick to tell me that he had loved doing the scene, had in fact contributed many of the trashiest touches to it, but was concerned about how it would affect audiences who had originally seen Casey Donovan in such a different context. He did, he reminded me, have Casey's reputation to think about.

One last *Back Row* story seems to reveal both Cal's consummate professionalism and his schizophrenic sexual intensity. There is a moment in that final scene when Casey is on his knees on the filthy floor of the men's room, giving head to the hard hat (Chris Villette, who had never made a film before). Casey is sucking cock as if he had invented the act, hungrily, energetically, totally focused on the shaft between his lips. The finished film cuts away to another shot at this point, but what actually happened was that Villette, quite naturally and instinctually, grabbed Casey around the neck to provide greater resistance to his heated thrusts—but in doing so, his arm blocked the action. Without missing a stroke, Cal lifted one hand, politely removed Villette's arm, and continued to give him the blow job of his life. Once his costar had come, Cal immediately turned to me and said, "Better get a cutaway, so you can cut out my moving his arm." It is one of the most treasured outtakes I own.

The last time I saw Cal, I was on my way to the post office one steamy day in the middle of 1987's sizzling summer. He had just been to the funeral of a well-known theatrical agent, and although he was as immaculately groomed as ever, and although he bubbled cheerfully about who had been at the funeral and what had been said, he looked haggard and gaunt. I asked him about his health, and he assured me, with the denial he maintained up to the moment of his death, that he was "fine."

The last time I spoke to him was on the day of Arthur Bressan's memorial service. Upon returning to my office from the gathering, Rob Richards and I called his apartment, which was only a few blocks away. He was fine he said, he needed nothing, but he didn't really feel up to seeing me. Rob later stopped over anyway, and within days Cal was taken in a wheelchair to a plane where he flew to his family in Florida. In subsequent calls to various friends in New York, he seemed his chipper, effusive self. Four days later he was dead.

Certainly, his films will long remain a significant part of the gay heritage, and he will long remain in my personal memories. But of all those memories that linger so vividly, one in particular stands out: In his dressing room one night before a performance of *Tubstrip*, I was giving him notes when he suddenly discovered a zit on one buttock. "Oh, my God," he gasped extravagantly, "a flaw! An imperfection on an otherwise perfect body." Then he giggled, checked himself in the mirror one last time, and hurried to the wings to make another entrance. I remember wondering at the time if I would ever get to know him.

Jerry Douglas
Los Angeles, 1998

INTRODUCTION

I'm planning to do my own book as a serious self-analysis—it's going to be by both Casey Donovan and Cal Culver. I want to do it as an interview between my two personas—getting into both my minds, so to speak—to explore both the wholesome, corn-fed boy and that other person who does all that wild fuck-stuff on film.

—From a September 6, 1984, interview with Rob Richards
published in the January 1985 issue of *Stallion* magazine

Cal never got the story of his life written. He did, however, have a firm grasp of the necessary approach. The man had two distinct—and opposite—facets to his personality: the well-spoken, preppie man-about-town who could converse knowledgeably about any subject and who could be at ease in any situation and the single-minded sleaze who could, and would, take on all comers—the man for whom no sex act was too outrageous, no sex partner too unattractive. For all his contradictions, or perhaps because of them, he was the quintessential hedonistic gay male of the era—sexually uninhibited, open to every new experience that life threw in his way, and unwilling to hide any aspect of his life from public view. He ultimately fell victim to his own excess, stymied in his career by the more-subtle forms of homophobia that supplanted the psychological and legal restrictions of earlier decades, isolated from intimacy in his personal life by his whole-sale acceptance of the credo of sex as a modern form of contact sport, succumbing at the end to AIDS-related complications. Through it all he remained poised, handsome, impeccably groomed, and sexually desirable—a secular icon of a way of life that is, to our post-AIDS sensibilities, almost incomprehensible.

Roger Edmonson
Seattle, June 1998

PROLOGUE

Birth of the Gay Adam

It all began in the summer of 1971 at a screening of the forgettable hard-core epic, *Highway Hustler*. Wakefield Poole—a dancer, choreographer, and director who was soon destined to become something of a porn legend himself—had been rehearsing an American Federation of Theater Arts showcase production in New York City. After more than a quarter of a century, he remembered the occasion vividly. "It was hot as hell, and the rehearsal was a disaster," he said. "Nothing we tried was working, and we needed a break." That break resulted in a trip to the Park-Miller, one of the city's two gay male porno theaters, because doing anything else that particular Friday night would have meant standing in interminable lines. So Poole and a quartet of friends paid five dollars apiece and filed into the humid darkness.

The Park-Miller was a sorry excuse for a palace to gay eros. It was filthy, smelling of stale sweat and solitary sex. The ripped upholstery was crusty with grime, and the wooden backs of the seats glistened with what could have been—but probably wasn't—slug trails. Poole and company took their places in one of the sparsely peopled rows and waited for their eyes to adjust to the images flickering on the screen.

As most visitors to such venues, Poole and his friends were willing to forgive the decor once they had been swept away by the filmmaker's artistry. They waited, but they were not swept away. The lead character had an exaggeratedly swishy speech pattern, the sex was far from convincing, and "June is Busting Out All Over" blared incongruously on the sound track. "It was a piece of shit we were looking at," Poole said. "I glanced around and saw that one friend was asleep and two of the others were nodding off. A man who wasn't in our party was jerking off, but his eyes were closed, so I hardly imagine he was finding his inspiration on the screen." Poole turned to his friend, Martin Sherman, the playwright who at the end of the decade would pen *Bent*, a powerful indictment of what the Holocaust did to gays, and told him that he "was going to try to make a porn film himself, just for the hell of it, just for fun."

*   *   *

Poole had his fun. From his casual remark sprang *Boys in the Sand*—what has come to be considered by many film historians as the seminal gay male porn movie. Made over three successive weekends on Fire Island for a cost of $8,000, the film almost singlehandedly managed to legitimize gay hard-core, bringing it out of the seamy purlieus of the Park-Miller to the 55th Street Playhouse, a theater that had never before screened an X-rated film of any persuasion. On the day that *Boys* premiered, gay chic was born.

"If I were going to do it, I wanted to do it right," Poole said decisively. "I wanted to create a film that gay people could look at and say, 'I don't mind being gay—it's beautiful to see those people do what they're doing.' The whole time I was doing it, I thought of the gay lib slogan 'Gay is Beautiful.'" *Boys* by intent avoided forced acts, sadism, and degradation—historically an important part of gay sex on film—concentrating instead on the pure pleasure of the sex and the beauty of the performers.

Part of doing it right entailed a media blitz unprecedented in the annals of porn. Poole and his partner, Marvin Shulman, commissioned artist Edward Parente to create the mustachioed bather with the sea shell bandolier draped across his bare torso and the lightning bolt on his crotch that became the film's emblem. *After Dark*, the magazine that for a number of years chronicled all things gay and beautiful in the arts scene, took up *Boys'* cause with great fanfare. The film was also promoted heavily in such mainstream media stalwarts as *The New York Times*, *Variety*, and *The Village Voice*. There were preopening screenings, cocktail parties, and brunches teeming with celebrities and members of New York City society.

As opening day approached, Poole and Shulman donned their coveralls and went to work on the theater itself. "We cleaned and painted, put towels in the johns, and replaced all the burned-out lightbulbs. We didn't want people who came to see the film to feel like dirty fags. There had been more than enough of that over the years. It was time for a positive change."

People noticed. "I'd never been to a film like that before," *Mel Sherman, a soft-spoken retired accountant from New Jersey confided in a telephone interview. "I saw the ads in the movie section of the *Times*—right alongside an ad for *X, Y, and Zee*, that Elizabeth Taylor film. The ad didn't say anything about *Boys in the Sand* being, you know, porn, but I knew it had to be. I mean, it did say it had an all-male cast and that it was for mature adults, so what else could it be?

"I cut the ad out of the paper and put it in a drawer, but I couldn't get it out of my mind. The artwork in the ad was just

---

*Denotes a pseudonym and will appear only on first reference to the individual.

beautiful." Mel paused for so long that I thought the connection had been broken.

"I was afraid. I…I was arrested once, back in the late '50s. I was out in Central Park, taking a walk, and this good-looking guy just fell in beside me and started talking. After a few minutes he asked me if I'd like to go somewhere private. I nodded, and he took me to this wooded part of the park I'd always been too scared to go into. He unzipped his pants and showed himself, and then he grabbed my hand and pulled it over onto him, and then he put the handcuffs on me. It was horrible. I lost my job and my apartment, and my folks found out about it. When it was over I swore I'd never even look at another man.

"But then I saw that ad. Well, I built up my courage for two weeks, and then I did it. I mean, I drove into the city to see it. The theater was near Sixth Avenue in a nice part of town, nowhere near the sleaze of 42nd Street. As I recall it wasn't far from where the American Ballet was performing at the time. I didn't feel the least bit unsafe. I parked the car, and I walked right up to the box office and bought a ticket. I did it all almost without breathing, so I wouldn't chicken out at the last minute." Mel sighed softly into the receiver. "That show was so beautiful. It really made me feel good. You can't imagine what it meant to me."

He wasn't the only one. On December 29, 1971, the opening day, Poole and Shulman were expecting only a handful of people to show up. "We went over to the theater just before noon when the doors were to open. Marvin was trying to hang a sign up on the door warning that the film was for mature adults when they opened the box office. Well, people just started pouring in. We both nearly fainted. If we had had 50 people there the whole day, we would have been delighted. The people in the box office didn't believe it either. They phoned the night manager in a panic and told him to 'get down here and take this money to the bank.'"

The take was astounding—$5,300 the first day, $24,655 by

the end of the first week. It beat out many mainstream films and maintained a place on *Variety's* weekly list of 50 top-grossing films for almost three months. *Boys* became a bona fide phenomenon—reviewed, analyzed, and discussed around some of New York City's finest dinner tables. Fashion designer Yves Saint Laurent was in the city to promote his new line at the time and is reported to have said that *Boys* was the thing he'd enjoyed most of all during his stay. Limos were seen spilling their tuxedoed and sequined occupants at curbside for late-night showings.

"It was incredible," said Kansas City attorney *Ken Phillips, who was just a youngster when he attended the film's first-run engagement. "I was in New York with my parents. I was only 17, but I looked older, so I managed to sneak in. I was so excited I could hardly sit still. I'd never had sex—except all by myself in the bathroom with the door locked—and there I was sitting in a theater, waiting to watch a sex film. If a sex film had ever crossed the border into Kansas, I didn't know about it. Anyway, the lights went down, and my heart started to pound. Then this Bugs Bunny cartoon came on. My heart sank. Surely they wouldn't show a cartoon as a prelude to a porn film. I'd made a mistake somehow. I wanted to leave, but I'd paid $5, which was a lot of money in 1972, so I sat there. And then it started. There was this classical music on the sound track, and a shot of a guy sitting on the shore in a grove of trees. And then *he* appeared and started to run right out of the water."

He emerged from the water like a gorgeous male version of Botticelli's *Venus* and stepped into the fantasies of an entire generation of gay men. Blond and blue-eyed with a taut, slender, golden body and a radiant smile, he exuded sex appeal and an irresistible charisma. "He was definitely one in a million," said Michael Kearns, one of his costars both off Broadway and in films. "All he had to do was look at you and smile, and you knew with certainty that you were the only person in the world who mattered. There was an aura about him that forced you to notice him. He had it—all the great ones do. It was immediately apparent to everyone that he was a star."

And not just any star. He was called the gay-liberated Robert Redford, the all-American male, a trim golden-blond Apollo—in short, the answer to a gay man's prayers. He was considered by many to be the man who would make the transition from porn to mainstream movies. And for a short time, it seemed that it would all come to pass. There were interviews, photo shoots, and national magazine covers. Then there were the roles onstage and in films. And projects in the works—big projects with the likes of Sal Mineo, Raymond St. Jacques, and Maggie Smith.

But as it turned out, *Boys in the Sand* became an albatross, defining him forever as the golden boy of porn. The legitimate projects never quite materialized, the only films were porn films, and the only dependable money came from his hustling. And still the man remained golden, his name a talisman embodying all things erotic. As door after door failed to open for him, he remained stubbornly optimistic, never failing to dazzle everyone with his smile. Who was this latter-day Candide, gay porn's first and most enduring superstar?

CHAPTER 1

The Early Life and Times of a Corn-fed Boy

On November 2, 1943, a son was born to Donald and Arlene Culver of East Bloomfield, New York. The boy was christened John Calvin and was taken home to live on a rural farm with his parents and his older brother, Duane. There was no way the Culvers could have known on that chilly November day while war raged in Europe and Asia that nature had taken a moment off to play a genetic joke, twining strands of their conventional DNA to fashion what was destined to become a flamingo, tucked into a nest of country wrens.

*　　*　　*

By the same token there was no way the U.S. government could have known that, as a result of its massive troop call-up during World War II, it had inadvertently rounded up the largest concentration of gay men and women in the history of the

7

world. When the war ended each of them returned to civilian life, no longer isolated, but part of a vast underground network. This knowledge unleashed a flood of feelings that—although fated to be bottled up for decades afterward—would ultimately be named gay liberation.

*　　*　　*

Young Cal thrived, growing up handsome, athletic and prone to mischief. His brother, Duane, seven years Cal's senior, viewed him with amused, if distant, tolerance. "We got along pretty well most of the time," he recalled. "He could be a little devilish. I remember he was very funny and would try anything he could to make you laugh. If that didn't work, he'd try to irritate you. He was pretty good at that too."

According to longtime friend Ted Wilkins, Cal's view of Duane was much less equivocal. "He adored his brother. He talked about him constantly. Duane was all the things that Calvin wasn't. Cal wasn't exactly masculine—in fact he could be a little nelly. Duane, however, joined the army when he graduated from high school and did all the things that 'real' men were supposed to do. Cal was always afraid that he didn't measure up, that his brother didn't approve of him."

The two boys worked hard alongside their parents to make a living. "My father worked a farm on shares with another fellow," Duane said. "I grew up driving tractors and teams of horses, doing all kinds of farm work. I remember we always grew lots of popcorn. Mostly it was for our own use, but we'd give it to the neighbors as well." Later, the family's income was supplemented with a tourist camp, which consisted of a cluster of cabins and spaces for people to park their trailers. "As he got old enough, Cal was mostly at the motel, mowing and trimming the lawns, and helping my mother make the beds and clean the cabins. I pretty much stuck to the farming side of things."

Life for the boys wasn't all drudgery. Cal's hardworking parents did what they could to provide recreational opportunities for their children. Duane fondly remembered some of their outings. "One of the things our parents did for us in our childhood when our motel chores were done in the evening was to take us to the amusement park on Canandaigua Lake for a few hours." There the boys played along the shores of the lake and rode the rides, the bright lights and the rousing music of the carousel conjuring visions of a very different world from the one they were used to back in East Bloomfield.

As Cal grew, so did the tourist business, providing an entirely new avenue for the young man's curiosity to explore. East Bloomfield is situated in the Finger Lakes region of New York state. The nearby town of Canandaigua, less than 30 miles from Rochester, had long been a popular holiday resort for city dwellers anxious to escape the heat and humidity of summer. After the hiatus created by the disruptions of World War II, people were once again able to turn their thoughts to summer vacations. With the new postwar mobility, the number of potential tourists far outran the number of rooms available in local hotels and boarding houses. Fortunately for the rising middle classes, mobility ran hand in hand with ingenuity.

Entrepreneurs began to manufacture small travel trailers suitable for hitching to the family car, and it was suddenly possible to visit an area without incurring costly hotel bills. All these folks needed was a place to park their temporary homes with access to basic services. Cal's dad quickly realized that tourists were an easier—and more profitable—crop than popcorn. In addition to the cabins already in place, he installed bathrooms, showers, and electrical hook-ups for the new-fangled travel trailers. That done, he put up a sign out by the road, advertising affordable peace and tranquility with all the modern conveniences. In short order the

Culver homestead became a full-fledged tourist camp offering cabins and landing pads for trailers. Young Cal found himself surrounded by an entirely new society.

The contrast between Cal's young life and that of the visitors must have seemed stark to the youngster. The region around his home had long been a hotbed of religious sectarianism, home to Perfectionists, Spiritualists, and most notably, Mormons. His parents carried something of this religious fervor over into their own lives, enough so that in later life Cal would describe his upbringing as puritanical and say that his adult life was in part a reaction to his background. Inevitably, perhaps, the gregarious youth was drawn to the rows of shiny trailers and their profane, city-dwelling inhabitants.

Children who traveled in some of these homes on wheels were willing, in return for a tour of the woods, to tell Cal of cities where buildings grew taller than the trees and people rode on trains under the ground. Even the adults were interesting. They were louder than Cal's parents, gaudy as tropical birds, given to laughing, drinking alcohol, smoking cigarettes, and sitting around in front of their trailers and cabins on hot summer evenings without many clothes on.

*John Billings, advertising account executive and self-described fox—"lean, fit, and hard as a rock where it counts"—met Cal as a client in the mid '70s and subsequently developed a friendship with him. They spent many happy evenings together sipping wine in front of John's fireplace talking candidly about any and every subject.

"Cal had an interesting childhood—at least his version of it was interesting. I always tried to keep an objective distance from his tales, but they were very seductive. When you consider the rest of his life, the stories he told about his youth make perfect sense. Besides, when I was 14 I seduced my best friend's father, so I was in no position to doubt him," he said.

"He told me about how he would sneak out of the house and wander down among the cabins and the trailers at his parents' tourist camp. He could often hear people through the flimsy walls, talking and snoring—and making strange moaning sounds as though they couldn't decide whether they felt good or bad. Well, since they were doing it every night, it didn't take Cal too long to figure out that whatever they'd been doing must have felt pretty good.

"Then he made the momentous discovery that people didn't just make those sounds in the trailers. Sometimes they did it out of doors, in the woods, under cover of darkness. Sometimes people who didn't live in the same trailers did it with each other. There were even occasions when two guys would do it with each other, which as you might imagine really fascinated Cal."

Even more fascinating was the big shower house used by the guests at the trailer park. "In addition to helping his mother make beds in the cabins," John recalled, "Cal emptied waste baskets and scoured the sinks in the shower house. He told me the showers were separated by knee-to-shoulder plywood partitions, and had canvas curtains that could be drawn for privacy, but not everyone bothered with them." Many young men, exposed to communal life in the military, had become quite cavalier when it came to matters of privacy. Young Cal was titillated by this disregard of the Victorian standards with which he'd been raised.

Cal's strong—some claimed obsessive—interest in sex was fully awakened by this constant exposure to a stream of naked strangers. "Cal knew at an early age what the birds and bees did," John concluded. The summer visitors at his parents' tourist camp extended that knowledge to the behavior of Homo sapiens as well. He began to develop his own rather extraordinary sexual techniques in this specialized atmosphere, benefiting from the expertise of many willing teachers.

Once puberty hit with its rush of hormones, it was inevitable that Cal would be initiated into the world of sex. He knew from many happy hours in woods and bathroom how good it felt to play with himself. It wasn't too great a leap to include playing with others as well. Cal was drawn to other men, although he would never have recognized the attraction as homosexuality at that point in his life. It was just that guys were less threatening than girls, and Cal was drawn to something about guys. Besides, he could sneak into the men's showers and look around without getting chased away.

Many of the male visitors were kindly disposed toward the slender, handsome youth with the dazzling smile and winning ways and were willing to stop and pass the time of day with him. They would often tousle his hair or put a friendly hand on his shoulder, affectionate gestures young Cal craved because it was nice to be noticed by grown men, to be treated like a real person. At some point along the way, Cal realized that the feelings these men aroused in him conjured a host of wild, forbidden thoughts.

*Sam McCarty, now a real estate agent in Rochester, New York, spent a memorable summer at the Culver's camp with his divorced mother. "I always remembered Cal even though I was only around him for one summer. I had just turned 14, and I think he was maybe a year or two older. He was mature for his age, or at least he looked mature from my perspective. He was tall, strong from the work he did around the trailer park, tanned and real good-looking. There weren't any other kids my age, so we gravitated toward one another—or at least I gravitated toward him. I was lonely, and I was drawn to him. He seemed to recognize my need and responded to it. He was like this really savvy older brother to me."

The two boys began to spend quite a bit of time together. Sam even helped Cal with his chores so that they could spend more time in the solitude of the woods. "He'd let me do the mowing sometimes. I loved the smell of the cut grass." As Sam remembered it, the payoff for the work turned out to be worth the effort. "One day I was late getting to the big rock where we always met. Well, when I did arrive Cal was sprawled back, naked, beating off. I was embarrassed inside out—I was still on the near side of puberty, much to my dismay—but Cal didn't miss a beat. He motioned me up on the rock and told me to drop my pants. I obeyed and got my first lesson in how to beat off.

"Cal kept telling me what to do and how to do it, and although it felt good, nothing much was happening—at least not on the scale of what was going on with him. As everybody knows from his movies, he had a big dick. Well, to my youthful, inexperienced eyes, it was huge. He also had pubic hair, which I envied. He kept stroking himself until he ejaculated. After that I started looking forward to puberty the way I'd always looked forward to Christmas."

A few days later, Cal opened young Sam's eyes even further. "We were talking about sex—what else?—and after Cal had given me a rundown on what men and women did in bed, he told me that guys could have sex together. Well, I just absolutely refused to believe him. Who'd ever heard of such a thing?" Who, indeed? When much earnest conversation had failed to convince his new buddy, Cal resorted to a firsthand demonstration to prove his point. It was a crucial moment in young Sam's development.

"There was this guy in a trailer in the row over from ours, and he was really something. I can remember him strutting around in nothing but a pair of shorts, flexing his muscles and flirting with all the women. I don't remember his name or anything, just that he was dark and hairy, and he wore a gold crucifix around his neck.

"So anyhow Cal pointed the guy out to me and told me that he could do sexy things with him. I just shook my head, but Cal told me to wait and see." Sam didn't have to wait for long, and he saw plenty. "Cal came around later that night and knocked on the window of my trailer. I sneaked out and followed him to the shower house. He hustled me into one of the stalls, showed me a knothole in the partition, told me to keep quiet, and pulled the curtain closed." A few minutes later Sam's sex education began in earnest.

"There were footsteps outside, then whispered voices, then I saw the shadow of legs on the floor. More than two legs. I crouched down and saw Cal and the hairy muscle guy, both naked. They didn't say anything, but they didn't have to. Cal got down on his knees and pushed his face into the guy's crotch. The guy sort of moaned and put a hand on Cal's shoulder. When Cal came up for air, the guy had a hard-on jutting out."

It was from that moment that Sam dated his knowledge of his own sexual orientation. "I had always known that I thought guys were more interesting than girls. When I saw that shiny cock sliding out of Cal's mouth, bobbing up and down in the air while he licked the head, I knew. I started getting all hot and sweaty and felt a funny tickling down between my legs, but I was afraid to move. After all, I had promised that I wouldn't make a sound.

"Cal kept sucking the guy, and I kept waiting for him to shoot off the way Cal had out in the woods that day, but that wasn't the way it went. All of a sudden the guy lifted Cal up and turned him around and pushed him up against the wall of the shower stall. Then before I knew what was happening, he leaned against Cal and started pumping. I wasn't sure what was going on, but then it dawned on me—he was fucking Cal.

"I was scared because I thought the guy must be hurting him. Then I looked at Cal's face and realized that he wasn't in pain. He was smiling. His face was transformed like he wasn't Cal anymore. He looked different somehow, like something wild. They went at it for what seemed like a long time, then the guy started groaning, getting really loud. He gradually stopped moving and just stood there panting while Cal jerked off. After a couple of more minutes, the guy left. Cal stuck his head through the curtain—his face all normal again—and winked at me, cool as could be. I went back to my trailer and stayed awake all night having these totally outrageous, sexy thoughts." Young Sam had seen what must rate as one of Cal's first public sexual performances.

The two boys shared other escapades during that long-ago summer, but none that remain as vividly etched in Sam's mind. "Thinking back I'd have to say that Cal spent quite a few of his nights hanging out with one or another of the men who were staying in the camp. I also know for a fact that we were out in the woods every day jerking off. Once I got the hang of that, I became a devotee. But Cal—I guess he was what you'd call compulsive. He couldn't seem to get enough. Sometimes he'd jerk off two or three times in a row. I was very impressed."

These sexual encounters provided Cal a closeness with other males, physical affection, occasional gifts, and always that intensely gratifying surge of orgasmic pleasure. It was a surefire way for Cal to gain approval. It was so easy to make a person happy, just as long as one paid attention. Cal paid very close attention indeed, mastering the techniques of sex, refining them, making them an art. The gratification was fleeting, as were the men who provided it. No matter. Cal quickly discovered that there was always another man waiting, ready to give him what he needed in return for what Cal was so willing to offer.

The years passed, and Calvin flourished in the midst of his uncomprehending family. He grew tall, strong, and handsome, obviously destined for something more than changing dirty sheets and renting plots of land by the week to urban escapees from the summer's heat. All that was missing was the catalyst—something, or someone, to start the reaction that would awaken him to the possibilities in the wide world beyond East Bloomfield.

*   *   *

There were factors in that wider world that would ultimately affect the course of Cal's life irrevocably. The liberalizing effects of the war years had given way to unprecedented repressions of gay men and lesbians. Throughout the decade of the 1950's, gays were systematically driven underground, barred from federal employment, purged from the military, and categorized as sick by the psychiatric community. Gays retreated deep into their closets, hiding their true selves from the world, simmering silently with resentment. For almost two decades pressure built, gradually reaching critical mass.

*   *   *

This government-sanctioned bigotry cast no more than a faint shadow over Cal's rural universe. His concerns were closer to home, centered around school and his chores at the tourist camp. In 1955 Duane graduated from high school and joined the military, leaving Cal alone with the folks. In the autumn of 1957, Cal was ready to begin high school himself. He attended the Canandaigua Academy, a venerable institution founded in 1795 that served as the area high school. After an undistinguished freshman year, he found himself enrolled in a sophomore English class taught by Helen Van Fleet. His life was utterly changed.

Mrs. Van Fleet was, by all accounts, an inspirational teacher. She saw that young Cal had intellectual potential and set about helping him realize it. Her role extended beyond teaching—she mentored him, opening his eyes to life's wider possibilities. She talked to him and gave him books to read. She was willing to sit and listen to him, to hear his thoughts, and to answer his questions. Because she was also the school's drama teacher, she encouraged Cal to explore his thespian talents. Cal flourished under her tutelage. Almost everything she shared with him stuck with him throughout his life.

According to her daughter, Alice, Mrs. Van Fleet was very gregarious. "She always welcomed all kinds of people into the house," Alice said. "Mom was a great influence. She encouraged people to be themselves and go their own way. She and Cal had a really wonderful rapport that extended beyond school hours. They were close friends until the day he died. He loved to hang out around the house, and Mom treated him like one of her own."

"I was a few years younger, and I came to think of him almost as an older brother. My mom became Cal's Auntie Mame. I suspect she had given him the book to read and that he took it to heart. Cal actually called her Auntie Mame and referred to himself as Patrick (Mame's nephew in the book). He took to calling me Agnes Gooch, even though I wasn't pregnant at the time. My mom was probably more accepting of Cal than his own parents were. I really don't think they understood him, especially his father."

Mrs. Van Fleet became Cal's mother of choice. As an adult he wrote to her constantly, detailing his travels and his life in the theater. Every time he was in a play, he would send her tickets. He took her backstage to meet Ingrid Bergman when he was in a play with the legendary actress. He took her to the Tony Awards, arranging for her to sit front and center in the audience. Alice was at home, watching on television. "She was right down in front, seated beside Helen Hayes, and every time they presented an award, you could see the back of Mom's head at the bottom of the screen. Mom had always loved the theater and everything associated with it. It was one of the high points of her entire life."

As their relationship took root, Cal continued to blossom. During his sophomore year he began working in the school library and joined the Academy Players, a high school theatrical group. That same year he was elected secretary and treasurer of his class, and he also began to take a leading role in the class committees that organized school activities.

Cal had discovered something very important, something that those encounters with the men at the trailer park had led him to suspect. People liked him, they liked to be around him, they responded to his smile, his looks, his humor, all in a very positive way. Much to his delight, he was quickly accepted as part of the "in" crowd of his classmates and became essential to the social life of his peers. It was another aspect of the skills he had developed while pleasuring the men at the tourist camp—the chameleonlike ability to become what people wanted him to be so that they would accept him. He cultivated the quality during his adolescence as a survival mechanism and employed it thereafter to make his way through life. Cal was a different person for everyone he ever met, always filtering his personality through the wishes of whomever he was with at the time. He was all things to all people, remaking himself into whatever was desired. Nearly the only constant thing about him was the seemingly timeless physical beauty that spun out a legend around him.

Those sessions in the showers and in the woods had taught Cal something beyond the pleasure/reward principle. He had learned that he was set apart, even in the midst of the laughing crowds that surrounded him, set apart by a fundamental quirk of his psychological makeup. He was gay, a fact that, to his everlasting credit, he accepted early on and never attempted to hide. "He was always a bit different. "You know—effeminate," was the assessment of Helen Van Fleet's son, John. "I was older than Cal, so we didn't pal around or anything, but I saw him around the house a lot because of my mom. He was witty and hip, into fashion and nice clothes. As I recall he was pretty open about his sexuality. There was no hiding it—it was just the way he was. I don't remember anyone ever giving him any grief about it."

Cal dated girls because that was what a guy did in high school in the 1950s—especially a popular guy. Especially a guy who loved to dance. And Cal was a dancer. For a while he dated a Filipina exchange student, and they formed a dance team, touring the fair and festival circuit in upstate New York. This provided an early taste of celebrity that was to prove almost as addictive as his need for sex.

Celebrity of another kind came to him when he tried out—and was chosen for—the varsity cheerleading squad during his junior year at the academy. This was in the autumn of 1959, a time when boys who wanted to be accepted tried out for the football team. It was a risk, but it worked for him, expanding his domain beyond theater and school government—he had been elected vice president of his class that year—and placing him on the periphery of the extremely masculine world of sports. Class jocks even expressed grudging admiration for his feat, admitting that it took "a hell of a lot of balls" to pull that off. By all accounts he made a success of it, enough so that he was chosen for the squad his senior year as well.

His senior year was a busy one. In addition to his cheerleading, Cal was involved with *The Cannon*, the school newspaper, and undertook a major role in the senior class play. He also helped to organize "senior day" and continued his work in the library. Because he planned to become a teacher like Mrs. Van Fleet, he was also a member of Future Teachers of America during his senior year.

In addition to everything else, he joined an athletic club because of a developing interest in gymnastics. Dancing had developed his legs, and the physicality of cheerleading wasn't that different from the moves of a gymnast. He took to working the parallel bars and the rings, pleased by the results. His lean adolescent torso gained bulk and definition, and he began to feel more comfortable around the brawny young men whose exploits on the playing field he so enthusiastically cheered from the side-lines.

Although he dated girls Cal's sexual antennae were always more attuned to the male of the species. It was clear to his peers, and it was clear to him. Many wonder what, almost a decade before Stonewall started the ball rolling for gay liberation, did a popular young man who happened to be queer do for sex.

"Don't get me wrong," John Billings told me. "The '50s were no sexual wonderland. Still we did manage to have sex, fun sex, usually right under the very noses of the adults who were responsible for seeing that we didn't have so much as a sexual thought in our young heads.

"Cal was a great conversationalist. Granted, that wasn't the original fantasy that led me to answer his ad in *The Advocate* and pay for his flight here to Chicago, but it ultimately became even more important than the sex. The sex was incredible, of course, but just being alone in the same room with him was the best part. I mean, you've seen pictures of him haven't you? That face! Those eyes! God, you didn't have a chance once he'd turned the force of those eyes loose on you.

"One night we were trading tales about our exploits as young-sters. I confessed my crush on one of the jocks in my school and told Cal that I'd stolen a pair of the guy's underwear and jacked off with them. Well, he got this twinkle in his eye, snuggled in deeper down at his end of the couch, then proceeded to tell me what he had done when he had a terminal case of the hots for a guy he went to high school with.

"First he told me about being a cheerleader, which completely blew me away. Hell, I spent my high school years struggling to keep my voice low and my wrists from fluttering. I flinched every time I heard anybody say 'faggot,' whether they were talking about me or not. And here was Cal, a cheerleader in high school in the '50s.

"He had a real crush on this guy who, to hear Cal tell it, was quite a looker. Tall, dark, furry in all the right places, typical gymnast's build—a real hunk. The two of them were in some athletic club, so Cal was around him quite a bit. It seemed that the guy was also very shy—so shy that he held back from showering until everyone else was done. So Cal took to waiting until this guy was alone in the showers, then joining him.

"Well, he said the guy wouldn't look at him for anything, but Cal wasn't the type to give up easily. He told me how one night he walked over to the shower next to the guy and started soaping up, watching the guy out of the corner of his eye. Soon enough, he saw the guy getting aroused. Then Cal stooped down like he was going to wash his feet but licked the head of the guy's cock instead, right there in the shower room.

John's voice dropped to a husky whisper. "When he told the next part, he was crouched at the end of the sofa, his eyes narrowed, looking for all the world like a big cat stalking a bird. If I closed my eyes, I could picture the whole scene—the white tiles, the steam rising, that humpy guy frozen there with Cal's tongue lapping the end of his dick. Cal said the guy gasped, but he didn't move a muscle, so Cal proceeded to blow him.

"I asked him if he was afraid he'd get caught. He just chuckled and told me that if someone had seen he would've made him wait his turn. I thought that was pretty ballsy, but he was a ballsy guy that way. Cal told me this years after the fact, but I always thought it had the ring of truth about it. It sure made a hell of a story. And I have to say that it sounded just like what I knew of him."

Another of Cal's youthful trysts spoke to me only after extracting my solemn promise to maintain his anonymity. "You're sure you won't use my name?" he asked uneasily. "I mean, I won't talk to you if you're going to use my name." I felt for a moment that I had been transported back in time to 1958, then realized that in many parts of the country attitudes hadn't changed much since that era. It was only one of many times that I encountered the dichotomy of people who wanted to talk but declined to be identified. I suggested that we call him David Hayes. He grunted his agreement.

*David Hayes cleared his throat and began to speak, his voice hoarse, spitting out night thoughts. "It was at a school dance. I was a senior, and he was a junior, I'm pretty sure. It was hot, and the girl I'd brought to the dance was spending more time in the bathroom with her girlfriends than she was spending with me. So I went outside to get some fresh air, and I saw Cal. I don't know whether he followed me out or whether he was already outside, but he was there.

"I knew him—everybody knew him. Every time you turned around he was up doing something in front of the whole school. He came over, and we started to talk. Then he asked me if I wanted a beer. I said sure. He said we should go out to the football field so that we wouldn't get caught. Once we were out there in the bleachers, he gave me a beer, and we started talking.

"Our talk got around to sex, which was sure as hell on my mind all the time back then. He was talking about it ,and the next thing I knew, he was down on his knees in front of me with my dick in his mouth. I know that guys usually say they'd bust a guy who tried that shit, but when you're terminally horny and you're all alone in the dark, it's a little different. Besides, it felt really good.

"After it was over he didn't act like he'd done anything wrong or anything like that. I remember that he asked me if I liked it, like he really wanted to know. Then he said thanks and went on back inside to the dance as if nothing had happened. I kept seeing him around school for the rest of the year, of course, but it never happened again."

Cal graduated with the class of '61, ready to test his wings on a larger stage. Armed with the social skills he had developed during his adolescence and with Mrs. Van Fleet's adjuration to be himself and go his own way firmly in his mind, he prepared to do just that. His first step was a small one, however. He didn't immediately flee to the bright lights of New York City so that he could discover himself. Cal had a plan—he wanted to be a teacher like his mentor.

*   *   *

As the decade of the '60s got under way, ripples began to disturb the placid calm that had prevailed during the previous decade. Blacks began to demand the rights of full citizenship, and the women's movement began to find voice and direction. Even gays were beginning, tentatively at first, to demand their civil rights. By the middle of the decade, students on college campuses across the country, radicalized by their opposition to the war in Vietnam, were prepared to foment revolutionary change against the status quo on all fronts.

*   *   *

Cal's rebellion against the status quo was not fated to be of the torn-jeans and long-haired variety. He began the decade with little more than a determination to complete his education. With that in mind he enrolled in the teacher's college at Geneseo, a small town about 30 miles from his home. It was a small school—there were only about 1,000 students when he attended—and he quickly established himself at the center of campus life. He was the class treasurer from his sophomore year until he graduated; he participated in dance, theater, and chamber singers; he was the president of the men's glee club; he was on the artist lecture series committee; and he was—once again—a cheerleader.

Amid these activities he somehow found time to major in elementary education and to work in the college cafeteria.

Cal made a real effort to cultivate his nascent interest in the arts. In addition to the artists who performed at the school, he was fortunate to be close to the city of Rochester, New York, which was then, as now, a major center of culture. The Eastman School of Music, one of the world's premier music schools, staged hundreds of concerts and recitals every season, and the city was also home to the highly renowned Rochester Philharmonic Orchestra. In addition there were many opportunities for evenings of theater and dance to help fill the long, cold winter nights.

*Richard Langford was in the glee club with Cal. "Everybody liked him. I guess everyone knew he was queer. He made no bones about it, but he didn't look the part at all. I mean, you know what he looked like. He was as far as it was possible to get from the stereotypical images the culture had reserved for a pervert. He drew people to him like a magnet, both male and female. Wherever Cal was, there was going to be a crowd. That you could count on.

"I remember he was nuts about music, always right there every time the doors of the auditorium were opened for a concert. Well, Geneseo wasn't enough for him, and he was always going over to Rochester with somebody to attend concerts at the Eastman School of Music. Sometimes he'd go with a coed, maybe double-date with another guy from the glee club. Other times he'd go all by himself or with another guy.

"One of the guys he'd go with was my roommate. This guy was on the swim team, expert in the backstroke and butterfly stroke, a real athlete. He was so straight he hurt, but he had a girlfriend who was totally proper. You know the type—nothing doing until the wedding night. The poor jerk was so horny he was cross-eyed. Well, for a while there, he and Cal seemed to be off to a concert two or three times a week. I was a little surprised because I had never thought of my roommate as being into classical music. I'd always sort of had him figured as a rock-and-roll man. Still, he and Cal seemed to really hit it off.

"Then one weekend I was driving to visit my folks over near Buffalo. My car broke down, and I ended up back in Geneseo late that same night. When I got up to the rooms we shared, Paul was entertaining, but it was no woman in his bed. He was packing Cal's ass, and they were both obviously loving it. I turned around and left them to it. I slept in my car that night. As far as I know, they never knew I'd seen them."

The dance-and-drama set at the school provided a compatible crowd for Cal to hang out with. Desiring to be thought of as sophisticated, most of his peers would have accepted Cal's freefloating, unorthodox sensuality without question. He cut a dashing figure onstage and was always willing to take on any role that needed to be filled. His ego and desire for attention did not preclude smaller roles—being onstage was enough.

Beyond the plays, there were also the occasional trips into New York City to see a play or a musical. The New York City theater was still in its golden age in the early '60s. Great musicals, dramas, comedies, and dance performances were available every night at prices even a frugal student could occasionally afford. And they provided a spectacle that was more than enough to dazzle a boy from a small upstate town who had a yen for fame and glory.

Cal would go and sit in the darkened theater and let the production sweep him away. How delightful it must be to be up there under the lights with all the glitter and glamour and adulation it implied. As he watched the performers, he couldn't help but think that he could be up there himself—on the stage, in the spotlight. After all, he could sing and dance and act—he'd been doing it throughout high school and was still doing it in college.

Granted, he was preparing to be a teacher, and yet…

According to friend and fellow thespian Miriam Bonner, "Cal was definitely stagestruck. He loved going to plays, and the more famous the cast, the better he liked it. He'd sit there, totally enraptured during the performance. Then once it was over, he'd head for the stage door. Of course, I followed. He loved to meet the performers, and I have to say, they liked meeting him as often as not. He was just so ingratiating, and his praise made it clear that he had really been paying attention during the performance. Actors find that quality hard to resist.

"I know I couldn't resist, even though I was never a serious actress. I guess, looking back, that I had a crush on him. I mean, he was so nice to be around. We used to go to quite a few plays and concerts during the course of the school year, and Cal always made me feel special, as though he really cared what I said and what I thought.

"He was a nice man. I never really saw him as a teacher, although that's what he was studying to be. I always thought he'd go on to do something with a little more glamour than teaching elementary school. I guess I was right, although I would never have expected him to do what he did. Not exactly, anyway."

"I came out right before my senior year in college," Cal said in a 1983 filmed interview, *Men in Film.* "The man was a teacher at my college." The admission more likely signaled a frame of mind than an actual fact. Cal was notorious for reorganizing the details of his life's time line as the need arose. For an interview Cal would give out the details of his life—real and imagined—that he felt would fit the picture he was trying to paint at that particular time. On more than one occasion, Cal said in print that he was through with porn at the same time that he was cranking out yet another feature. In one particularly egregious instance, he said that his first exposure to fisting occurred when Al Parker filmed a scene with him in 1978. The film evidence firmly pushes the date back seven years. The truth, as nearly as it can be reconstructed, is that it was from this moment in 1964 that Cal fully and freely began to feel comfortable with his orientation.

Miriam Bonner chuckled at the idea that Cal was just coming out. "If Cal dated his coming out from that point, then he was the last person on campus to know. He was always so comfortable, so happy, so totally himself. To the best of my knowledge, he certainly wasn't living a double life. He was always attentive, polite, and charming, but there was never that 'I've-gotta-get-in your-panties-or-die' desperation that straight guys exude in college. He dated a few coeds—hell, he dated me—but nothing was ever serious."

"The professor he 'came out' with? That I don't know. Sorry. I saw Cal with any number of professors over the years, but it was a small school, and it wasn't uncommon to go to a professor's home for tutorial help, or just to hang out, drinking cheap wine and talking about the meaning of life. If any faculty member had anything to do with a student, he would've had to be really discreet about it."

And so Cal's life on campus continued, with classes completed and new stage roles memorized and performed. And always there were concerts to attend, plays to see, people to watch, and dreams to dream.

CHAPTER 2

Assault on New York: The Early Years

Cal graduated from college in the spring of 1965 armed with a contract to teach a sixth-grade class in Peekskill, New York. Peekskill, a once-bustling factory town situated at the southern end of a spectacular rocky gorge known as the Hudson River Highlands, had lost its industrial base and was already beginning a long, slow decline into obscurity. Cal hadn't chosen the place for its social life or its historical associations with the Revolutionary War, however. He viewed the situation as a convenient staging area.

Peekskill was within easy striking distance of New York City, a place that had long held a distinct fascination for Cal. After shepherding his charges through their world history and mathematics, he would go back to his apartment, change clothes, get in his car, and drive two hours into Manhattan—often several times a week. There he was able to indulge two of what were rapidly emerging as the great passions of his life—culture and sex.

Here at last Cal was able to indulge fully his lifelong addiction to the arts. He made it a point to see every play in New York City, whether it was a major Broadway production or a one-man show presented in a loft in the East Village. He also haunted the concert halls and opera houses, spending every free moment soaking up high culture. Between performances he would go to museums, art galleries, and photography exhibits determined to learn all he could about this glamorous world he was beginning to explore—and that, some fine day, he hoped to conquer.

New York City had more than culture to offer—and Cal was eager to sample it all. Rob Richards met Cal in 1981 through an interview Richards was writing for *Topman* magazine. The two men became friends and often talked about Cal's early years in New York City. "After he first began spending significant amounts of time in the city, Cal frequented public restrooms, movie theaters, hotels, parks—the classic cruising spots in the mid-to-late '60s. That wasn't the least bit unusual because there weren't many bars, so those public spaces were the standard gay meeting venues. It was the best way for a young man of Cal's orientation and gargantuan appetites to explore his sexuality."

*Jay Smith was a struggling artist when he met the not-yet-famous golden boy. "I was living in SoHo. I had a studio in one of the old cast-iron buildings on Prince Street." SoHo—short for the district south of Houston Street—was just starting to come to life in its new guise as a haven for artists. The rents were cheap, and the high-ceilinged spaces made great studios.

Jay had made the space in an old storefront below his studio available for an impromptu opening for a photographer friend. "There was a wall full of glossy prints under Plexiglass, a couple of jugs of cheap wine, and a box of crackers. Other than a knot of friends, I don't think more than 20 people had wandered through during the course of the whole evening. I was just ready to lock the place up and call it quits when this really handsome guy wandered in. He was impeccably dressed, and he was carrying a program from one of the Broadway shows that was big at the time. He jumped right out at you because he was the only person in the gallery wearing a suit—not to mention the fact that he was drop-dead gorgeous."

After a few minutes of desultory conversation, Jay asked his guest upstairs. "I was living in my studio. It was the thing to do in SoHo back then. We just added plumbing and heating and made ourselves at home. The guy really seemed delighted by this gypsy approach to life. I showed him my sketchbook, and he was very excited by some nude studies I had been working on. He asked me if I wanted to draw him.

"Well, I'm no fool—of course, I said yes. He stripped and was exquisite—beautifully proportioned, tight without any unnecessary bulk, completely delicious to sketch. He was totally uninhibited and obviously got off on the idea that I was getting off on him. I made a couple of quick sketches, then tossed pad and pencil aside and proceeded to make him. He was a willing and an accomplished partner. He was also insatiable. We grappled until it was almost dawn. We could have continued, but he told me that he had to drive a long way home so that he could get to work."

Jay and Cal didn't repeat their interlude, but Jay never forgot the sexy visitor to his studio. "There was something about him that stuck in my brain like a burr. It wasn't just his looks or his sexual vitality—although that was damned near unforgettable. There was just something about him that got under my skin."

A few years later when Jay picked up a copy of *After Dark* magazine, he got a pleasant surprise. "There was a gorgeous shot of Cal, naked from the pubes up, advertising a porno film he had just made. I checked the papers and hightailed it to the theater. It was him all right, big as life and sexier than ever." Years later Jay saw Cal's "escort" ads in *The Advocate* but could never bring himself to call. "I was afraid to spoil the fantasy. Besides, I'd had it for free, and I wasn't into paying for it."

*   *   *

A gallery was as good a place as any to meet a man in New York City —or in any other major metropolitan area in the mid 60s. In the city itself there weren't many bars left to hang around in. That had been seen to when the allegedly liberal mayor, John Lindsey, authorized a "cleanup" campaign to get the "undesirables" out of Washington Square Park in the heart of Greenwich Village, aiming to sanitize the city's image prior to the 1964 World's Fair. Gay gathering places were raided and padlocked throughout the city. At about the same time, in a related burst of social progressivism, the New York state legislature voted overwhelmingly to keep the sodomy law criminalizing homosexual behavior on the books.

Banished to the great outdoors, gay New Yorkers displayed their accustomed ingenuity and hardiness. "The rambles," a heavily wooded area in the middle of Central Park, had long been a gay cruising ground. Now gay men set about organizing it and making it as safe as possible for their revels by watching out for the police and for each other. Someone had devised a system whereby if a policeman was spotted, a stick was beaten on the ground or the trunk of a tree. This was the signal to climb back into your clothes so that when the police arrived all they would find was a group of men standing around and enjoying the night air—an activity the legislature had neglected to forbid. Central Park became, for a time, gay New York City's living room, the place to go when you wanted to meet a man and invite him to come home with you.

Cal was seen around the rambles by more than one man in the mid 60s. *Joe Raines was a salesman in the men's section at

Bloomingdale's department store by day, a devotee of park cruising by night. "I knew him well—biblically," Joe said. "The woods there were full of hot men, and he was definitely one of the hottest. In the winter we would generally meet there and then wander off to some place a bit warmer for sex—unless you were just there for a quick 'maintenance' blow job. In the summer, however, things were much wilder and more open. It was an orgy every night of the week in Central Park."

"After a while you got to recognize some of the regulars. In the summer when it stayed light late, you could often see who was up to what and with whom. Well, he was up to a lot. Sometimes he'd just be with one guy, sometimes with a group. He could manage a crowd quite well. I know this because I've always liked to watch. Given the chance, I'd position myself so that I could see what this hot young hunk was up to. Hell, he knew I was watching him. He loved it.

"One evening after we'd seen each other maybe half a dozen times, we got together and started messing around. He pulled my cock out of my pants, and I think he was surprised by the size of it. I don't want to brag, but most men are," Joe said. "He got this look in his eye, like something wild was possessing him. It would've been scary if it hadn't been so sexy. Well, he proceeded to give me the workout of my life that night. He did everything with my dick but let loose. It was intense.

"I remember doing a double take later on when I'd come across a picture of him in the papers, modeling clothes, looking like an aristocrat. It was such a shock when I was used to seeing him on his hands and knees, taking it up both ends. That was a trip. Years later I started seeing him in glossy porn magazines and on film. He was very hot, but I think he was even hotter in the park in the moonlight, doing it just for fun."

Cal was exposed to kink at this juncture—and took to it immediately. Joe had a pal who was an expert in such things. "Mike was a hard-core leatherman from way back. He wore full regalia even back in the '50s when you could get arrested for walking the street in a black leather motorcycle jacket. We were comparing notes about tricks one night over a beer and concluded we had both had him.

"I asked Mike what he thought, and he told me he thought the guy had potential. That made me take notice because Mike was one serious dude. I bought him another brew and started pumping him for info. He told me he had been walking down the street one evening when this good-looking guy dressed up like an ad for Brooks Brothers started following him. Mike was a no-bullshit kind of guy, so he stopped and waited for the guy to catch up.

"He walked right up to Mike and asked him if he was for real. Believe me, that took some balls because Mike was one mean-looking dude. When Mike nodded, the guy looked up at him, all submissive like, and asked if he'd be willing to show him what it was all about. Hell, Mike couldn't wait. He told me he figured the guy would take one look around his dungeon and head for the hills."

Cal wasn't the least bit intimidated. "Mike told me his eyes just lit up when he saw what was in store for him. He wanted to try out everything—cock rings, tit clamps, dildos, restraints, butt plugs, you name it. Mike put him through his paces, and he came through with flying colors. I actually think Mike was impressed—and believe me, that impressed the hell out of me."

Cal approached the New York sexual scene with the same avidity that he displayed in his assault on the cultural resources of the city. He embraced all that was new and unknown to him, sampling everything, finding little that wasn't to his liking. It was all a part of his ongoing education process, honing skills that would serve him well as his life path became less and less orthodox.

*　　*　　*

The long commute back and forth from Peekskill to the city eventually began to take its toll. It was also becoming clear that the regular grind of being an elementary schoolteacher in boring old Peekskill wasn't to Cal's taste, so he chose not to renew his contract for a second year. It was time to take the plunge and make a frontal assault on New York City.

Cal applied for a teaching position at the Ethical Culture Fieldston School, a private institution on Central Park West, and, much to his delight, he was accepted. The school catered to the children of celebrities—"Harry Belafonte's kids, Steve Lawrence and Edie Gorme's kids, Eli Wallach and Anne Jackson's kids," as Cal once gushed to an interviewer. Throughout his life Cal was dazzled by celebrities, and the idea of teaching their children took some of the drudgery out of that task. With his new contract in hand, Cal packed his belongings and made the fateful move. There would be no looking back, no return to the bucolic safety of life in a small town upstate. He wanted to see New York City—and he wanted New York City to see him.

*　　*　　*

While Cal was tending to the needs of the offspring of the rich and famous, the world all around him was in ferment. Pressure was building for change that would ultimately catapult Cal, and all that he came to represent, to prominence. It was a change for which he—the least political of creatures—would become a sort of poster child. It was ironic that throughout his career as a gay celebrity his every move would be seen as a kind of political act. He was not a radical or a conservative but a member of the "hedonist's party," that huge group of pleasure-seeking gays who by and large dominated the gay scene in the 1970s and early '80s.

In retrospect it seems only logical that this would have happened—that the march would have been stolen from the serious activists who had put it on the line in earlier decades. Older generations of gays were acculturated to the closet and found it difficult to trust the changes that were taking place. Cal, although not officially a "baby boomer" was most definitely a hedonist at heart, ready to burst forth into the light once the doors of liberation had been pried open. He was an embodiment of the pleasure principle, which for better or worse was to preoccupy gay culture until the specter of AIDS changed everything.

*   *   *

As the atmosphere of the '60s became increasingly confrontational, homosexuality became increasingly difficult to ignore. Despite the raids, the ordinances, the witch-hunts, gays persisted in becoming increasingly visible. It was not an easy time. Police harassment and entrapment was commonplace—on the streets and in the parks and public restrooms of major cities and small towns. It seemed for a time as though the main job of the police in the United States was to prevent adult homosexuals from engaging in consensual sexual relations.

Cal undoubtedly knew of these things—in 1967 and early 1968 New York City's finest were entrapping more than 100 men per week—yet he continued to explore all avenues of gay life. He was either more discreet, or luckier, than his fellows, for there is no record that he was ever arrested on charges of homosexual solicitation. Of course, Cal didn't fit the stereotype of a "degenerate" for whom the police would have been looking. Neither effeminate nor a long-haired radical, Cal would have been invisible to the vice squad.

*   *   *

On the other hand, gay men and lesbians were making progress—glacially slow, some thought—on several fronts. By the mid '60s, there were dozens of organizations representing gay men and lesbians forming across the country. Gay groups began picketing—they went after the State Department, the Civil Service Commission, the Pentagon, and even the White House, calling for civil rights for gays. By 1968 the North American Conference of Homophile Organizations was able to boast that no less than 26 gay groups had attended its annual convention.

*   *   *

Meanwhile, Cal was experiencing some job-related troubles. Teaching the children of celebrities had its drawbacks as well as its glamour. A number of these children—bright, undisciplined, spoiled—were real brats, and putting up with their temper tantrums wasn't quite the same thing as attending the theater to watch their parents emote. One day at the beginning of his second year, something snapped. He grabbed an unruly student and gave her a swift kick in the butt.

The student was Eli Wallach's daughter, Roberta. By all accounts she had been disrupting the class and richly deserved her punishment. Be that as it may, she ran to the office and complained bitterly. Cal was called into the office and confronted by nervous administrators. Seeing no point in lying, Cal answered their questions truthfully. As a result, he was summarily fired, bringing his teaching days to an ignominious close. He turned in his keys, cleaned out his desk, and left the school. He had gone only a few blocks before fate intervened, and an entirely new vista opened up.

Shortly before his death, Joe McCarthey, a friend of Cal's from those early days, told the tale to writer Jeffrey Schmidt. "Poor Cal was really distraught about losing his job. He hadn't managed to save any money, and his rent was coming due in less than two weeks. It was the middle of the school year, and nobody was hiring. He was in deep doo."

While he contemplated the depth of this "doo," Cal noticed that a late-model, red Cadillac convertible was pacing him as he walked briskly along 72nd Street. Cal turned and looked at the driver. "He was an older guy, well-dressed, gray at the temples, craggy-featured—from the way Cal described him, he was quite good-looking. So Cal smiled, and the man smiled back. The guy pulled over to the curb and stopped. Cal walked over, leaned against the car, and started a conversation."

One thing led to another, and Cal opened the door and settled into the plush leather upholstery. As McCarthey recalled, Cal was really despondent over losing his job and thought that motoring around the streets of Manhattan in a big car might just lift his spirits. After they had driven around for a couple of hours, cruising through Central Park and up and down the quiet streets on the Upper East Side, the man, a doctor from Riverdale, New Jersey, suggested that Cal should come up to his hotel room with him where they could have a drink and pursue a more private, intimate conversation.

"Since the Doc was fingering his cock through his trousers, Cal knew exactly what he wanted," McCarthy said. "He was just starting to explain to the guy that he really wasn't up for anything sexual right then when he stopped dead in his tracks." The good doctor made it quite clear that he was proposing a business transaction—an exchange of money for sexual services rendered. "Cal quickly figured that the amount the doctor had mentioned would be very helpful in making up for his rent shortfall." He agreed to spend the afternoon with the doctor at his hotel, and so he first initiated himself into a profession that would in later years stand him in good stead.

Cal had his own take on the art of hustling. He added something to the mix that had in most instances been missing—flair and a sense of style. With his collegiate good looks, his Harris tweed jackets, crisply ironed shirts, conservative ties, and highly-polished Florsheims, he looked more like a young executive than a sex toy. There was nothing sleazy or unwholesome about him. He wasn't someone to be picked up in a dark alley, then discarded before the harsh light of day could expose the transaction for what it was. He could, and did, walk into any hotel, gallery, museum, or restaurant in the city. There was never a danger that he would be cornered by security or a disapproving headwaiter and escorted out the back door.

*   *   *

Although he was now on his own in the big city without a job, Cal refused to admit defeat. Teaching was no longer in the cards for him. He had signed up as a substitute after his dismissal from Ethical Culture, but the experience had been disastrous. He was called to sub at a public school in the Bronx. "I went in on the first day, and I immediately felt like Sandy Dennis in *Up the Down Staircase*," he once told an interviewer. Reading his account of the battleground schools were becoming at that time, one can easily imagine his exasperated tone of voice. "It's being a zookeeper. It's horrible! There was no way. I called them up the next morning to let them know I wasn't coming back. I loved teaching, but that was ridiculous."

This encounter with big city reality sent Cal off in a totally different direction. He had always been enamored with the theater from both sides of the footlights. After appearing in all those high school and college productions, he thought he was ready to try his hand in a more professional capacity. In time-honored showbiz fashion, Cal packed a bag and headed for what had long been a proving ground for young talent—summer stock.

He went to New Hampshire where many of the towns had a summer theater set up in the town hall or a schoolhouse, or even, in some cases, a barn. Cal landed a position with one of the most reputable of these, the Peterborough Players in Hampton. There along with other young, untried thespians, he worked as an apprentice. Apprentice was a euphemism that covered building sets, painting scenery, and, if he were really fortunate, a walk-on part in a play.

Here, Cal was once again among those summery throngs with whom he had grown up. Summer stock not only drew the tourists but also attracted New York City theater people—famous actors and directors who wanted to get out of the city for a few weeks to avoid the summer heat and soak up the ambiance of New England. Cal was, of course, drawn to the celebrity and glamour of it all. In turn, there is little doubt that any celebrities who were so inclined would have been drawn to the astonishingly handsome young man hovering on the periphery of the action, watching, listening, taking it all in.

Cal had gone up to New Hampshire on a lark and wasn't getting paid much of a salary beyond his meals and a place to stay. Luckily for Cal, he really didn't need cash in his pocket. He had other assets that were far more valuable than mere currency. The handsome, impeccably dressed young man was careful to insinuate himself into the right circles, circles where all that was required of him was to smile and say the right thing at the right time. Cal could talk about theater. He had most likely seen all the New York City plays the visiting stars had appeared in last season. What, after all, could be more pleasant for a jaded actor than to sit across from someone who looked like Cal while he gushed about how wonderful that actor had been in his last role?

*Don Stevens worked as a stagehand at the theater with Cal. "I don't remember the play, but I do remember him," he recalled, his voice hoarse with too many years of tobacco. "It was after a performance when we were all milling around, waiting for some-body to decide to make his place available for a party. I'd had my eye on the guy just because I couldn't believe how good-looking he was. I was getting ready to talk to him when the star of the show, a famous guy who had just completed a run on Broadway, stepped out of his dressing room. Cal noticed it right away like he had radar for that sort of thing."

"He walked right up to the guy and started telling him that he'd been in the front of the house and had watched his perfor-mance. He piled on the praise, but he was so smooth about it that it didn't seem phony. Well, the guy wasn't averse to hearing his praises sung, so he invited Cal out for a drink. You could tell that Cal was thrilled. He was practically glowing. He obviously really got off on this guy, even though the man was way past young and not particularly handsome. He was a damned good actor, however. They spent quite a few evenings together during the course of the run."

Don had other opportunities to observe Cal. "We became friends. I did get him in the sack once, but we got beyond that. He actually wasn't my type, believe it or not. So anyway, we hung out—the techies and apprentices—creating our own society. Most of the locals saw us as just a little too bohemian, so they ba-sically avoided us, except, of course, for the stagestruck among them. The directors and big names who came out to do the star turns were generally polite but distant—except where Cal was concerned.

"Every time the bill would change, and a new group of celebri-ties would show, Cal would check them out carefully. I'll be damned—if anyone could be had, Cal got him. There was this one young actor, drop-dead handsome, macho as hell, who'd just had a huge success on Broadway. A couple of years later he made a big splash out in Hollywood.

"When he arrived with a gorgeous female companion in tow,

Cal got that hungry look in his eye. I said to him, 'No way,' but he just flashed me this little grin and nodded. About a week later, I'm backstage wrestling with a piece of scenery, and I see Cal and this guy talking. A few minutes later the guy's done rehearsing his scene, and I see him heading back to his dressing room. Then I see Cal drop whatever he's been doing and make tracks in the same direction. He knocked on the dressing room door, and the guy let him in. Maybe ten minutes go by, then the gorgeous female companion makes the scene. Well, when she knocked the door didn't open. She gave it a couple more taps, then roared out of the place in a righteous fury. Two days later she blew town, and Cal was having quiet suppers with the guy. He was an operator."

Don considered for a long time before he answered my last question. "Hustling? I don't know, really. I don't think so. It wasn't as if he ever had more money than the rest of us, and we were all pretty much broke all the time. Any time we passed the hat to buy a jug of cheap wine or a pizza, Cal would empty his pockets like the rest of us. I don't ever recall him being particularly flush. It seemed to me that the thrill of having dinner with one of his celebrity dates was all he needed to get out of it. That and the dinner. Besides, I doubt if those guys would've been too pleased if he had put his hand out after they'd spent an evening together. Ego, you know."

After Cal returned to New York City from his stint in summer stock, his theatrical career actually began taking off. He ran into a woman he had met when he first arrived in the city. She was an actress and had exciting news for Cal. "She was in *Pins and Needles* at the Roundabout Theater, which was a house off Broadway," Cal later said. "There was this guy who was leaving the cast to join the company of *Hello Dolly* with Pearl Bailey. Somehow or other I was chosen to replace him." The play, which had received decent reviews when it first opened, ran for a respectable number of performances and gave Cal his first chance to wet his feet in the New York City theater scene.

Second-tier theaters didn't—and don't—pay lavishly, so Cal had to keep scrambling to stay afloat. He kept himself going in the time-honored fashion of most out-of-work actors, dabbling in any venture that might prove lucrative. He worked in sales at Saks Fifth Avenue for a time, then took a doorman's job at Cartier's during the month of December. "It was great fun. They bought me a fabulous Pierre Cardin suit, shirts, ties, the whole bit." Cal was up at the front of the store in all his burnished blond glory watching the well-heeled come and go.

As was so often the case, the well-heeled were also watching him. "I wasn't even shopping," retired Merrill-Lynch executive *Ken Barnhart confided. "I was walking back to the office from lunch when I saw him. I just stopped in the middle of the street and stared. I didn't know how I was going to manage it, but I knew I had to have him." Have him Mr. Barnhart did. He walked into the store, bought an expensive cigar case, and arranged to have it delivered to his Fifth Avenue address. "I tipped the sales clerk generously to make sure that he got the package delivered by the right person. Cal was the doorman, so he wasn't really supposed to be delivering packages. I didn't care, and by the time I finished tucking $20 bills into the clerk's breast pocket, neither did he. Afterward, I stopped by the office to cancel my appointments, then went home to wait. Five minutes after he arrived I knew I had given myself the perfect Christmas present."

After the holidays Cal got a job as a waiter at Serendipity, a New York eatery favored by the beautiful people in the late '60s and the '70s. He worked there off and on for a couple of years. As remembered by Holly Woodlawn in her autobiography, *A Lowlife in High Heels*, "Serendipity was basically an upscale ice cream parlor. It was nestled in the very chic Upper East Side and was largely patronized by the fashion set from *Vogue* and

Harper's Bazaar. The fashions were divine." It was also frequented by Jackie Kennedy, who brought her children in for ice cream sundaes.

The restaurant was a great place for Cal to work. Calvin Holt, one of the owners, took a shine to him and was kind enough to let the young man have extended "leaves" when the need arose. The need arose more than once during the course of his employment as Cal began to fulfill what would become another lifelong obsession—travel.

These weren't just little trips to the beach. This was real travel—to Europe and Hawaii—destinations that were much less commonplace in the mid '60s than they are now and, although less expensive then than now, certainly not free. It doesn't require a degree in accounting to determine that these jaunts weren't financed solely by Cal. He had taught for only a year before moving to New York City. He had spent most of the subsequent time doing summer stock for peanuts, working as a waiter, and scrambling for poorly paid, often unpaid, theatrical gigs. So who paid?

As we have seen, Cal had already begun to engage in what would become his financial mainstay through the years—hustling. His physical beauty, style, and intelligence enabled him to attract men interested in more than a one-night stand—men who could easily afford to pay for it. These men bought Cal perfectly tailored suits and provided chauffeured transportation to elegant dinners in discreet hotel dining rooms, as well as all-expense-paid holidays to Europe.

Cal was employed by an escort service—"hustling occasionally through a madam" as he told an interviewer years later—long before he became famous as Casey Donovan. There is no record of who directed him to this service, but it was discreet and high-class, catering to wealthy gays who wanted more than they could find on even the better streets of the city.

One of these clients, a retired businessman, wanted someone

to accompany him to Hawaii. It was February, the weather was terrible, the expenses were paid, the client was a gentleman—naturally, Cal jumped at the chance. A month in Waikiki was a difficult thing to resist, and Cal wasn't a man to resist pleasure.

A few postcard vignettes hint at a visitor's first glimpse of paradise—palm trees, beaches like warm sugar, first-class living in a hotel on Waikiki. A more in-depth picture emerges when talking to someone who was there and met Cal on the beach. Terry Morgan was a travel agent at the time, taking advantage of a promotional trip organized by a recently opened hotel.

"The first time I saw him was out on the beach," Morgan said. "I was on a beach towel, soaking up some rays, when one of my friends nudged me and told me to check out the goods that were coming along the beach. I propped myself up on my elbows and watched as this really spectacular number strolled by. He was chatting with this older guy, carrying a bag and a beach umbrella. There were quite a few good-looking guys laid out on the sand, but he didn't bat an eye. It was clear that he was devoting every bit of his attention to his companion.

"Well, about two hours later he came wandering back and spread out his towel. He started talking to this really handsome guy, and a few minutes later they packed up and left. The next day, at about the same time, he was back, putting the moves on someone else. As the days went by, he picked us off like birds sitting on a fence." As it turned out, the older guy took a long nap every afternoon, and Cal was putting his time off to good use.

"I saw them together several times, and Cal was always dressed impeccably when he and the older guy were having dinner or sipping cocktails. He was just the perfect gentleman, hanging on every word the older guy said, never letting on that he had the least bit of interest in anyone else in the place. He had style. You could tell that from a mile away. He also had more sexual energy than any one man had a right to."

Cal returned to the mainland tanned and rested. He was also in possession of a nice "thank you" check from his businessman friend. He picked up his tray again and waited tables for a few months, but his wanderlust was not sated. As summer faded into autumn, Cal decided to treat himself, to make the grand tour and see the great cities of Europe.

A number of young American travelers were beginning to descend on Europe, bringing nothing but a guidebook, a backpack and a spirit of adventure with them. This was definitely not Cal's style. Although his spirit of adventure could hardly be faulted, his tastes were far too patrician to be satisfied with a loaf of bread, a jug of wine, and nights spent in a crowded hostel. He had set his sights much higher and prepared himself accordingly.

He may have tucked in one pair of jeans, just in case, but his suitcase was filled with carefully chosen shirts, ties, slacks, and jackets—clothes that would make the right impression on the right people. He purchased his ticket, converted his savings into travelers checks, and set off on yet another adventure into the great world.

Cal had dreamed of just such a trip ever since Helen Van Fleet had opened his eyes to the possibility when he was in high school. He had read about Europe—the history, the art, the architecture, the food—and now he was going to see it for himself. The plane touched down at Heathrow Airport, and Cal hit the ground running.

"Saw Trafalgar Square, Buckingham Palace, Hyde Park and walked along the Thames this morning," he wrote in a postcard. "Visited the Tate Gallery in the afternoon. Tomorrow I plan to launch an assault on the British Museum. So far everything surpasses my wildest dreams." He attacked the London scene with a vengeance, determined to take in everything. Nothing was too grand or too humble to attract his notice. He visited galleries, elegant shops, and palaces during the day, then sat in working-class pubs in the evening, rubbing elbows with the locals as he watched and listened, soaking it all in.

While exploring in the vicinity of Westminster Abbey, he attracted the attention of a well-dressed British man who engaged him in conversation and invited him to a nearby club for a drink. Cal had done his homework well—he chatted knowledgeably with the man about art and music. The drink extended into dinner. The conversation still flowed, and Cal was duly invited to the man's London flat.

Everything clicked—Cal saw to that—and the evening stretched to a week. There were trips to the theater, private homes in the city, even a weekend in the country. Cal was introduced to the man's friends and made an excellent impression. He made many connections that were useful later in life.

When it was time for Cal to continue on his journey, he was given names and numbers of people to contact in other places. Cal's well-heeled host had many well-placed friends—the son of a German industrialist, an expatriate school chum now living in the south of France, an Italian count with a palazzo in Venice— and Cal made plans to visit them all.

And so the tour continued, from capital to capital, sampling all the best that every place had on offer, all of it made more delightful as a result of his "insider" status. He was seeing Europe intimately, experiencing it like a native, not like a tourist. That was easier in the '60s before Americans had clogged every important city and site on the continent. Americans, especially handsome, cultivated specimens like Cal, were rare enough to be considered interesting. They were also refreshingly uninhibited, even in the days before liberation was fully under way. Add to that a degree of naivete, an unjaded enthusiasm for everything that was offered him, and enough sex appeal to vanquish a regiment, and it is easy to understand Cal's appeal. Wherever he went he fit in perfectly. It was as though he absorbed the surroundings, took them in through his pores, and managed to become totally at ease. He had it all—the looks, the charm, the manners—and his trip was a triumph.

Upon his return from this whirlwind of travel and culture, the reality of his life in the United States must have been a bit of a shock. Fortunately, Cal was never one to sit idly by and complain about his situation. He stepped back into his life, got busy, and he found another occupation for which he was imminently suited, an occupation that brought him into close contact with the beautiful people he so greatly admired.

One of his "clients" had suggested that he try his hand at modeling and had steered him to the famed Wilhelmina Agency. It was instantly apparent that he came alive in front of the camera. The flaws in his facial structure—nearly nonexistent cheekbones, and an aquiline nose that curved like the beak of an eagle—faded away, and what remained was the golden boy. Cal Culver photographed as the boy next door, that wholesome, corn-fed icon of all-American male beauty.

His modeling career was almost immediately successful. He pulled down $60 an hour—a princely sum in the late '60s— and did everything from print ads that appeared in *Reader's Digest* to taking flights to Rome to do the Valentino fall collection. He was in mail-order catalogs, *The New York Times* Sunday magazine, on record jackets and book covers, in filmed spots touting the beauty of the Bahamas, and on upscale underwear boxes. As the '60s came to a close, Cal's face was poised to become the face of a new era.

*   *   *

That era was officially inaugurated in the predawn hours of June 28-29, 1969. There was a full moon. Judy Garland had been buried that afternoon, and gays in Greenwich Village were not in the mood to be messed with. The Stonewall Inn at 51 Christopher Street was a dark hole in the wall with a long bar along one side that featured go-go boys in bikinis dancing on either end. It also had a small dance floor and a jukebox. The bar attracted an eclectic crowd—butch guys, preppy boys, older men, a few lesbians, and some so-called "straight" trade for good measure. It was also frequented by streetwise drag queens who had courage, a strong sense of life's injustices, and nothing much to lose.

When the New York City vice cops forced all the patrons out onto the street and attempted to close the place for the illegal sale of alcohol, they were set upon by an outraged crowd of queers, dykes, and street queens who attacked the police with pennies, beer cans, rocks, and even parking meters. After a pitched battle that lasted about 45 minutes, the police retreated inside the bar, which was then set ablaze by the crowd. After the blaze was extinguished and reinforcements were called in, it took several hundred cops two hours to secure the area from a crowd of upward of 1,000 gays. The mayhem was repeated the following night and the modern gay liberation movement was officially launched. A month later gays were marching in the streets beneath banners emblazoned with the slogan "gay power." Gay life—for better and worse—would never be the same.

*   *   *

Street drama wasn't really Cal's thing. He preferred his drama within the confines of the stage. Cal's affinity for the theater was the acting out of a classic gay fantasy à la Ruby Keeler: young man escapes the restrictive life of the small-minded town of his youth and flees to the glamour, sophistication, and bright lights of Broadway where he makes it big. There it didn't matter if you were gay or straight—all that was important was that you had talent and looks. And Cal knew he had both.

*　　*　　*

Gays had been flourishing on Broadway for decades. Playwrights Tennessee Williams, William Inge, Edward Albee and Doric Wilson created many of the milestone works by which the American theater is judged today. In addition, choreographer Jerome Robbins, composer Leonard Bernstein, and lyricist/composer Stephen Sondheim added their genius to the mix through their work on many of the great Broadway musicals. Along the way, these men had long been trying to make points—elliptically, of course—for gay life.

Then in the late '50s and early '60s, there was a backlash against gay playwrights. American culture was on the brink of a social change of unprecedented proportions. Everything that had been viewed as social and political dogma during the former decade was now being openly questioned and, as often as not, rejected. Those who wanted to hold back the forces of change were looking to pin the blame on someone. The arts community was no exception.

Because it was common knowledge that gays were involved in the arts, and because the arts had an important influence on everyone, it was a (barely) credible stretch to suppose that gays were responsible for this unprecedented warping of American society. There was even talk of what some critics styled a "homosexual mafia" controlling the arts world. Formerly sympathetic critics turned on Albee, Williams, and other talented artists, accusing them in so many words of undermining the heterosexual way of life and attempting to subvert American culture.

The artistic response was the creation of a new venue. In addition to the increasingly hostile attitudes of critics and producers, production costs for the mainstream shows had become too exorbitant for their financial backers to take any risks. This had begun to kill the innovative spirit on Broadway. Off-Broadway theaters—galvanized by the Circle in the Square's critically acclaimed 1952 revival of Tennessee Williams's 1948 Broadway flop *Summer and Smoke*—began by presenting revivals and foreign plays. Heartened by early successes, they went on to present plays that were too political or too avant-garde to play uptown. This would soon come to include a great deal of gay-themed theater.

Gay theater really all began when Mort Crowley, a young man from Mississippi, rose to the challenge of Stanley Kauffmann, a straight critic who said the homosexual playwright should "write truthfully of what he knows, rather than try to transform it to a life he does not know, to the detriment of others." The result was his epochal 1968 success *The Boys in the Band*.

That off-Broadway play, despite the pervasive self-loathing of its gay protagonists, was honest and open in its treatment of a certain segment of gay life. It humanized gays, making a plea for understanding and acceptance. It also pried open the closet door, unleashing a subsequent flood of other gay-themed plays. In October of 1969, as his modeling career began to burgeon, Cal was hired as understudy for *And Puppy Dog Tails*—one of the first of these gay-themed plays to hit the boards. Although the play was poorly received by the critics, it ran for 141 performances.

*   *   *

As 1970 rolled around, Cal was modeling full time for Wilhelmina. This, coupled with a bit of flesh peddling, paid the rent, but Cal still wanted to be on the stage—or on the screen—in the spotlight, where he could be seen and admired in the flesh by more than one person at a time.

He pored over the ads in the trade papers, one of which led him to the part of Rodney David Allworth II in the film *Ginger*. The movie, a low-budget James Bond knockoff, had plenty of sex, violence, and a female heroine who spent much of her screen time frolicking in the buff with her equally naked costars. All of the exposed flesh was not, as it turned out, enough to make the film a success. On the bright side for Cal, he managed to garner *Variety's* only positive mention: "Only Calvin Culver as the thrill-seeking jet set blackmailer shows any indication of better things to come." Cal later joked that the mention was nice, but none of those "better things" ever happened to him as a result of the film. "I mean, I couldn't get anybody to go see it. No one would go because it was so bad."

Well, there was one person who went to see it. Cal enjoyed telling the tale of how his mother came down to the city from upstate New York for his film debut. The film's producer was worried that the unworldly Mrs. Culver might be offended by her son's on-screen nudity and took her aside in an attempt to soften the blow. He mentioned the nudity and explained that there were certain explicit things in the picture that might be shocking to her. She looked at the man and replied—"Shocked? I doubt it. Bored, maybe." In fact, she seems to have taken it all very well. "So when I came on the screen nude, she laughed a lot," Cal told an interviewer after *Boys in the Sand* had catapulted him to stardom. "And when it got to the part where I got my balls cut off, she thought that was very funny." Cal's matter-of-fact mother was never particularly impressed by Cal's forays into the glamorous life of stage and film.

Cal didn't have much leisure to think about the dubious quality of his first film. His efforts to break into the business were bearing fruit, and he was working steadily. In March of 1970 he made his Broadway debut in the Robert F. Kennedy Theater for Children production of Joseph Golden's play, *Brave*, at the Anta Theater. This show was a mixed program of music, dance, and mime memorializing the Native American. It was shut down by a newspaper strike after only six performances, so unfortunately, no critic had time to commit his opinions of Cal's Native American impersonation to print.

In April, Cal scored yet again at an audition. Jerry Douglas, best known today as the award-winning director of a number of explicit gay films, was then involved with the off-Broadway theater scene in New York City. He had been called in to rescue an ailing production of *Circle in the Water*, a gay-themed play whose opening-night performance had been so bad that the patrons had stormed the box office to demand their money back. Douglas was frantically rewriting, redirecting, and recasting, and Cal was one of the replacements he hired. Douglas felt that Cal was ideally suited to play the costarring role of a popular young athlete whose physical beauty brings the unspoken sexual tensions among a group of closeted young cadets at a Michigan military academy to a head.

Throughout chaotic weeks of wholesale rewrites and restaging, Cal impressed Douglas as being very professional. "He was never late to rehearsal, was the first to know his lines, and was enormously popular with the other members of the cast." The handsome young actor was also something of a mystery to Douglas: "There was an easygoing charm and affability about him, but he always vanished promptly after each performance, not to be heard from until his next call."

Cal disappeared into his increasingly busy life in New York City—into the photo shoots, the auditions, the bouts of steamy sex with paying customers and with handsome strangers who caught his eye on the streets and in the parks. And when not being admired by the eye of camera, audience, or trick, he was haunting the theaters, concert halls, and galleries, admiring culture, beauty, and the lives of other people, vicariously and alone.

CHAPTER 3

The Birth of Casey

Shortly after *Circle in the Water* closed on June 28, 1970, Cal decided to celebrate a day off from his increasingly rigorous modeling schedule to enjoy a day at the beach. In those days the beach most accessible to gay Manhattanites was at Jacob Riis Park, about an hour's journey by subway and bus. Guys would load up the cooler, take a beach towel, and make a day of it. While he was there that day, Cal met the man who, barring adolescent crushes and youthful flings, would become one of the two major love interests in his life.

"He was frolicking in the waves when I first spied him," retired theatrical agent Ted Wilkins recalled. "I got up off my blanket and went into the water as well. I saw him, he saw me seeing him—and so it went as we rode the waves and cruised. We began chatting, exchanging pertinent information, gauging potential. I was about 13 years older than Cal, which was a plus in his book. He was gorgeous, which was certainly a plus in mine. In short, we became lovers for two years, then remained lifelong friends after that.

"Cal was modeling when we met. And he was still working at Serendipity restaurant, which with its celebrity clientele was perfect for him. He loved rubbing elbows with the rich and famous, but he was just as personable and engaged when he was talking to people at the local market. He could fit in anywhere with ease."

Cal and Ted settled comfortably into an urban lifestyle. Work occupied their days, leaving evenings free to pursue a shared passion—the theater. "We went to the theater a lot," Ted said. "Cal was a great fan of Steven Sondheim, and we always made a point of attending any show that Sondheim had a hand in." When those possibilities had been exhausted, the pair just went right down the list. "I particularly remember a performance of *Pippin* because that was when I first introduced Cal to a man who would later play a very important part in his life. The Tryons were friends of my family, although Tom and I were never close. I heard about him when I was growing up, of course, and met him at functions attended by both the families, but I never knew much about him. We had both been extremely closeted as young men, so there had been no communication on that level.

"During intermission that day, I saw him in the lobby. He came over to chat, and I introduced him to Cal. Cal was with me, and Tom was talking to me, not to Cal. I don't think they exchanged more than a few words. Neither man appeared to be particularly taken with the other." That would come, but later on.

Ted Wilkins realized early on that his relationship with Cal would have to be an open one. "He was totally driven sexually. It was a strange dichotomy. On the one hand he was a very conservative guy; on the other he was an absolute sexual libertine. Shortly after we got together, we were at Riis Park, sunning ourselves on our blanket. Cal got up and told me he was going to the bathroom. Time passed, but he didn't come back. After an hour I got up to go look for him. I was afraid that he might be ill.

"I walked into the bathroom and saw that there was a lineup

of men outside one of the stalls. One fellow walked out, and the next in line walked in. I went over and looked in. There was Cal, sitting on the can, servicing all comers. I have to admit, I was a bit dismayed. Afterward he told me, quite matter-of-factly, that he had done such things before and probably would again. He didn't seem to have much control over it. He was the only person I've ever known who could have a sexual experience with someone for money, then go out immediately afterward looking for more sex just for fun and relaxation."

*   *   *

As the '60s gave way to the '70s, gays, once an invisible minority, were suddenly popping up everywhere—in plays, in books, and on film. For decades, gays had been banned from stage and screen, except for occasional appearances as comic relief. Then as the '70s dawned, homosexuality became box-office chic. Well, chic it may have been, but normal it wasn't. Gay characters were portrayed as disturbed, degenerate, psychopathic, or as comic foils to heterosexual characters. It was to be an entirely different type of film that provided gays with their first cinematic hero.

*   *   *

This hero—in the person of Calvin Culver—would, given the chance, be willing and able to fill the bill. In the late spring of 1971, that chance arose. "I originally did it for the money," Cal admitted to an interviewer in 1973. "I was desperate, and I needed bread, and it was a lot of money at the time—$125 a day. That's a lot of bread. A lot of people are lucky to make that in two weeks."

It all started when Cal got a call from a woman he had worked with in *Ginger*. "She'd do anything for money, and she and her boyfriend were very into fuck movies. And she called one day and said she knew a guy who was making a porno film, and the guy who was supposed to have the lead (who was to play a character named Casey) chickened out at the last minute, leaving the director in a fierce mess, and she thought I'd be perfect for the movie. She asked me if I'd be interested in reading for the part. I mean, I had no money—no money—at that time." There was money to be made, so Cal said yes.

What he agreed to was *Casey*, a low-budget, gay hard-core film, shot on location in suburban New Jersey. He said yes on Tuesday, and the film was to begin shooting on the following Saturday. Cal went to meet the director in an apartment on the West Side. "I read through the script, just dialogue; he never asked me to take my clothes off or to see any part of my body. And while this was going on, a girl who had been one of my students at Ethical Culture burst into the room. She and her mother lived in the apartment, and this gay man who was making the film was staying with them. Small world, huh? Anyway, I got the part—$500 for four days work. That's how 'Casey' was born."

As it turned out it was a rather difficult birth. Ted Wilkins was on hand to watch. "*Casey* was a real trip for Cal. He didn't really know what he was getting into. He would come home at night and talk about performing in front of this crew, all of whom were really straight. He had to do sexual things both to and in front of straight guys, and I think it was a bit overwhelming for him."

The other cast members were extremely inhibited about performing sexually in front of a camera, and it was left up to Cal to encourage them. "Now I had to produce a hard-on and perform, really fuck for my supper. One kid turned out to be married and was very straight. I don't think he'd ever been involved with a guy before and was obviously doing it for the money. And I thought, 'Wow, you know, come on, if you're going to do it, be into doing it, because if you're not, you're gonna look terrible.' But he was cast, so what could I do? And there was another guy who was very uptight, and the problem was my having to make them look good." The inhibitions show—most of the sex is simulated—and Cal provided most of the hard-ons seen on the screen.

And the result? Aside from Cal's timelessly watchable good looks, there was his performance. It was a tour de force of its type. Cal not only plays the callow hero, but he also plays the role of Wanda Uptight, his own fairy godmother. "It was madness on that set. I played my alter ego; I played my fairy godmother in drag. I looked just like Doris Day shot through linoleum, it was just incredible." Incredible it certainly was—our hero in a cheap brown wig, a rhinestone tiara, and eyeliner. He played the role to the hilt without a trace of embarrassment, making it one of the more memorable star turns in the history of porn films.

In *Casey*, Cal portrays a man who has grown bored with sport-fucking his way through all the available male flesh on the eastern seaboard. He gets all the sex he wants, but he's looking for something more fulfilling. When he wanders into the bathroom to clean up after a JO session and smokes a joint, Wanda, his flamboyant alter ego, appears before him and offers to grant him his most cherished sexual wishes. "Perhaps," he suggests modestly, "someone who will like me and someone I will like."

"So," Wanda asks him, "what do you want?" Casey replies that he wants to be recognized. Wanda generously grants his wish. "Everyone will recognize you. Everyone will want you." Wanda waves her magic wand, and within minutes he has them coming through the doors, literally. Menacing music fills the sound track, and a faceless man in rubber boots makes the scene. The two sit opposite one another in the living room, then Casey makes a dive for the man's crotch. The plot indicates that the intimacy is nil, leaving poor Casey more alone than ever. In actuality, the sex is nonexistent—the rubber-boot man fails to achieve erection, and the money shot looks suspiciously like hand lotion.

Reinforcements, however, are on the way. Moments later another young man arrives on the scene delivering potatoes and beer to Casey. He announces that "potatoes make me horny," and falls to the floor with Casey for a frantic roll in the spuds. Almost immediately after they finish, the rubber-boot man returns and simulates anal intercourse with Casey. "Would you like me if you couldn't fuck me?" Casey asks plaintively. "You talk too much," the rubber-boot man replies gruffly, defining at least one of the views of romance espoused by gay hedonists as they blazed the trails of sexual emancipation.

Casey soon goes back to Wanda and asks to be irresistible. He almost immediately finds a devoted lover. In an interesting bow to topicality, the lover is a young hippie who has taken a vow of silence until the Vietnam War ends, a plot point that is almost immediately jettisoned. The pair settle into a summer of domestic bliss. Unfortunately, this state of grace palls just as everything else has, and Casey convinces his lover that they need company. During the ensuing orgy with the boot man and Mr. Potato, Casey is the center of attention, at least for a time. All of his former conquests converge to show him what tender loving care is, yet ironically Casey is left all alone in the living room at the end, a victim of his own promiscuity. The film turns out to be a parable of the dilemma that would be faced by many gay males in the 1970s—settle down in a monogamous relationship or play the field, moving from man to man like a bee in a field of clover? It was a conundrum that helped shape the course of the era.

Cal walked away from this project with some explicit film experience under his belt and with the all-important $500 in his pocket. He had also acquired the name that he was soon to make famous. "I wanted another name to use for these hard-core jobs because I was modeling by then, and, of course, there was my family to consider. I didn't want to blow anything at that point." He knew full well that his folks and his brother wouldn't care to have the family name emblazoned above Cal's erect penis. They had all seen him cavorting naked onstage and on-screen in non-explicit performances, but there were limits.

The last name came to him first. "One day when we were filming, the radio was on and this Donovan song came on the radio. I thought, 'Donovan, that's kind of a neat name.'" He tried it out in the credits of *Casey*, appearing as Ken Donovan. Once the film itself had been completed, he took the name of its eponymous hero. It was, after all, more or less all about Cal and his lifestyle, so why not? And so Casey Donovan was born.

The movie, which got widespread distribution only after the release of *Boys in the Sand*, actually received serious critical attention in the gay press. It was considered one of the better efforts in the genre up to that time. A March 1, 1972, review in *The Advocate* called it, "a serious attempt to produce the definitive fuck film for gays." Another reviewer gave it a "three hard-on rating" and yet another claimed that "in the final analysis, it can be said that *Casey* offers a fuck film well above what has thus far been available." That, given the tepid sex play, the ghastly sets and—with the exception of the star—the zombie level of the acting, seems a bit hard to believe. Some context may make these reactions more understandable.

*   *   *

The gay sense of the erotic is not solely a product of the post-Stonewall era. Erotic photographs of naked males posed singly and in pairs begin to crop up as early as 1850, only a few years after the invention of the camera, and sex films followed soon after the first public showing of moving pictures in 1894. Gay-oriented photographs cover the entire spectrum of gay eroticism—young boys in classical poses, rough workingmen, men in drag, depictions of autofellatio, anal and oral intercourse, group sex, and nearly any other species of gay eroto-pleasure that can be imagined. There are many fewer films, however, and their range is much more limited.

A "stag film" has been defined by gay-film historian Tom Waugh as "an explicit sexual narrative, produced and distributed, usually commercially, to clandestine, non-theatrical male audiences…principally in Europe and the Americas." In the early decades of the century, there were traveling projectionists who went from town to town in the United States showing films, usually to men's clubs such as the Shriners at one of their "smokers." These evenings often served as the initiation of young, heterosexual males to the world of sex. For young men in the audience with same-sex longings, the exposure to gay sex techniques would have occurred only as a matter of chance.

Of the approximately 2,000 stag films that were made between the year 1908 and the hard-core theatrical explosion of 1970, about 15 depict a significant amount of male-on-male sexual activity. In these films the gay subplots are secondary to the main attraction, which is almost invariably heterosexual intercourse. In *The Exclusive Sailor* (1923-25), for example, an officer sees a sailor having sex with a lady and demands to fuck both of them as a punishment. Neither of them objects to this arrangement. In a French film, *Le Telegraphist* (1921-25), a husband catches his wife and the telegraph boy making it. The husband joins the fray, fucking the boy after the boy sucks him. In these and other similar scenarios, the gay subplots are rooted in rigid role-playing and often incorporate the idea of active anal intercourse as a sort of punishment of the passive partner. For the record, however, the passive partners show no distress and take their "punishments" quite gamely.

One of the reasons for this state of affairs is the lack of an organized gay audience for sex films during the early years of the century. Gay culture was almost exclusively underground, and even in large cities with substantial gay populations such as New York and Berlin, the audience was not large or stable enough to permit its becoming a viable market for anything as relatively expensive as a stag film. Wealthy patrons for gay films may have existed, but organizing a large-scale showing of a gay film would have been too dangerous to contemplate. The pickings were slim and not available to most gay men.

The necessity of a closeted existence in the decades prior to Stonewall made some needs—particularly sex—even more urgent. What couldn't easily and safely be enjoyed in person would be sought in other ways. Hard-core pornographic materials—visual and print—were difficult to obtain, often of dubious quality, and dangerous to possess. There are virtually no records regarding the production and marketing of commercial gay hard-core during this era, except to say that it was disorganized, unprofitable, and usually hit-and-miss. Explicitly sexual photos were rare compared to physique nudes and beefcake. Although illegal, heterosexual sex films were tolerated. Homosexual hard-core, however, was not. Aside from the explicit home movies now in the possession of the Kinsey Institute and the very few fleeting images of gay sex in the stag films, cinematic sex between males prior to 1960 was largely nonexistent. From the decade after 1960, about 30 all-male stags have come to light, most of which were most likely sold for home consumption in eight-millimeter versions, rather than seen in public venues.

What emerged in its place was a gay-oriented cinema that suggested sex but didn't show it. Enter Bob Mizer and the "Athletic Model Guild," which he founded in 1945. "I wanted a great build," he once told an interviewer. "I couldn't get one, so I set out to glorify guys with great builds." Mizer popularized the view of the ideal male not as a lithe youth or pensive scholar but as a butch, tightly muscled young man who bore no resemblance to the effeminate queen who kept on getting his unfortunate ass arrested in the real world when he dared show his less-than-butch face. It is this view of the male as an amalgam of swollen muscles—and organs—that has dominated gay erotica ever since.

Mizer began with photography, then moved into the world of the eight-millimeter silent short film. A typical Mizer feature required two or three fresh-faced, well-muscled hunks, dressed in whatever tight-fitting or skimpy costume had caught Mizer's fancy that day. These men then wandered onto a slapped-together set reminiscent of a locker room, a Roman bath, a college dormitory, or a construction site. The cameras would roll, and within two or three minutes, the actors would be peeled down to posing straps, smiling and wrestling in invariably erotic poses. Perhaps his greatest claim to genius was his ability to recruit incredibly hot young men for his films—mostly avowedly straight men who likely wouldn't have recognized a homosexual if one spoke to them—and then cajole them into playing at being gay themselves. Even the most naive among them can hardly have failed to realize what was going on by the time the director had wrapped up a shoot. There were some risks involved—a California fireman actually lost his job over a series of physique photographs—but the pool of available men was dazzling.

Mizer was fearless, shipping his films through the mail to his list of customers at a time when gay freedom of expression was at its nadir. When vice cops, city attorneys, and homophobes tried to stop him, he took them all on and ultimately won, paving the way for all those who followed him.

Another pioneer of the gay erotic cinema was Richard Fontaine, the man behind Zenith Films. He created short silent films with gorgeous men and coy bits of dialogue on reader cards—"I'm really stiff," one muscled hunk complains to a buddy.

"I'll rub you down," his equally buffed pal replies—that pointed those in the know to the subtext underlying the innocuous plots.

Physique films were the order of the day and had evocative titles such as *Days of the Greek Gods, Slaves of Empire, Shore Leave Olympiad, Cellblock,* and *The Captives.* Greek gods, models, sailors, and athletes were the subjects, flexing and posing, their muscles glistening with oil, their genitals cozily tucked into posing straps. The men stare and strut and posture, their hidden cocks and balls more potent than if they had been visible.

In the earliest of these films, the men appear alone, sleeping, stretching, and dressing and undressing for exercise and showers—lots of showers. Bare butts are legal and are often the point of focus. The forbidden cocks are almost-but-not-quite visible at least twice a minute, hidden only by split-second lifting of towels, turns of body, cupping of hands, changes of camera angles. It is the ultimate tease, delicious as a buildup, but incredibly frustrating when served as the main course. One can almost hear the lonely men who purchased these shorts in the '50s gnashing their teeth in frustration as the reel comes to a close. The only solution would have been to spin a continuing fantasy with the handsome man from the film emblazoned in the imagination.

As time went by, solo appearances gave way to groups, still often disguised as Roman centurions, Greek gods, or noble captives destined for the slave markets. This made some sense of one man stripping another down to his posing strap, then performing an up close examination of his nearly naked body from every possible angle. Another popular scenario called for a lonely guy who couldn't get to sleep to call up a buddy and invite him over for a bit of wrestling. Over comes the buddy, and off come the clothes, revealing the ubiquitous posing straps. After a session of grappling on the floor, belly to belly, biceps flexing, ass cheeks twitching, the guys would shower to cool off, then sprawl back on a bed to share a beer and a coy glance.

The tension in some of these shorts is palpable as these men touch, rub, and wrestle, flesh on flesh, cock separated from belly or thigh by only a scrap of fabric, never seen, never hard. The camp costumes and Styrofoam columns in the films patterned after the Hollywood epics fail to detract from the distinct eroticism of the situations. Although nothing overtly sexual ever occurs, the undercurrent of sex makes it quite clear what happens after they walk off into the distance arm in arm. It was painfully obvious to those left behind in the dark that when the cameraman stopped cranking the fun was just beginning.

Many of these homoerotic shorts explored the imagery of fetish, depicting leatherboys and street toughs who frequently got their comeuppance at the hard, heavy hands of a half-naked, hairy-chested, muscle-bound, macho-daddy type. A few of these films, such as Jean Genet's *Un Chant d'Amour* (1950) and Kenneth Anger's *Fireworks* (1947) and *Scorpio Rising* (1963), went on to attain true cult status. *Scorpio Rising* was especially important because it was the first film that reflected the artistic sensibilities that soon gave rise to pop art. Andy Warhol was particularly indebted to Anger.

In the early '60s several court rulings were delivered that had a definite impact on gay erotica. In June of 1962 the Supreme Court decided the case of MANual V. Day. The magazine *MANual* was being sued for publishing obscene pictures, and the court ruled that "these portrayals of the male nude cannot fairly be regarded as more objectionable than many portrayals of the female nude that society tolerates. Of course not every portrayal of male or female nudity is obscene....[The material was] dismally unpleasant, uncouth, and tawdry...[but] lacked patent offensiveness."

Although it wasn't openly stated, the ruling recognized that homosexuals were a legitimate audience for erotic magazines. This ruling called off the censors at the U.S. post office and helped to ease the paranoid atmosphere surrounding the whole idea of gay erotica. The ruling also opened the door for magazines to become increasingly explicit and, in some cases, downright raunchy.

In 1965 full-frontal nudity appeared for the first time in magazines and mail-order photos. In 1967, the year in which Colt Studios was founded, the last legal skirmish took place before the floodgates were finally opened. A magazine was prosecuted for frontal nudity, and all charges were dismissed. The judge determined that the material wasn't obscene simply because it might be aimed at a gay audience. The judge offered this groundbreaking opinion: "The rights of minorities expressed individually in sexual groups or otherwise must be respected. With increasing research and study we will in the future come to a better understanding of ourselves, sexual deviants and others."

In 1967 Richard Fontaine put a graceful period to this coy era of filmmaking with his 15-minute silent drama, "Cellmates." Although it has full-frontal nudity, it sticks very closely to the old physique formula. The protagonists meet when the younger man is tossed into the cell with the older man. Foreplay consists of a slow strip and a vigorous series of push-ups performed by the younger man at the feet of his new cell mate. The climax is reached when the older man pulls the younger up to the bed, and the two of them share a lingering kiss. Although neither man achieves erection, their cocks grow noticeably before the fade-out. The touch, the kiss, the tumescence—it was the final hurrah for a way of eros that had kept the flame alive for more than two decades.

*   *   *

Pat Rocco, known as the Cecil B. DeMille of male films—not to mention the king of the "danglies" (full-frontal nudity, but no erections)—was instrumental in helping to develop a theatrical audience for gay porn. In June of 1968 at the Park Cinema in Los Angeles, the first exhibition of a gay film in a theater took place. Although laughably tame in light of today's almost clinical hard-core, the premiere was seen as so sensational that it was covered by *Variety*, hyped by klieg lights and limos, and attended by Rocco's own mother.

Rocco didn't make porn, or even approve of it, but he provided the stimulus for much of what followed in the '70s. He created gay films that were designed to show off the beauty of the youthful male physique. "I started a whole new revolution in films, and other people jumped on the bandwagon, started making films with male nudity...People couldn't believe it was happening...Nobody thought that anybody would go into male films." At the time, the very idea of two males kissing was considered so daring that on the opening night of a film celebrating just that, Rocco had lawyers present in the audience.

In general, his films dealt with the concept of coming out and the acceptance of being gay. They were designed to help the men who "kept thinking that not just gay life but they themselves were dirty for being what they were. I've tried to present in many of the films that it's not so. You're a human being like everybody else, and you've a right to enjoy life in your own lifestyle as you please."

On September 30, 1970, the Commission on Pornography and Obscenity, which had been authorized to investigate the topic by the U.S. senate in 1967, came back with its verdict. The commission recommended that "federal, state, and local legislation prohibiting the sale, exhibition, or distribution of sexual materials to consenting adults be repealed." President Nixon and the Senate rejected the report in horror, but the floodgates were opened, and the hard-core porn industry grew rapidly.

*   *   *

With the advent of the "danglie" films, there was more reticence on the part of many actors to perform nude, and young street kids were often recruited to fill the void. According to Barry Knight of Jaguar Productions, a major hard-core film studio from the early '70s, central casting in those days—at least in Los Angeles—was The Gold Cup, a restaurant on the corner of Hollywood Boulevard and Las Palmas. When a filmmaker needed an actor, he would drop by and check out the available talent. The other reliable source of youthful performers was the huge pool of hitchhikers who poured into Los Angeles in the late '60s and were looking for ways to make a quick buck. Their youth and enthusiasm recommended them to many, but these youngsters didn't really embody the accepted fantasy of gay "man sex" as it had been developed by Mizer, Fontaine, and others during the course of the preceding decades.

The underground gay hard-core that began to proliferate in the late '60s was generally devoid of any artistic or sexual energy. Many of these productions are painful to watch, featuring furtive performers hiding behind dark glasses or pulled-down hats, pitifully anxious to get their rocks off so that the whole sordid mess could come to an end.

There was definitely a gap in the fantasy fabric of gay life. When Cal/Casey came along—an adult, handsome man of 27—he found his niche and helped to fulfill this pent-up demand for mature, masculine-acting, porn actors. This was at least a part of the reason for his spectacular success and his meteoric rise to gay superstardom.

*   *   *

After his brief break in scenic suburban New Jersey, Cal returned to his life in Manhattan—still chronically short of cash, still looking for fame. He was continuing with his modeling and waiting tables. Ted Wilkins was doing his best to help, making it a point to introduce Cal to people who were able to boost his budding career.

One of the men Wilkins introduced Cal to was Roy Blakey, one of the photographers responsible for the luminous photographs of Cal that would soon appear in *After Dark* magazine and elsewhere. It was Blakey who would ultimately create Cal's all-time favorite image of himself, one he used on his business cards in later years and marketed as a poster in the late '70s.

Interestingly, for a man to whom image was everything, Cal didn't initially display much interest in being photographed. "We met before *Boys in the Sand* made him famous," Blakey told me. "Ted had filled me in, so I knew a little bit about him. When we met, I also realized that I had seen him at a party on 72nd Street. It was a huge old apartment. Everyone was dancing. He was down in the middle of the dancers, standing out like a peacock in a field of crows. I left because I thought the floor would collapse. I was really struck by him. He was dazzling, so charming and boyish. Years later, in the mid '80s, I was walking along Tenth Avenue, and I saw this gorgeous young man approaching me. As he got closer, I saw that it was Cal. I was struck at the time by his seeming immunity to aging and change. It reminded me a bit of Oscar Wilde's tale of Dorian Gray." Cal actually once joked in an interview that he sometimes felt like Dorian Gray and that he was "afraid to see my picture up in the attic."

Wilkins introduced the two men. "Ted said to Cal, 'You know, Roy should do some pictures.' Cal smiled politely but he certainly didn't jump at the opportunity," Blakey recalled. He changed his mind not long thereafter, and Blakey produced a series of shots that captured Cal's special allure—that of the boy next door who needs only a quick caress to transform himself into a high-powered, insatiable sex machine, capable of fulfilling any man's wildest fantasies. These images capture the Casey

Donovan mystique—the lean, taut physique, coupled with the boyish gleam in the eye, that conveyed Cal's sheer delight that his fate has landed him in the midst of all this glamour. It was an innocence that he never totally lost throughout his career as a sex object to the masses.

Blakey recognized this quality in Cal. "He was naive for a person who made porn and led the lifestyle. One of his favorite things was a coffee-table book of Norman Rockwell paintings. He really loved that sort of art. He somehow remained untouched by the porn world he was a part of."

*　　*　　*

Untouched Cal may have seemed, but he was just about to burst on the scene and shake the porn world to its very foundations.

CHAPTER 4

Boys in the Sand

Shortly after finishing work on Casey, Cal was out on Fire Island with Ted Wilkins. "We were off to the beach again," Wilkins said. "We had some friends who had taken a share in a house at Fire Island Pines for the summer. They asked Calvin and me if we wanted to buy two weeks of that time. We said sure. I took my vacation, and Calvin got time off as well."

Almost immediately after they arrived, Cal was involved in a project. Calvin Holt, one of his bosses at Serendipity was producing a little film comedy. "It was called *Dragula*," Cal told Rob Richards years later. "I played the son of Dragula in it." Ted remembered the episode as well. "I even remember the house where they filmed the piece. It was in Cherry Grove, the last house on the beach. It was a takeoff on *Dracula*, of course. It wasn't pornographic, but Cal may very well have appeared naked in it. I don't remember ever seeing the finished product." It was, by all accounts, basically a home movie.

Of much greater importance to Cal's future was another "home movie" looming on the horizon. On one languorous, sultry evening while Cal was wandering along the beach, he saw Joe Nelson, a friend and former trick who was then dancing in the Stephen Sondheim musical *Follies,* and they started talking. During the course of their conversation, Joe casually mentioned that he knew someone who was working on an experimental film. "It's just a home movie. They need some bodies." Cal had the body, and the idea of appearing before the cameras again intrigued him. Cal now had his modeling career to consider, and it was clear that a porn film was *not* the type of exposure he needed. Nevertheless, he took the filmmaker's name and phone number, then made what proved to be a fateful call. After all, it was only a home movie.

*   *   *

This little "home movie" was fated to set many forces in motion. The legal hurdles to film pornography had been dismantled by the courts in the previous few years, and nothing remained but some catalyst that would start the reaction. Directors had been churning out heterosexual soft-core for years, beginning with nudist films in the 1950s and moving on into the Russ Meyers era of the "nudie-cutie" films that featured lots of bare flesh but no sex. Director Radley Metzger, who would soon work with Cal, upped the stakes with his lushly produced soft-core films, often featuring artistic lesbian encounters. What the erotic movie audience wanted, however, was movies that showed real, not simulated, sex. Needless to say, the gay audience wanted that to be homo sex.

Ever since the 1969 explosion of gay hard-core, gay film had been in search of a direction. The original hard-core loops were indisputably sleazy. These features had been quickly and cheaply made, and it showed. There was little imagination and certainly no art in these early efforts. The fact that the acts portrayed were same-sex was incidental to the mechanics—erection, insertion, money shot—and there was no effort to portray any of the psychological ramifications of homosexuality.

There had been a few notable attempts to break out of this mold. In 1970 the classic soft-core film *Song of the Loon* was released. An earnest tale of love and brotherhood among men, the film made a real effort to validate same-sex affection. In that same year *Meat Rack*, a series of sexual encounters between a bisexual San Francisco hustler and his clients was released, giving a fairly honest portrayal of life in gay San Francisco at the dawn of the Stonewall era. The following year, *Pink Narcissus* hit the screen. This hybrid cross of gay porn and underground art details the erotic fantasies of a teenage boy poised at the threshold of manhood. The film, although sympathetic to its protagonist, draws its tone and motive force from an era prior to gay liberation. What was needed was a good, modern, message-positive gay film that would plant the hero firmly on the side of the new values that were being spoken aloud.

*   *   *

Poole provided that homo sex in a classy wrapper. "I think, without tooting our own horn, that we're responsible for half of the revolution that's going on now," he told an interviewer at the time. "I think everything is a progression, and we were just that little tiny cornerstone. *Deep Throat* couldn't have happened without us. I firmly believe that." His film hit streets that had been cleared by the courts for action. It was one of the opening shots in an unprecedented assault on the great gray wall of moral and social conservatism that had set the standards to which everyone adhered. If it didn't blow this wall down, it certainly marked it. Gay sex was suddenly out of the closet, captured on film in a sizzling how-to-do-it piece that helped to define the era's hedonism.

*　　*　　*

Wakefield Poole was born in Jacksonville, Florida, during the 1930s. "I don't know the exact year," he once told an interviewer. "I don't think about that anymore." Although his film experience was virtually nonexistent prior to his precedent-setting directorial debut as the force behind *Boys in the Sand*, Poole was certainly no stranger to show business. "I was a performer since I was about 4 years old, singing, dancing, acting—all that stuff."

After he graduated from high school, Poole got it into his head that he wanted to be a ballet dancer. He proved to be a quick study—after only nine months of classes in New York City, he joined the Ballet Russe de Monte Carlo. He performed with that troupe for the 1958 and 1959 season, then joined Rod Alexander's "Dance Jubilee," a dance company that toured Asia under the auspices of the State Department.

When he returned to New York City, he gravitated to Broadway, dancing in such shows as *The Unsinkable Molly Brown, Tenderloin,* and *West Side Story*. He also danced in summer stock and on television as a regular on the *Garry Moore Show*, a popular variety program that gave Carol Burnett her start in the business. Other television gigs included a couple of appearances on *The Ed Sullivan Show* and a special he staged for famed American ballet dancer Edward Villella using six videotape machines, something no one else had ever tried before. He also worked as a choreographer on such shows as *No Strings, George M,* and *Do I Hear a Waltz;* directed the London production of *No Strings;* and staged Phyllis Diller's television show for 26 weeks.

Although he was a gay man, there was nothing in his career to suggest that Poole was destined to become the godfather of contemporary gay pornography. "I had it in my head that I was going to be a Broadway director-choreographer, and that's what I was striving for. I knocked around the theater for a long time, trying to get a break, trying to get a good property." Not an easy task without all the proper connections, especially at a time when the Broadway theater scene was so markedly homophobic. In the summer of 1971, Poole "was really at the end of my career as far as I was concerned." At the end of one phase of his career, perhaps, but already poised to begin another.

Poole had at least a nodding familiarity with film. He had shot more than 25,000 feet of it during his State Department–sponsored dance tour of Asia on a home-movie camera and had learned to edit film while doing shows at New York City's Triton Gallery in 1970-71. Still he had never thought of himself as a filmmaker. "This thing had been there all the time...but I had those blinders on. Suddenly all this came bubbling to the surface, and now I can relax. I can just make movies."

All it took was a single viewing of *Highway Hustler*, a dreary bit of homosexual hard-core, to put Poole over the edge and into the history books. After two hours in the stale confines of the Park-Miller theater, Poole felt as though he had been taken. "There was no challenge to the head at all—I was not allowed, or not asked, to bring anything to that film. I was only there to open my eyes and look." What he saw wasn't particularly pretty—"it was a piece of shit we were looking at"—so Poole set out to see if he could do better.

At first it was to be nothing more than a joke—a short home movie to prove to his friends that he could indeed exceed the level of heat generated by the likes of *Highway Hustler*. With that in mind, Poole and his lover, Peter Fisk, enlisted a third man and headed to Fire Island with a camera. The script was only an idea in Poole's head. It was to be a ten-minute film built around a gay encounter—hard-core eroticism with a bit of suspense thrown in for good measure.

"It was really just done out of fun, you know?" Perhaps, but the fun looked great on film. So good in fact that Poole and his friend Marvin Shulman formed Poolemar Productions with the idea of shooting two more segments. If all went according to plan, they looked forward to the possibility of a theatrical release.

Two more segments required more actors, so Poole put the word out among his friends. "Joe Nelson turned me on to Cal. I told him what I was up to, and he said he had just the person I needed. He and Cal had tricked, so Joe knew how hot Cal was." During a party out at The Pines on Fire Island, Poole showed the raw footage of the original first scene featuring his lover. Cal was there that night and was entranced.

"It was just fabulous," he later told an interviewer. "It was incredible. Brilliantly done, so lush and so tasteful, the most different thing I'd ever seen. I was impressed." So impressed, as Poole remembers it, that he stood up and shouted: "I love it! I'll do anything you want me to do." Cal later said he told Poole that he didn't have to be paid, although he was paid—including a $500 bonus and a check every time the film grossed an additional $12,000, which had been the original cost of the movie and promotional expenses.

What Poole originally wanted was for Cal to costar with Tommy Moore, who is featured as the black telephone repairman in what ultimately became the final segment. As Poole was preparing to shoot this scene, the fellow who had costarred in the first episode learned that the film was to be distributed theatrically and wouldn't sign the release forms. "He suddenly pulled a whole switch; he wanted a lot of money that we didn't have. He'd get paid for his work, but he suddenly saw a chance to demand 20% of our profits." Poole was not going to have any of that. "So I said, you know, 'Fuck you. I'll do it over, you know, double fuck you.'" He scrapped the original "Bayside" footage and reshot with Peter Fisk and Cal.

The results were delicious—by turns artistic, tender, and incredibly sexy. Cal was so good that Poole was struck with a new inspiration: "I decided to use him for the other two scenes to make a connecting line, and it worked." A near-disaster was averted, and Poole's perseverance resulted in three hot sex scenes that would define industry standards for decades to come.

As *Boys in the Sand* opens, the waves are lapping at Casey Donovan's name, which has been crudely carved into the sand with a stick. The music of Debussy plays on the sound track, and Peter Fisk, lean, brunet, and sexy, is seen walking along a boardwalk, out to the wooded shore. There is a lyrical quality to the film as the camera moves deep into the shadows of the woods. Fisk sits on the shore, alone and pensive, and looks out to sea. The camera pans to the water, and at the point where sea and sky merge, the figure of a man appears, golden and naked. In that moment Cal Culver as Casey Donovan achieved a kind of immortality.

Cal runs to the shore and couples with Fisk. The two men, one dark and smooth, the other blond and hairy, are perfect foils, their lean bodies fitting perfectly in every position. The camera dances around them as they kiss, the intensity building slowly as they begin to devour one another with eyes and mouths. There is a definite voyeuristic sense that the camera has happened upon two men having sex, not that they are performing for the camera. It is quite clear that the two are turned on—in the extreme—by each other. There is nothing furtive in the scene, absolutely nothing faked.

Whenever the camera focuses on Cal's face, one is startled by the sheer beauty of the man. The intensity of his gaze makes it clear that he is totally involved in the sex and in his partner. The pulse of the scene quickens as Cal mounts Fisk. The actual coupling is brief, then Cal straddles his partner's chest and shoots on his face. Afterward, Fisk puts his own cock strap on Cal's wrist and runs back out into the sea. Cal, left alone, dresses in Fisk's clothes and walks back to the reality of the boardwalk.

"Poolside" with Danny Di Ciccicio is the central episode, a humorous scene with less romance and more raunch than the opening. Cal, alone and lonely, sends for mail-order fulfillment. It arrives in the form of a large pill that, when tossed into Cal's pool, becomes a long, lean, tightly muscled man. Cal's delighted expression when Di Ciccicio emerges from the water makes one believe that the magic in that pill was very real indeed.

This time the sex is rawer, more frantic. The camera jumps around, spying on them through bushes and deck chairs as they couple in every possible combination. Their lithe bodies twine together in carefully choreographed poses that betray Poole's background. The stylized effect of the perfect symmetry is aesthetically quite pleasing. They take turns topping one another, then slide back into the pool. There is no sign of the now-obligatory money shot from either man.

In "Inside," the third and final scene, Cal and Tommy Moore almost set the world on fire. The sex is straightforward, raw, and spectacularly hard-core. Shot indoors, there are no shadows to mask the bare bodies as they couple. Based on their physical responses, there is no doubt that the two are totally aroused by one another.

Once again Cal is alone. He sees Moore out in the street beneath his bedroom windows and begins to fantasize about him. As he snorts poppers and fondles a long black dildo, Cal imagines sex with Moore, devouring his prick and invading every orifice of his slender body. Then Moore turns the tables. For one brief scene lasting mere seconds, he fists Cal. The expression on Cal's face—eyes wide, teeth bared—reveals the animal behind the classically handsome face. The scene switches, and the two men stand and fuck, generating a level of sexual heat rarely equaled on-screen. The film ends as the repairman appears at Cal's door in the flesh, allowing the viewer to imagine whatever delights he chooses.

This last sequence was quite controversial at the time and remained one of Cal's favorites in all of his films. "It was very relaxed and very hot. It worked so well because there was a lot of trust between us. When the film came out, here I was, the Mary Pickford of porn, the new star, the all-American boy, having hard-core sex on-screen with a black man. Some people were outraged. It hadn't happened on the screen before, and a lot of people at the time couldn't handle the fact that this blond, blue-eyed 'preppie' was getting it on with a black man."

Through it all, Cal's partner Ted Wilkins was remarkably unruffled. "Every morning I'd pack his lunch for him, and he'd go off to do *Boys in the Sand*. It's true. He'd come back in the evenings, and we'd be together at night." Cal confirmed the odd story in one of his interviews with pal Rob Richards. "Ted tells the story about how I would leave in the morning, kiss him and say, 'Goodbye, dear, I'm off to work,' and away I'd go to make one of my little porno films. He was wonderful—just the best attitude! He never made a big thing of it because he understood I was having fun."

The three sequences of *Boys* were created on three successive August weekends, none of it scripted out in advance. In fact, Poole improvised everything he wanted to do. "The night before I was going to shoot, I'd go off by myself, maybe cook a lot of food because I think best when I'm doing something." Much of the success of the film was based on this casual approach to the filming and to the obvious chemistry between the performers. Cal was wildly enthusiastic about his costars. When he learned that Poole had asked Danny Di Ciccicio to do "Poolside," he was ecstatic: "My God, we've cruised each other for two years—finally, I'm going to get that guy in bed!" Cal and Tommy Moore had tangled before as well, but both were obviously more than ready to go at it again. "Tommy and I had fucked privately a couple of weeks before, and he was so hot that I recommended him for the job."

Poole was quick to give Cal a lion's share of the credit: "He was so natural, never rushed anything. I could tell him something to do, and it was done very slowly and deliberately. He had a sort of magic that made it all work. He was genuine and real, and he had a wonderful quality about him. He loved sex—there's no doubt about that when you see the film. He loved doing it on-screen." Cal was equally quick to respond, praising his "marvelous working relationship with Wake. I knew where his head was at. I knew what he was trying to do. I really owe it all to Wakefield. I simply trusted him. And I think that's why it worked, because I did have this great trust in him."

Even after the footage had been shot, there was no clear-cut plan to do anything with it. Cal returned to New York City with Ted and resumed his modeling career and his work as a waiter. Poole set the film aside, not even looking at it until the end of September. When he did pull it out and looked at the rushes, he realized that he had captured something extraordinary in his camera's lens. Poole started cutting the film, hoping to piece it together into a viable whole.

He soon realized that he needed professional help. He took the film to a lab and asked for their help. "I said, 'Look, I've got a movie here, and I don't know what to do with it.' I told them it was already cut, and they blanched. They said, 'You mean you cut your original footage?' and I said, 'Yeah,' and they said, 'You've got some balls.'" Luckily, the men were sympathetic to Poole's admission that he didn't have a clue what he was doing, so they took his work on as an interesting project. "They put it together for me. They were very nice to me."

The completed film needed one crowning touch—a title. Each segment had a title when it was conceived, but none seemed appropriate to the whole. Poole knew the title was crucial so that his opus didn't sink into the indistinguishable mire of *Highway Hustler* or *Sex Pigs on the Subway*. Poole had friends who were porn aficionados, and they told him that the biggest recent heterosexual X-rated hit had been titled *My Bare Lady*, playing off the name of the mainstream Audrey Hepburn/Rex Harrison vehicle. A friend suggested *Boys in the Sand*, a reference to Mort Crowley's hit play and movie *Boys in the Band*. Poole and his actors began referring to the film by that name, and it stuck.

Poole was quite clear as to what he wanted to achieve. First and foremost, the picture was to be silent. As long as the situation could be explained in cinematic terms, dialogue was unnecessary. With the memory of the main character's swishy speech mannerisms in *Highway Hustler* still firmly in mind, Poole was determined to avoid that pitfall. "Sex is all involved with fantasy anyway, so the person watching it could see Casey's face and look at the glint in his eye and imagine him saying whatever he wanted." It was a brilliant ploy as it turned out—each guy in the audience imagined Cal/Casey as the perfect man and imagined that he was looking at, and speaking directly to, him. Casey and *Boys* seemed to appeal to the whole world of gay men.

In order to give the film the start Poole felt it deserved, he and business partner Shulman blazed new marketing trails. Never before had a pornographic film been advertised in the mainstream media, but they took out ads in the Sunday *New York Times* and *Variety*. They persuaded *After Dark* to run ads as well—the magazine's very first for an X-rated film. As a crowning touch, Poole put his name on the finished product. "I think that gave it validity, the fact that I put my name on it. I'd done a few things in the theater, and even though I wasn't well-known, people in the industry knew me." Those people included some big names. A month before the opening of *Boys*, he had done a multimedia show at New York's Triton Gallery with Leonard Bernstein, Hal Prince, Alexis Smith, and Steven Sondheim. He was clearly a man with talent and connections. Although his theatrical friends were somewhat horrified that he had lent his name to a piece of porno, Poole stuck by his decision. As a result, his life, as Cal's, was irrevocably changed.

As opening day approached, the hype continued. Poole convinced friends to stage a series of events to promote the film. There were private screenings, brunches, cocktail parties—everything one might expect to accompany the opening of a much-heralded, star-vehicle, big-budget film event. Cal's picture began appearing in print media, advertising his presence in the film. "He was a model, so his face was widely recognized. He went to the parties and mingled with the guests. He was a celebrity—a star."

*   *   *

There were a few individuals who were able to resist Cal's star quality. Ted vividly remembered one man in particular with whom Cal fell from grace. "I definitely remember him," Ted said when I mentioned the man's name. "He absolutely hated Cal. They had met in London in the late '60s. In fact, he was the man who introduced Cal to London society. The two of them had quite a thing going while Cal was abroad, and the fellow wasn't ready to let go of it. When he found out that Cal and I were a couple, he was very miffed. He got very upset and never had anything to do with Cal again. I remember he was out at The Pines the summer that Cal was making *Boys*. It's a rather small place, actually, and it was inevitable that their paths would cross. The man was like an angry cat, hissing and posturing and cutting Cal dead. He was rather a bitter British queen," Ted concluded dryly.

*   *   *

Never shy with the lads, Cal was quick to put his time in the spotlight to good use, as waiter *Jason McNamera found out to his great pleasure. "I was doing a catering job for a private party, maybe 40 people in a very big, very grand apartment near Central Park. It was the usual collection of society types—skinny women and closet-case gays who eyed the help like dogs seeing a bone for the very first time. Then there was him.

"He really stood out. First off, he was better looking than any of the others. Then there was his attitude. He looked you right in the eye and smiled and said please and thank you. I just figured he was somebody's son home from college for the holidays. Boy was I ever surprised.

"After people were through eating, the lights went down, and this projector started to whir. Well, I was expecting home movies of the host's trip to Europe." What he got instead was the first reel of *Boys*. "I figured it was somebody's idea of a joke at first, then I noticed that none of the high-brow types were flinching. They were all sitting there taking it in. Then I figured out who the guy who was running through the water up to the shore was.

"I looked from him to the screen and back again. I didn't believe it, but it was him, sitting in the room, dressed to kill, watching himself up on the screen, giving head like a pro. I just kept looking at him. Finally, I caught his eye. He smiled and winked at me.

"Afterward, when the party was over, and I had helped pack everything up, I left. The elevator opened in the lobby, and he was sitting there waiting for me. He came over and asked me if I had enjoyed the film. All I could do was nod like an idiot. He asked me if maybe he could come back to my place with me. You can guess what I said."

Cal adored this celebrity. He took his moviemaking every bit as seriously as a Hollywood hopeful would have done. He was not at all abashed by what he had done on film. What he did, he did well. Where was the shame in that? He couldn't have been better suited for the role he was to play—the ideal, out-of-the-closet, sexually liberated gay male. He was the man everyone wanted. He was the man everyone could have. There would be no dark glasses and pulled-up collars for this man. Instead there was that sunny, open, I've-got-nothing-to-hide smile that reflected back every man's most secret fantasy.

*   *   *

At last the great day dawned. On December, 29, 1971, at high noon, the 55th Street Playhouse threw open its doors, and a moment of gay history was made. The theater filled, the projectors rolled, and soon the word was on the street—*Boys in the Sand* was a hit, a phenomenon, an epochal event. The critical response was startling, especially since this genre had never before received any official attention from the media. "There are no more closets," *Variety* trumpeted breathlessly. "Everyone will fall in love with this philandering fellator," *The Advocate* said enthusiastically. "The Gay Adam," was *Gay Sunshine's* take on him. "It is impossible to ignore Casey's magnificence or to minimize his impact...I adore him," *The Gay Insider* gushed artlessly.

The film itself garnered a more mixed bag of reviews. Some critics thought it was too arty—all those leaf shadows obscuring pertinent body parts—others carped that the three segments didn't hang together as a whole. For the most part, however, the response was to view it as an art film, close cousin to Anger and Warhol and the European avant-gardists, who were no strangers to disjointed narratives and handheld cameras.

Everyone who saw it seemed to have an opinion—and everyone seemed to have seen it. The first week's gross proceeds paid all expenses related to production and promotion. After the second week Marvin Shulman, Poole's business partner went out and bought a new Mercedes. By the summer of '72, the film had pulled in more than $140,000. It was knocking mainstream films off *Variety*'s top 50 box-office list. Poole couldn't leave the house without hearing something about it from someone. He was at the baths one day in Manhattan when he "overheard two queens in the booth next door to mine, talking about the movie, critiquing it, and getting it all wrong. I remember thinking that this had to stop."

SIZE 39R
HEIGHT 6'
WEIGHT N8
WAIST 30
INSEAM 32
SHIRT 15-34
HAIR Blond
EYES Green
SHOE 9½
HAT 7
GLOVE 8

S.A.G.
EQUITY

MODELS

TMI LE 5-0500

Talent Management International, Inc.
333 East 65th St. • New York, N.Y. 10021

CAL CULVER

A head shot from Culver's modeling portfolio. He had the look and was starting to pull down big money when his career was scuttled by his spectacular debut as gay porn's golden boy.

Culver at ages 1 (*left*) and 4 (*below*), already showing his affinity for the camera. "He could be a little devilish," his brother, Duane, recalled.

Culver (*above*) was Canandaigua Academy's first male cheerleader. And whether in high school (*below, left*) or in college (*below, right*), he was the quintessential boy next door.

Opposite page: Culver with Ingrid Bergman. He said, "She taught me everything I know about being a star."
Above: Cal backstage during the run of *Captain Brassbound's Conversion*, poring over *Variety* in search of his next big break.

Cal's impeccable penmanship on display in one of a lifelong stream of postcards from "Patrick" to his "Auntie Mame."

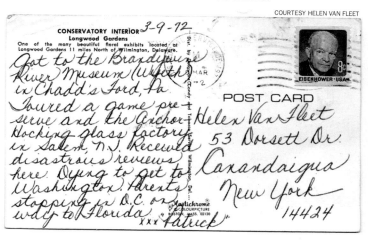

Above, left: Culver advertising the benefits of sex therapy for *Newsweek*. *Above, right:* With Tom Tryon during a mellow moment in their troubled relationship. *Below:* Culver aboard a canal boat in Amsterdam while taking Europe by storm.

Culver on tour with Hanns Ebensten's agency (*clockwise from top, left*): in the Inca ruins of Sacsayhuaman, near Cuzco, Peru; at the Summer Palace in Peking dressed in the robes of the last empress dowager of China; and praying outside the the Temple of Heaven in Peking.

Culver at Casa Donovan (*above, left*), the money pit that devoured almost every penny he made. Mature but still golden (*above, right*), Culver poses on Fire Island. Culver and Joan (*below*)—just a couple of perverts—strike a pose in Spain.

CHAPTER 5

Annus Mirabilus—1972

"Then I realized that if one movie, one *After Dark* cover, and a few stills and shows for Valentino could make people react that way to me—think what it must be like to be Bette Davis!"

As 1972 dawned Cal found himself in a new, and to him, enviable position. He was soon well-known in New York City, and, as *Boys in the Sand* opened around the country, he became something of an underground national celebrity. "It made me *immediately* recognizable in New York, and as it opened around the country—a national celebrity. There was nowhere I could go in the cities it was showing in that people didn't do double takes. I loved it—I got off on it...It made me feel really special." He began to check out the competition in the world of X-rated performers and discovered there really wasn't any: "They were so dreadful, they were terrible. And I thought, 'Jesus, I'm sure doing a hell of a lot better than this number.' And the word of mouth on it was just wonderful. My God, everywhere you went people were talking about it. 'Did you see *Boys in the Sand*?' I mean, it was really incredible. There was even a blurb on me in the *Johannesburg Star* [in South Africa]. It said 'Calvin Culver, who was seen in *Boys in the Band.*' Obviously somebody thought it was a typographical error and changed it. But as the guy said, it doesn't matter what you're seen in as long as you're seen."

*　　*　　*

Cal could be touchingly naive about his own celebrity. A friend recalled attending Bette Midler's Central Park concert in the summer of '72. The legendary entertainer got her start in the basement of the Continental Baths on 74th Street singing her heart out for towel-clad gay boys and the few clothed straight couples who had sought out this temple to decadence, a New York City bathhouse, to check out this formidable new talent.

Midler was, of course, a phenomenon, and her star had risen rapidly, taking her out of the baths and into Carnegie Hall on her way to superstardom. During a break in the concert, Cal leaned over to his friend and remarked that he remembered watching Midler perform at the Continental. "Isn't it neat? Bette Midler and I becoming stars at the same time. Who would've thought?"

*　　*　　*

And so Cal became, if not a star, at least a very marketable commodity. After the movie was released, he was besieged by callers who wanted to meet Cal—or, rather, Casey. "People would call or write and ask for Casey Donovan for a party, and I would pass the information on to Cal," Wakefield Poole said. "At first I think he hesitated to take advantage of the offers; then later he did."

Cal did accept at least a few of the early offers, one of the more memorable of which was an invitation to an orgy in New York

City early on in his miraculous year of 1972. Cal was practically breathless with excitement when he got back to Ted with the details. "Rock Hudson had been there," Wilkins recalled. "Cal was very pleased and suitably impressed." Cal and the macho film star definitely made contact at the orgy. Their relationship allegedly continued on a professional basis for a number of years. Hudson was only the first among the roster of Hollywood clients whom Cal would eventually acquire.

Cal's "celebrity" status as a result of the notoriety of *Boys* was, in his mind, already beginning to pay off. It brought him in close contact with real stars, people who had made it—gay people at that. What Cal never considered was the fact that people like Hudson had made it by hiding their sexuality from the world, not by flaunting it on-screen. It was an oversight that would cost him dearly.

For the time being, there was no thought of cost or consequence. He was, as he had admitted, getting off on his new-found celebrity because it was, after all, "kind of fun to be up there on the screen. You can kind of become a fantasy figure for a lot of people. I sort of get off on that. Look at how many people fantasize on Clark Gable or fantasize on Marilyn Monroe. I mean, I think if people don't fantasize about you as a movie star, you're not gonna be a star. And a lot, a lot of people have gotten off on Casey Donovan."

*   *   *

*Darryl Ferris, slight, bespectacled, balding, was another of those people who called Wakefield Poole and left his number. To Ferris's complete surprise, Cal returned his call. "He was very professional. Friendly, but businesslike. I was floored that he was calling. I was even more floored when he agreed to come to my place to meet me and some of my friends. Believe me, as soon as he hung up, I got on the horn and called up everyone I knew.

"I don't know exactly what we were expecting—I guess for him to show up at the door naked and soaking wet with seaweed in his hair." In any event, that wasn't quite the way it happened. "This really gorgeous, really preppy guy appeared, shook hands with everyone, and began chatting. I'm not sure what he talked about, but I seem to remember that it had something to do with a gallery opening or a Broadway show. It was funny because all of us were ready to take turns licking the sweat off his balls or something, and there we were, all standing around, sipping cocktails and talking about the state of the theater. He was holding court as if he were one of the grande dames of the silver screen, rather than being this hotter-than-hell porn performer whose sexual expertise was a matter of public record."

A bit later in the evening, Darryl got another glimpse of Cal's chameleonlike personality. "Everyone else had gone home. I started picking up dirty glasses and carrying them into the kitchen. We had discussed payment for the evening earlier over the phone, but I hadn't given him any money. I was about ready to go to the bedroom and get my wallet when he came into the kitchen with a tray of dirty dishes and started helping me to wash up. It was really strange standing there with Casey Donovan and having him dry while I washed. We talked about the party and about my friends, just basically a postmortem of the evening the way you'd have with a good buddy.

"Then when we were done, he came on to me. I mean, really climbed all over me as if I were the hottest thing in the city—which I wasn't—and he couldn't wait another minute to get into my pants. From my perspective we damn near melted a hole in the kitchen linoleum. It was the most intense sexual encounter I ever had in my life. I told a couple of my best friends about what had happened that evening after they left, and they gave me this 'oh, Mary, please!' look, meaning I had just lost a lifetime of credibility. I knew what happened, so I didn't really care. I saw him on the street a few weeks later, and he smiled and spoke to me. He even remembered my name. He was quite a gentleman."

*   *   *

In relatively short order Cal began to believe in his own publicity. And for the whole delirious year he had every right to. He was, it seemed, unstoppable. Early in 1972 Cal's attention was caught by a casting call in *Variety*. Cal went, turned in his resume, did his audition piece, smiled—and was hired. The part was not a starring one. It amounted, in fact, to little more than a couple of walk-ons. He understudied a speaking role, but he never went on as his character. Basically, he and a coterie of handsome, physically fit young men were required to fill the corners of the stage around the main character. But this was not just any actress Cal would be providing a decorative backdrop for; this was someone special.

Ingrid Bergman had already achieved icon status on the screen by the time *Captain Brassbound's Conversion* was staged. The play, by George Bernard Shaw, had originally been written as a vehicle for Ellen Terry, a famous English actress at the turn of the century. Less a play than a showcase for the female lead, *Brassbound* has very little to offer the supporting players. According to the reviews the only reason to watch the proceedings was Bergman, who was basically playing herself. Fortunately, she made a star turn of it and dazzled all comers.

Most dazzled of all was Cal, now finally onstage, in a handsomely mounted production with one of Hollywood's most luminous stars. As he did his series of bits night after night, he watched her avidly, trying to learn what it was that made her so special, what gave her that ineffable star quality that he so desperately aspired to have as well. In the publicity photo where Cal appears onstage with Bergman, he looks like a youngster who has just been told that he will be receiving a pony on his birthday. Throughout his life, that photograph was one of his most treasured possessions, and he often told people that "everything he knew about being a star" he had learned from her.

Longtime friend Jake Getty first met Cal during the run of *Brassbound*. Another aspiring young actor, he had also been cast as living scenery. Jake liked the affable young man, but he had no idea that Cal was Casey. "He was just a young actor like everyone else. Nobody in the cast knew about his other persona. This wasn't a crowd who went to those movies. It was a totally different world."

It was a world that gave Cal time to put aside, for the moment, the sexual superstar role that had been so unexpectedly thrust upon him with the success of *Boys*. Even so, there was still a distance between him and other members of the cast. "During the tour of *Brassbound*, Cal always stayed off by himself," Jake recalled. "He didn't stay at the same hotel as the rest of the cast. We would all socialize and shop and eat together, then Cal would go off to his own lodgings, which, as often as not, were in the local YMCA. The rest of us doubled up in cheap hotel rooms to save money. Not Cal. There was always something hidden about him, something that the rest of us didn't know about. It was clear that he didn't want everyone to know his business. I'm convinced that it gave him a chance to go out and pick up men without having the whole cast know what—or who—he was doing. Cal always seemed to know people wherever we went. I never asked, but in retrospect I suspect that he was hustling."

Not all of his solitary time was spent in pursuit of sex and money. While *Brassbound* was touring, preparatory to the New York City opening, Cal was using his spare time in a characteristic way. In a postcard to Helen Van Fleet, mailed during a short run of the play in Wilmington, Del., Cal reported his off-stage activities: "Got to the Brandywine River Museum in Chadd's Ford, Pa., to see the Andrew Wyeth exhibit. Toured a game preserve and the Anchor-Hocking glass factory in Salem, New Jersey." Only then did he mention, briefly, that the play had received "disastrous" reviews. He ends by mentioning that his parents would be stopping in Washington, D.C., to catch their son onstage.

Cal's quest for culture was repeated at every stop along the way. "When the troupe pulled into Washington, D.C., the first thing Cal did was go to the National Gallery," Getty said. "He had read about a special exhibit and couldn't rest until he'd seen it." This time alone remained important to Cal throughout his life—the more so as he grew older. It gave him a chance to escape for a time from the various personas that he presented to the public. Alone in a gallery, he could shed all the images—the porn superstar, the golden model, the aspiring serious actor, the gregarious social animal whose name was beginning to appear on every notable party list—and become for a time the quiet, shy, unassuming scholar, the former teacher whose lifelong quest for knowledge and culture was almost as all-consuming as his quest for sex.

After strutting his stuff for the folks in Washington, D.C., Cal and the company headed to Toronto, Canada, for a week, then returned to New York City for a two week run at The Barrymore Theater at 243 W. 47th Street. Cal was onstage with Ingrid Bergman every evening, but it was a very different type of theater that would soon be taking up every spare minute of his time.

*   *   *

Jerry Douglas, his *Circle in the Water* director, approached Cal with an idea for another hard-core film. Oddly, even though *Boys* was such a resounding success, opening in new cities almost every day while still playing the 55th Street Playhouse in New York City, it hadn't brought any offers of work for its star from other directors of gay hard-core. The industry was still in its infancy, and most of the men who were shooting gay porn weren't quite up to using a star as dynamic as Cal.

Here, as at other points in his hard-core career, Cal was fortunate to come into contact with a man of talent who knew what he was doing. He knew and respected Douglas from their earlier theatrical association, so he was intrigued when he heard the director's vision. *The Back Row* was to be a total contrast to the summery, green-leafed pastoral of *Boys*. It was dark, wintry, neon-lit, indoors, urban—highlighting totally unexpected aspects of porndom's golden boy.

The Back Row casts Cal as a toilet-cruising, sex-addicted sleaze, a man who ought to know better, but who just can't seem to help himself—in many ways the quintessential gay man of the '70s and early '80s. Cal plays himself here, in one of his many chameleonlike manifestations. The viewer senses that he is totally at ease in the milieu, an impression only partly attributable to his acting ability.

Almost all the action takes place in the 42nd Street Theater, a sleazy porn house that oozes authenticity. Cal flits around in the darkened auditorium watching, but not participating, as a young man services a nervous sailor. The smooth camera work is quite effective, gliding around the pair as they have sex in the narrow confines of a row of theater seats. A great deal of expertise was lavished on the production, and it shows. The film is without dialogue, relying on pantomime and an excellent musical score that highlights the psychological state of the characters and their situations.

After the first scene draws to a close, Cal hits the streets and soon encounters George Payne, a young man who successfully personifies youthful innocence and allure. Perhaps the only false note in the film is the fact that Cal can resist this young man for even a moment, let alone keep him waiting throughout the film while he humps every other gay sex-cliche who crosses his path. Such, however, are the vagaries of individual taste.

After a short fantasy interlude in which Cal models various pieces of leather gear and test-drives a dildo—a scene that fore-shadows the raunchy finale in the theater's toilet—both men re-turn to the theater. There, after they indulge in fantasy sex with each other that is intercut with the action on the screen, they proceed with their game of sexual cat and mouse. Cal cruises and smiles and beckons, but whenever the young man comes near him, he withdraws, opting for toilet sex instead of romance.

The central scene in the film is of down-and-dirty urban boys engaging in toilet sex in the bowels of the porn theater. The set-up is so raunchy that you can practically smell the sweat and poppers. The sex is immediate and raw. For better or worse, it opened the eyes of many a gay man to the possibilities of leather. In 1972, outside of a rather limited subculture, all of this leather gear was a relatively unknown quantity. Even a contemporary re-view in *The Advocate* found the demonstration of "what those gadgets are used for" quite titillating.

Big-city boys may have known all about such things, but their more sheltered brothers in the heartland could hardly have failed to be dazzled and more than a little aroused. When Cal was har-nessed and cock-ringed and cuffed, it all looked just a little more glamorous than before. The boy next door, it seemed, could not only suck and fuck in the woods, but he could also get kinky in a public toilet. The film ends with Cal in the arms of George Payne, the sweet, young innocent. But the implied romantic close is undercut as Cal looks over Payne's shoulder to cruise yet another guy with a hard-on who passes on the street.

So with only three explicit films to his credit, Cal had already managed to star in pioneering examples of what were to develop into the two main branches of gay male porn during the next 25 years. He had made it clear that handsome, wholesome, well-built guys could have gay sex, lots of sex, of every kind imaginable. He became the model for the humpy, tanned, blond-haired California dreamer—as well as for the pale-skinned denizen of New York City's urban jungle of back rooms and warehouses.

Cal was already quite conscious of his image and his most recent screen transformation startled even him. After he had filmed the toilet scene in *The Back Row*, he took director Douglas aside and voiced his concerns. "He was worried that 'Casey's fans' might not buy the golden boy as sleaze pig. He was quick to tell me that he had loved doing the scene, had in fact contributed many of the trashiest touches to it, but he was very concerned about how it would affect audiences who had originally seen Casey Donovan in such a different context. He did, he reminded me, have Casey's reputation to think about."

Cal's doubts didn't end on the set. He went home to Ted and shared his concern. "He hated that film," Ted recalled. "I went to see it, and I had to agree with him—it was a terrible film." Cal expressed himself even more strenuously to a journalist who interviewed him not long after the film was released. He said the film was too trashy, and he was worried about its effect on his image and modeling career. "A lot of it is really, really bad. And that's very disappointing. The film is better than a lot of other films that've been done, but people really, really hate it. It's a very trashy movie. It's like really dirty sex, a whole different trip…it's Casey Donovan in the johns, and it's very grubby. A lot of people are offended by it because they don't want to see that sort of aspect. Still, I mean, it's in its twelfth week. I thought it closed last week. I couldn't believe it; I thought that turkey closed."

*   *   *

Casey needn't have worried. *The Back Row* did get a few good reviews, but Cal's golden-boy status remained unchanged. *Boys* continued to play across the country, bringing more and more acolytes to Casey's temple. He had also come to the attention of *After Dark*'s editor in chief, William Como, a man who was in a position to give his career quite a boost.

After Dark magazine was founded in 1968 on the ruins of its forerunner, a ballroom-dance magazine. Although originally conceived as a magazine dedicated to coverage of dance, it quickly expanded to cover—or uncover—all the arts. Centered on the New York City scene, the magazine functioned as one of the first aboveground, widely distributed, gay-friendly publications in the country. Under the guise of "art," *After Dark* was able to photograph acres of supple flesh and present it unadorned to the public. Although women were certainly never excluded from coverage, the emphasis was always on the male form. Few men who posed for its pages could resist the temptation to remove their shirts. Many bared all.

The democracy of the flesh dictated that the nudest man won. This meant that the cover was often adorned with an unknown, notable only for a chiseled face and lithe physique. The magazine itself never disappointed its many gay readers—there were always photo spreads of the latest in theater and dance, invariably featuring barely clad young males, often caught in sinewy embrace with one of their comely fellows. It was heady stuff in the early '70s. It was the sort of magazine that could safely be left out in the open. After all it did feature articles about Bette Midler, Peggy Lee and Maggie Smith in addition to all those delectable shots of gorgeous men. This was art.

The success of the magazine was assured by the quality of the photography. Top-notch professionals like Jack Mitchell, Kenn Duncan, and Roy Blakey provided their considerable talents to the transformation of near-naked young men of often question-able thespian talent to iconographic status. In a radical departure from other media of the day, a search was made for all things gay—no gay play was too obscure to be featured in the magazine's pages, especially if at least one scene featured male nudity. The world of the dance was always represented—and as the liberated era's costumes became skimpier, the photo spreads became longer. *After Dark* served as a wish book for gay men around the country.

The man behind all of this was William Como, a man whose stated goal was to take "an exciting and sexy look at the arts." He was already succeeding in a stunning fashion when he found a new and daring face to grace the cover of his magazine. The combination of theatrical legitimacy and porn chic that Cal brought with him were irresistible to a man who enjoyed tweaking the more straight-laced members of the New York City arts community.

Cal was perfect for a crossover from the world of *Boys* to that of *After Dark*. He had the face, the body, and the charisma. He also had a modest resume of theatrical credits, which fit in with the magazine's stated purpose as a chronicler of the arts. Cal had come to Como's attention when Wakefield Poole came in with his original advertising artwork and a request that *After Dark* promote *Boys in the Sand*. It was the first time that Como had agreed to advertise an openly pornographic film, and once he had embraced the idea, he became an enthusiastic champion of the star.

The campaign began modestly enough—a head shot of Cal with a brief caption in the February 1972 issue, followed in March by a pubes-up body shot that again mentioned *Boys* and that makes an erroneous reference to his appearance at the Garrick Theater in *Dragula*, calling the work a stage play, rather than a film. Judging by the Roy Blakey photograph, the box office for the Garrick's legitimate stage was probably inundated with requests for tickets.

Even as the folks at *After Dark* proceeded with plans to expose Cal in a truly spectacular fashion, the young man was getting ready to set off on another adventure. This adventure would unsettle his local plans, a disruption that would lead to many changes when he returned home. "During the summer that Cal was filming *Boys*," Ted Wilkins said, "we had met a couple of guys who invited us to spend some time together with them. We really hit it off, and they asked us to share a house with them the following summer. When the time came Cal and I packed up our things and started to move in to the Fire Island place. Then all of a sudden, Cal decided to return a call to someone. When he hung up I could tell that he was really excited. Director Radley Metzger had offered him a featured role in his latest film, *Score*. It was clear to me that he couldn't say no to the chance, although it would take him away to Yugoslavia for most of the summer."

While Cal was waiting for this new adventure to begin, he was far from idle. The Wilhelmina Agency had been using Cal steadily for the past couple of years, finding him an easy sell. He wore clothes beautifully, he had an air of class about him, and he exuded that indefinable allure that could make people buy the clothes he modeled. Whether the customers subconsciously wanted Cal—or just aspired to look like him—didn't matter a whit. The final result was that he made the fashions he modeled extremely popular.

When the folks at Wilhelmina fielded the prospect of a shoot for Italian designer Valentino, Cal was more than eager to go. "I suspect that the work for Valentino entailed much more than a fashion shoot," Wilkins observed dryly. "To be quite honest, I don't recall any photos of Cal in Valentino fashions around that time." And so off to Italy Cal went. He breezed through the assignment, whatever it may have been, with his usual aplomb and had a few days to kill before he was set to meet his next deadline. Never at a loss, Cal traveled to Rome, took a room near the Spanish Steps, and began touring the city, revisiting favorite haunts, exploring new sites, and, as always, meeting people.

There were plenty of handsome Italian guys for a hot blond American to meet in the summer of '72. Several decades behind the extremely liberated New York City scene, Rome was—and in many respects still is—a very repressive place. Sex was rampant but clandestine, which presented no obstacles to an inveterate cruiser of Cal's caliber.

He loved it all—the antiquities, the beating sun, the ubiquitous stray cats, the delicious, dark, liquid-eyed Roman men who prowled the streets in their tight trousers, their sex outlined beneath the fabric like poorly concealed weapons. It could be bliss indeed to play languid games of cat and mouse among the columns of the Roman Forum, then stroll with your prize to the ruins of the Coliseum where those in the know would seek out a hidden spot in the vast structure for a bit of open-air dalliance. There, with the tourists strolling in ignorant bliss just below, daring pairs of any sexual predilection could couple beneath the azure Roman sky as the tour guides droned their tales of ancient glories.

In the evenings Cal turned to the cafes for his entertainment and socializing. One evening Cal was sitting out at a table in the Piazza Navona, sipping Campari and soda when a tall, handsome, elegantly dressed man strolled by. He caught Cal's eye and nodded. Cal smiled and watched as the man made his leisurely way toward Bernini's spectacular *Fountain of the Four Rivers* in the center of the piazza.

Cal sat there for a long time watching the man as the evening shadows purpled the stones of the piazza. As he told a friend years after the fact, "I loved the way he moved. He was long and lean, and his pants were tailored to show off every curve of muscle when he walked. I wanted him, and I thought at the time that it was important for him to want me as well. So I waited to see what he would do." Finally Cal finished his drink, gathered up his glasses and guidebook, and went inside the restaurant to pay the check. When he stepped out into the piazza, the man was nowhere to be found.

He experienced a moment of panic as he looked frantically up and down at the groups of tables that spilled out of the doorways of every cafe around the piazza. There were many handsome men, but there was no sign of 'his' Italian. After his second circuit of the piazza, a dejected Cal gave up the search and prepared to make his way back to his hotel near the Piazza Di Spagna.

As he stepped out onto one of the surrounding streets, he saw a small red sports car at the curb. The man driving turned and nodded. It was him. Cal stepped to the curb, opened the door of the car, and slipped into the soft leather upholstery. The dark man of mystery popped the car into gear and whisked Cal through the streets of Rome, out into the star-studded night beyond the suburbs.

Roberto turned out to be royal—well, a minor count, in any case. He was from an ancient Italian family with social connections and pretensions to nobility, sporting a pedigree that reached far into the dim past and possessing a decaying estate with a villa so old it had transcended run-down and become "romantic." Cal was swept away by the romance and glamour of it all. The man brought him into a cavernous salon, plied him with brandy, and seduced him. Or perhaps Cal seduced the handsome count. No matter—the evening stretched out over a series of delightful days during which time Cal was whisked up north to Venice—that improbable floating jewel of a city. They arrived on the final day of the feast of Santa Maria della Salute, which ended with a spectacular fireworks display. Cal's friend arranged for a private gondola so that they were floating on the Grand Canal, drinking wine under a flickering canopy of red, sapphire, and gold fireworks, "the likes of which you've never seen," as he assured Helen Van Fleet via postcard.

There were other pleasures—introductions to other elegant Italians and dinners in the still-fabulous palaces moldering along the Grand Canal. Cal took it all in, reveling in every glamorous moment and, it must be said, contributing his own not insignificant glamour to the proceedings. The idyll continued right up until it was time for Cal to go. He would have liked to stay and absorb more of the languid, aristocratic aura of life among the Italian glitterati, but duty called. He had an obligation, and it just wouldn't do for him to be late.

*   *   *

Under the auspices of Jerry Douglas, his *Back Row* director, Cal had been cast to appear in the film version of Douglas's off-Broadway play *Score*. The producer-director was Radley Metzger, a man who had already made his reputation with *Carmen, Baby*, *The Lickerish Quartet*, and *Therese and Isabelle*, glamorously photographed, heterosexual films featuring European-inspired soft-core porn touches. Metzger had already explored lesbian sex as a means of audience titillation and was now ready to exploit the possibilities of sexual couplings of gay men.

"Jerry knew Cal and had recommended him to me," Metzger continued. "He told me that I should go and see *Boys in the Sand*. I ran down to the theater where it was playing, put down my money, and saw the picture. I sat through only half of it. I remember thinking at the time that it was junky—jerky camera work, no dialogue, very amateurish. I know now that my thoughts were based on ignorance. I didn't realize where it fit into the canon of gay porn. It was only later, when I mentioned my take on the film to Cal when we were on location, that I gained perspective on it. Cal explained that most gay porn audiences hadn't even seen anything in color."

Metzger might not have thought much of the film, but he was quite taken with Cal. "I was impressed with his looks and offered him the role in *Score*. He had another offer on line at that time, but he told me that if I ever needed an aging blond, I should give him a call."

Cal's other commitment failed to materialize, and he gave Metzger a call. "I was delighted. He was exactly what I had in mind for my movie. In the original play none of the actors were really very glamorous. I was looking for more of that quality for my film." Cal simply exuded that glamour. And his aura of free-wheeling sexuality was also an asset. Metzger was savvy enough to realize that, "but I wasn't exploiting his notoriety as a gay porn star. At that time he was keeping the two personas separate as much as he could. He was still striving to break into the mainstream at that point. My film was not X-rated. It was art, not pornography, although the two areas were beginning to blend. He was becoming something of a superstar when I met him, and *After Dark* was beginning to market him heavily."

Cal was a natural choice to play Eddie, the closeted lust-object of the film's male lead, Gerald Grant. At the outset, the swinging bisexual couple Jack (Grant) and Elvira (Claire Watson) are discussing their ongoing game of keeping score of their same-sex conquests during a summer in Europe. Jack is one up on Elvira and is taunting her to concede the game because her six-month time limit to even the score expires at midnight. She has had her eye on Betsy (Lynn Lowry), Eddie's young wife, and plans to bed her before the deadline. The jaded pair separate the young couple, then spend most of their time seducing them—female to female, male to male. The sex play is quite explicit for its time, especially considering that *Score* was released for the mainstream theatrical market.

The acting is quite accomplished, and the dialogue is witty

and fast-paced. Watson and Grant are particularly good as the predatory swinging couple, trading jibes with each other in their scenes together. Watson and Lowry are both quite physically attractive and play their erotic scenes with considerable grace and restraint. Cal and Grant are both quite memorable in their erotic scenes as well—although restraint is hardly the operative word here.

The two men are nicely matched—Grant dark and furry, Cal the blond golden boy, an image enhanced by his newly shaved torso, which emphasized Cal's youthful appearance. After Grant spends the requisite amount of time enticing Cal into a "scene," the action heats up. The sex in *Score* may be soft-core, but there is nothing soft about either Cal or Grant as they trade artistically lit blow jobs. Equally hard are the glimpses we get of Grant's cock as he plows Cal's backside. Soft-core couldn't be much more explicit than this. It may be Cal doing the dialogue, but Casey definitely takes over when the sex heats up.

According to Metzger, Cal was a joy to work with. "He had gone on to Europe ahead of the rest of the cast. He had gone to Italy for a fashion shoot for Valentino. By the time we met up with him in Yugoslavia, he had the entire script letter perfect. He was a consummate professional who took direction very well.

"What we were doing—giving movement and energy to what had originally been a stage play—took some critical staging. I actually handled the camera myself on *Score*. Because of the type of lenses we were using, I required an incredible precision in the actual physical moves the actors made in every scene. It's like dancing partners—the director leads, the actors flow with him. It's a very special relationship. The burden was definitely on them to play the scenes exactly as choreographed. They could make it look good, or bad. This was true even—or maybe especially—in the sex scenes. Cal really measured up. He hadn't had much professional experience at that time, but he took to it very well."

Cal and Grant make their on-screen couplings appear very authentic. "Off the record, I don't think there was anything between them off the set," Metzger theorized, scotching several rumors to the contrary. "Gerald Grant had been in the theater business for a while. Both he and Cal were pros. They were gay, and they really had a feel for the material. Grant was the predator; Cal was the innocent lost in a grown-up world. They had a firm grasp of their characters and extended that knowledge into the sex scenes.

"Those scenes flow very nicely. There is no change in terms of who they are when they are doing the sex scenes. I think that what you see on-screen is a testimony to their professionalism rather than an expression of their personal relationship. It took us three full days of shooting to get those sex scenes. All of that time was put into getting those shots just right. If they are effective, that most likely accounts for it."

The film was being shot in Bakar, a tiny town on the northern coast of the Adriatic south of Ljubljana. Life on location in Yugoslavia, as Douglas remembered it, "was a violent culture shock for many of us in the company, especially the homophobia of that iron curtain country." They had been warned that—officially—homosexuality didn't exist. They were there for nine weeks, the only English-speaking people in the vicinity. The cast was working day and night, and the work was really exhausting. There were hardly any opportunities for sexual release, and members of the cast spent much of their free time bemoaning the fact that no one was getting laid.

Cal spent many of his evenings writing postcards with a zeal that Metzger found quite amusing. "He had the biggest Rolodex I ever saw in my life. He spent many evenings writing cards and letters. Damn near everyone in the world must have gotten a card from him during the shooting of that film."

Cal wasn't really spending all of his spare time writing postcards. He was also checking out the local talent, not an easy feat in Tito's Yugoslavia in the early '70s. This was back in the bad old days of communism when good communist countries didn't harbor anything so decadent as a homosexual. Such aberrations were officially forbidden, and Western tourists were definitely not encouraged to entertain themselves by corrupting the locals.

Cal apparently couldn't help himself. Douglas tells the tale that within days of his arrival, Cal had already made a conquest. One of the locals Metzger had hired to assist during the filming was a swarthy, well-built fellow with the beard-stubbled good looks usually associated with swashbuckling gypsy brigands. The man's swaggering, macho sexuality and well-stuffed crotch caught Cal's eye, and they began to flirt. Cal's smile and demeanor spoke "sex" in any language, so the local stud wasn't left in doubt for long regarding Cal's intentions. The fact that the man often brought his wife and children along with him to watch the filming did not stand in the way of their liaison.

Despite the claims of communist ideology, Yugoslavian men were no strangers to gay sex. The country had been a battle ground between the religious and cultural forces of East (Islam) and West (Christianity) for centuries, and customs outside the major cities were often influenced by Islamic social structures. This meant a strict segregation of the sexes outside the bonds of marriage. This, in turn, led most young men to experiment sexually with other young men, religious proscriptions to the contrary be damned. No doubt Cal's Yugoslav lover was one of those men. Whatever his exact circumstance, he had no scruples about leaving his wife and children alone on the set while he dallied with the dazzling American.

As time passed, it is likely that Cal fraternized with the locals as much as he dared. At that time Americans—especially American actors—were a novelty in communist countries. Men hung out in the traditional bars and coffeehouses in the town, bantering with one another as they discussed work and life. By tradition, these were exclusively male-only gatherings. Respectable single women were at home closely guarded by their families. Married women were at home caring for their families. Prostitutes—officially nonexistent like other corruptions of capitalist life—were visited as the need arose. For socializing it was just the guys doing what guys do when gathered together in fellowship—most likely talking about sex.

Enter Cal. Handsome, charming, outgoing, charismatic—even with the language barrier there were ways to communicate. A few rounds of drinks purchased, a few packs of cigarettes distributed, a few discreet gropes in shadowy corners—desire could easily be communicated and responded to.

Metzger recalled one instance during a break in the rigorous shooting schedule when Cal had an opportunity to meet some willing men. "A visiting dance troupe came to Bakar from another part of Yugoslavia. I know that Cal made some contact with some of the male dancers." There was even a rumor of a liaison with a woman who was a part of the company. More than a rumor, according to Ted Wilkins. "Cal was very lonely and wrote to me frequently during the filming of *Score*. In one of these letters, he confided that he had had a sexual experience—his first ever sexual experience with a female—with one of his costars. He was quite pleased with himself about it, I think. At least it eased his loneliness. It made me feel a little less anxious about the situation that had developed with me back at home."

*   *   *

When Cal returned from his sojourn in Yugoslavia, everything had changed on the domestic front. Ted Wilkins had been getting on with his own life. "When Cal left town to do *Score*, I decided to go ahead with the summer rental on Fire Island. I had promised our friends, and I felt obligated. I also know how miserable Manhattan can be in the summer. To make a long story short, that summer I fell in love with another guy who was staying in the house. Walter and I have been together ever since. I wanted to write and tell Cal, but I kept getting these letters from him telling me how lonely he was and how much he missed everyone back in New York. I just didn't have the heart to write him a Dear John letter.

"That same summer, a good friend of Cal's died. He just dropped dead on the beach. It was a really scary experience for me. Well, I didn't want to have to tell Cal about that either—not in a letter. So when he and the cast sailed back to New York from Europe, I had to tell him that his friend was dead and that I was in love with Walter.

"Cal was stunned. I remember that he was very upset with me. He left, and I didn't see him for quite a while. He got over his hurt eventually, and we reestablished our ties. He was quite fond of Walter. I think he really understood how tough it was to have a relationship with a sexual athlete like him. I know that I found it extremely difficult to be seriously involved with a guy who made fuck films during the day. It was my old New England puritan streak asserting itself, but there it was. Cal bounced back very nicely."

*   *   *

A part of that bounce happened because Cal returned to New York City and discovered that he had become a major media celebrity. While he was away, the July 1972 issue of *After Dark* had hit the newsstands, and it was a sizzler. Cal is featured on the cover in a very '70s swimsuit—something white and stretchy with suspenders that frame his physique and pull his basket up into sharp relief. He was definitely delicious.

He appears inside the magazine in a photo shoot along with other young hopefuls in the theater world, modeling more swimsuits, caftans, and other trendy leisure wear while romping on the beach. Immediately following this is an article just about Cal, featuring two full pages of our boy wonder naked on a trapeze, every muscle perfectly flexed, his radiant smile promising all manner of lewd wish fulfillments. In the space of a couple of flashbulbs popping, Kenn Duncan immortalized Cal's gorgeous ass for all the world to see. And what a great ass it was.

If the reader could tear his eyes away from the photos long enough to notice, the text fawned over Cal's assets as well. Written by the editor in chief Como, the article accompanying the trapeze spread gushes about all of Cal's thespian accomplishments to date and theorizes on his future success as an actor. Cal makes no attempt to hide that he has done porn; rather, in the article he talks of it as a building block in his career. "I can never put down having done those three films because they were a fantastic chance for me to play in front of a camera. I've learned so much about myself from those films—the little subtleties of expression with my face and body. It's difficult to let yourself go—to be relaxed and natural."

It emerges clearly here and elsewhere that Cal really believed that the porn wouldn't hurt him, that he could sail right past it and into a legitimate career. "Raymond St. Jacques (an actor and director) wants me to play a role in his new film, *Book of Numbers*. He told me, 'You have a charisma that Robert Redford had when he first started. You've really got to get it together and get into films. It's where you belong.'" Cal clearly believed this, and Como's article pushes the theory as well. "Yeah, but can he do dialogue?" is the question Como poses in the title of the article. His final line put him squarely in Cal's camp: "Mother Nature and I are betting he can." The bet was fated to be lost, but for now at least, Cal was riding the crest of the wave. It was his golden moment, and he worked to make the most of it.

* * *

When Cal returned to New York City, he instantly realized that his life had changed utterly. "It was the talk of New York," Cal enthusiastically told an interviewer, referring to the cover shot and feature story in *After Dark*. He had gone out to Fire Island for the weekend upon his return and discovered that he was a bona fide celebrity. "In a way it was like being a new face, but not exactly a new face. But it was really incredible that first weekend back—everybody knew who I was. It was really frightening. I went through the whole recognition trip, people doing numbers, and people sort of stopping and doing double takes. And I thought, 'Wow, now I really realize why people in Hollywood want their privacy, and why they don't go out in public, and why they don't like to sign autographs, and why they don't like to be recognized, and why they want to be left alone.'

"And the intimidation of people was incredible like how afraid people are to come up and talk to me. I mean, they'll see me in a bar or restaurant or on the street or in the subway. And you see them, but sometimes I play it very cool, and I pretend I don't see it. But I'm taking it all in, 'cause it's really a hoot.

"Sometimes it's a great deal of fun, and sometimes it can be a bummer. Sometimes it's annoying, you don't want to be bothered. And I really realized what a price you have to pay to your public. And I thought, 'Jesus, if this is happening to me, think what Bette Davis has gone through all these years, or Robert Redford or Paul Newman, the letters and the phone calls and the kooks that must come by.'"

He was indeed taking it all in and enjoying it all. Based on an amusing anecdote related by pal Jake Getty, most of his annoyance stemmed from people not acknowledging him. "We were coming back home from some event we had attended. We were on a subway platform. There was this good-looking guy who kept watching Cal, but who was making a huge deal out of pretending not to notice him. It was totally obvious to me—and to Cal—that he knew exactly who Cal was. Naturally, Cal was looking back—he just couldn't help himself—but every time he looked, the guy turned away. You could see Cal doing a slow burn as the minutes ticked by. Finally, as the train was pulling into the station, Cal put his hands on his hips and called out to the guy. He said, 'I haven't got time for this. You'll just have to die with your secret, honey.'"

On the other hand, if a person happened to be young, gorgeous, and interested, Cal was quick to forgive any lapses in the man's celebrity knowledge. Actor John Burke fit that bill in spades. "It was 1973 when we first met. I was 21. We were out on Fire Island on the beach. We cruised, we met, we talked, we went to a secluded area and made love. I really didn't have a clue who he was.

"Afterward, we exchanged phone numbers. It was great because Cal had a tiny pen tucked into his small swimsuit. He told me I might know him as Casey Donovan. I just smiled and shook my head. He wasn't offended in the least. He actually seemed to be rather charmed that I didn't know who he was, that I was attracted to him just because he was a hot guy on the beach on a beautiful summer evening.

"When I got back to the place I was staying, my friends all wanted to know why I was so late getting back. I was new to the scene and that was the very first time I had done it on the beach in the great outdoors. They quizzed me for details, and I told them I had met a gorgeous man. 'You might know his name,' I said. 'I guess he's a porn star.' Everyone was incredibly excited and couldn't believe I was so naive as to be unaware of the magical Casey Donovan's identity. I had never seen a porn film, so I didn't know. Still, I was the one who had just made love with him on the beach, so I didn't waste much time feeling too stupid."

*   *   *

Soon, even folks in the hinterlands who had never thought about pornography or the New York City art scene were exposed to Cal. His face was on the cover of the November 27, 1972, issue of *Newsweek*, the "New Sex Therapy" issue, which was the second-biggest seller of the year. On it, a rapt Cal—perhaps still basking in the afterglow of his conquest of a real female in Yugoslavia—is nuzzling the neck of a ravishing blond woman. Whatever the therapy touted by the accompanying articles, it appears to be working.

In addition to all of this, Cal found time to appear in *Fun and Games*, a film shot in New York City by writer/director Mervyn Nelson. One of Nelson's previous efforts, *Some of My Best Friends Are...*, was panned as "a painfully cliched depiction of gay stereotypes." Set in a Manhattan gay bar on Christmas Eve, the film was of the "it's a lonely, pitiful life for a faggot" genre. *Fun and Games* was billed as a sex spoof, and Cal portrayed the male half of a prototype swinging couple, a relatively small speaking role in the film. The plot, what there is of it, revolves around a conservative suburban couple who get caught up in the sexual revolution after placing an ad in *Screw*, an underground paper of some renown in the '70s. The rest of the story is primarily a series of vaudevillian blackout sketches poking fun at the excesses of contemporary sexual attitudes. As a reviewer put it: "The cast conducts itself like the movie was a whole lot of fun in the making...but the result is definitely not as much fun for the audience as it apparently was for the participants." Not exactly a thespian triumph for Cal, but at least he got paid for his time.

*   *   *

Cal's miracle year was crowned with one more glorious gift from *After Dark*. A gorgeous head shot of him by photographer Jack Mitchell graced the December cover. "He was a lot of fun," Mitchell said. "He was sent to me by *After Dark* to photograph for that cover shot. I did a couple of shoots with him. He was definitely a very hot number. He was also a very nice person. I remember once when I was doing a color shoot with him, I screwed up. I put the wrong film in the camera, and the pictures all came out too blue, so we had to do it all over again. He was very gracious about it."

Inside, another full-page photo of Cal with *Score* costar, Lynn Lowry displays Cal's boyish torso—and a look of almost impossible innocence. The accompanying text trumpets Cal's latest triumph, "that he has signed to play a major role in Robert Fryer and Steve Fellouris's production of the Mary Renault novel, *The King Must Die*. Maggie Smith…and Jack Clayton will also appear in this version of the Theseus legend."

This was indeed heady stuff to find his name coupled with serious movie stars. Cal bought up numerous copies and distributed them to friends and family. His star was at the zenith, and the future was bright.

CHAPTER 6

Riding the Crest

Cal floated into the new year on a cloud. Things got off to a rip-roaring start when he managed to snag a grand new apartment. Actually the place had been Wakefield Poole's. He had run into Poole on Fire Island the previous autumn, and during the course of their visit, he learned that Poole was going to move to Los Angeles. Poole asked Cal if he wanted the place. Cal recruited pal Jake Getty as roommate, and they took possession in January 1973.

The apartment was a vast, high-ceilinged barn of a place totally devoid of furniture. Cal and Jake, naturally enough, decided to throw a party. They opted to make it a "rent party," charging every guest a dollar. Cal and Jake started putting out the word, and soon the great day arrived. It was, by all accounts, a dynamite party, one that people talked about for years afterwards. More than 400 people showed up including Sylvia Miles, Rex Reed, a slew of Wilhelmina models, and a liberal dose of gay boys. Getty still recalls the event vividly. "We were at the front door collecting the money. At one point I turned to Cal and whispered, 'Who the hell are all these people?' Cal just shrugged his shoulders and kept taking the cash." As it turned out none of their bounty went to pay rent—it was all used up paying for the beer the thirsty crowd soaked up.

Among the crowd that day was Tom Tryon. The 48-year-old ex-actor was tall, dark, and extremely handsome. He had been brought to this raucous party by his pal, Richard Deacon, the portly, bald actor who played many character parts on film and television, and who is probably most widely remembered for the role of Mel on the old *Dick Van Dyke Show,* which also starred Rose Marie and Mary Tyler Moore. Deacon had previously met Cal as a "client," and the two had struck up a friendship. Deacon had responded to Cal's party call and had alerted Tryon.

The spark that had failed to strike when Ted Wilkins had introduced the pair during the intermission of *Pippin* ignited now. When Cal first saw Tryon that day, the older man was at the center of a rapt group, quite obviously dazzling them all. Tryon felt the intensity of Cal's gaze and looked up. Their eyes met. Tryon smiled. Cal smiled back. The atmosphere crackled with mutual electricity. They both separated themselves from their respective groups, approached, shook hands, acknowledged their previous meeting. The chemistry between them asserted itself instantly. Their up-and-down relationship—initially on a pay-to-play basis, gradually transforming to true romance—would last for almost five years.

Tom Tryon, born in 1926, was directly descended from a former governor of colonial New York. After a stint in the Army during World War II, Tryon went to Yale University, where he earned a bachelor's degree in fine arts in 1949. After studying to be a painter in New York City, he got involved in the theater. He was painting scenery in a theater in Cape Cod when actress Gertrude Lawrence took him under her wing, advised him to study acting, and directed him to the New York City stage, warning him to avoid Hollywood. He followed her advice for a number of years, playing bit parts in a number of productions but never making much headway.

He eventually gave in to the lure of Hollywood, where his career still failed to take off, leaving him bogged down in a number of lackluster roles, including that of a monster in Paramount's 1958 film *I Married a Monster from Outer Space*. In that same year Tryon was chosen by Disney Studios for the title role in their hourlong television series *Texas John Slaughter*. He acquitted himself well on the series, but still no great offers were forthcoming.

Tryon continued making mediocre films until 1962 when he had a featured role in Darryl F. Zanuck's *The Longest Day*, a gripping historical account of the Allied invasion of Normandy on June 6, 1944. Shortly after that he worked with Marilyn Monroe on her last film, *Something's Got to Give*, which was never released because of her untimely death.

Finally in 1963 Tryon got the role that gave him his widest recognition as an actor. His experiences during the filming of *The Cardinal* also gave him a nervous breakdown and heightened his resolve to get out of film work. Director Otto Preminger was reportedly a monster to work with. On the first day of shooting, Preminger fired the actor in front of a huge crowd of people, including his parents, then hired him back within the hour. Subsequent battles with Preminger during filming managed to ruin the acting profession for Tryon, leaving him with nothing but a burning desire to get out and do something else for a living. Roy Blakey remembered a story that Tryon told much later about the experience. "I remember Tom telling this incredible story about an occasion when Preminger had him so rattled that they had to tie him to a chair to keep him from shaking during the filming of a scene."

The memory remained vividly imbedded in Tryon's mind. He

later told an interviewer that at that point, he "had to get out. Had to find something else to do. I was totally shattered after *The Cardinal.* I came down with hepatitis and everyone was saying how Preminger had put me in the hospital. The rumor was that they put me away in a funny farm."

While he was recuperating, Tryon began to dabble with writing. He discovered that he liked it much more than he liked acting. He applied himself and wrote *The Other*, an eerie horror novel. The book was on the best-seller lists for seven months after its publication in 1971, then was optioned as a screenplay and made into a successful film. When Cal met him, he had just finished *Harvest Home*, a gothic thriller. *Lady*, a character study of the relationship between a young boy and an older woman he idolizes followed in 1974. In 1975 he began *Crowned Heads*, a series of four interrelated novellas. Cal would be intimately involved with that project.

Tryon was perfect for Cal in many ways. Not only was he the prototypical older man but he was also a real celebrity—part Hollywood star, part best-selling author. And he had connections—in Hollywood and in the New York City theater and publishing scene. He was plugged into the middle of everything. He was what Cal aspired to become—a bona fide star.

Tryon knew people—important, glamorous people whom Cal wanted very much to meet. Cal had rubbed elbows with many of them at the flashy parties he had attended in New York City, but most of them had viewed him as a sex toy, not as a man to be seriously reckoned with. All that would change, of course, once he had settled down with Tom.

Tryon found Cal as delectable as the younger man found him. Tryon was a hot man who liked his sex slightly raunchy, and he found the darker side of unbridled sensuality that Cal represented very attractive. Cal was, of course, absolutely perfect from that standpoint. In the abstract the idea of having a porn star at his beck and call excited Tryon—even though he was terrified that someone might make the connection. Although by all accounts Tryon was obviously gay to everyone but himself, he was deep in the closet. It was one of the problems that would ultimately prove to be the pair's undoing.

*   *   *

The few people who might not have recognized Cal's face prior to that December 1972 *After Dark* cover recognized him now. He was definitely an item. Those X-rated movies of his were still running in theaters all across the country as well, and it didn't take men who were interested long to put two and two together. The magazine exposure had also revealed his real name and the fact that he lived in New York City. He began to get fan mail—"it doesn't come flooding in by the hundreds every week, but every once in a while I get a letter…I've saved all of them…"—and he occasionally answered it.

*George Kanter was living in St. Louis and working as a buyer in his father's department store. "Looking back, I can't believe I did it. I was a closeted guy in my mid 20s, and I was totally infatuated with Casey Donovan. I was like a teenage girl about it. I wrote a letter to him. And he wrote back, a real letter, not just a form answer to fan mail. He told me that he was going to be in St. Louis to do some modeling for a wholesaler and that he hoped he'd see me. That was rich—he wanted to see me.

"Well, I went to the center where the show was being held, and sure enough there he was in the flesh, more gorgeous than in the movies. I think I ended up ordering a gross of everything he modeled during the runway show. Anyway, after the show I gathered my courage and went back to the dressing rooms and waited for him. I saw him come out and walked up to him and introduced myself. I'll never forget his reaction—he just lit up as though he had suddenly run into a long-lost friend. He smiled and looked into my eyes and told me how glad he was to have a chance to meet me.

"I was totally dazzled. My heart was going 90 miles an hour. He was so incredible to look at, and he was acting like he thought I was something special. Believe me, I wasn't. I was just a scared, nerdy guy with a dumpy physique, thinning hair, and a major crush on someone unattainable.

"So I invited him to dinner. And he accepted. But the catch was that I had asked him to my home. Well, I was living with my parents, who were wonderful, but who didn't have a clue that there were gay people in the world, let alone living in the same house with them. And I'd just invited a major porn star home to meet them. I couldn't believe I'd opened my mouth, but by then it was too late.

"I was a nervous wreck for the rest of the day, and by the time dinner rolled around, I was practically ill. What had I been thinking, inviting a porn star to meet my folks? I guess I was convinced that he was inevitably going to do something pornographic in front of them. It turned out that I didn't have a thing to worry about. He was perfect. He was wearing a blazer and a tie and looked like he'd just stepped out of a very upscale magazine. He'd even brought flowers, which he presented to my mother. She was charmed. So was my father.

"During dinner Casey was the one who kept the conversation going. He found out that my mother was on the board of the opera guild and took off on a discussion of opera that thrilled her to no end. It turned out that he knew one of the artists who was coming to sing in St. Louis that year. Then my dad asked him how he liked the wine we were drinking with our meal, and he took off about that subject as well, telling my father all about some vineyard he had recently visited when he was in the south of France. He was amazing. By the time he left that night, my parents were ready to adopt him.

"He'd taken a taxi to my home, and so naturally I offered to drive him back to his hotel. As we went by Forest Park, he asked me to drive through. Then he asked me to pull over for a minute. Then he scooted across the front seat and put the make on me. I mean, really came on to me. Not that I was objecting, of course. I thought I'd died and gone to closet-case heaven. I couldn't have devised a fantasy better than what happened in that car. Afterward, I drove him back to his hotel. I never saw him again, but he sent my mother a lovely thank-you note the next day. He had beautiful handwriting."

*   *   *

Oddly enough, for a man who had made three soft-core erotic features and appeared in an equal number explicit of films where no holds were barred, Cal was very concerned about his public image. He confessed to an interviewer that he had to keep a vigilant eye out for anything that might tend to cast him in a bad light and thereby become a stumbling block on his path to stardom. "Somebody wanted to write an article about me, and it was so incredibly tasteless and tacky that it would have absolutely ruined my career. And I can't go to bars that much, and I have to play it cool when I do go. I mean, I'm certainly not going to walk in and be outrageous, because the talk would be all over New York the next day. I'm afraid tongues would be wagging. Friends of mine are always telling me stories of conversations that they hear. And my name comes up all the time, and that's kind of frightening because I don't want any bad rumors to start going around, you know, anything tacky, because the word spreads fast. You really have to play it cool."

Cal most likely overestimated the importance of his sex life in providing grist for the gossip mill. He was, however, talked about among his peers, and not all of what was said was flatter-ing. The modeling game was, and is, a cutthroat business with many people fighting for a very few slots at the top. Cal hadn't yet reached the top, but he was close. He was going to exotic lo-cales for photo shoots, and his face was appearing everywhere.

Neither of his careers, considered separately, caused any prob-lems in the liberated—some would have said licentious—atmos-phere of New York City in the early '70s. What bothered some was the ease with which he could slip from one career to the other. A friend of Cal's met one of these young models at a party and later reported all the grisly details of the encounter. "This kid started rapping about me to my buddy," Cal told an interviewer with obvious relish. "'Well,' he said, 'anybody who's done mod-eling in New York just doesn't go around, just doesn't go out and make a *fuck movie!* I mean, how can anyone dare do that?' The guy started carrying on, and he's doing this whole number say-ing, you know, 'You just don't do that,' and finally he says, 'Well, you know what, that son of a bitch did it and got away with it.' And that's sort of the attitude a lot of people have had. They think it's sort of fascinating that I've been able to make it work." And sort of irritating, by all accounts.

When asked how he managed to get away with it all, Cal re-portedly said with a straight face, "My charisma." At that time it actually appeared to be the case. He was so charming, hand-some, poised, and eager to please that it looked very much as if he would pull it off—that he was going to be able to balance the two worlds and make them both work to his advantage.

*   *   *

Cal Culver was certainly the first and the most likely—and perhaps ultimately the only—gay porn star who ever had a chance of crossing over into the mainstream. He came along early on, took the media and the public by storm, had the brains and the savvy to charm big-name producers, actors, and directors, and he certainly had that ultimate necessity, star quality.

Michael Kearns worked with Cal onstage and on-screen in mainstream work and in porn. He knew the man and was able to watch him up close. "I've been part of the mainstream, and I've dabbled in the other side as well, so I know what I'm talking about. He was the first. He was really, seriously talked about as potentially crossing that invisible line into the mainstream world of Hollywood films. His acting was immaterial. He was a star. He had that ineffable quality of 'love me, I'll love you back.' He most definitely had star quality."

Gay men and lesbians were no strangers to Hollywood. The list of famous names rumored or known to be gay—Tyrone Power, Rock Hudson, Barbara Stanwyck, James Whale, Rainer Werner Fassbinder, Charles Laughton, Cary Grant, Randolph Scott, Montgomery Clift, George Cukor, John Geilgud, Agnes Moorehead, Greta Garbo, John Schlesinger—goes back to the beginnings of Hollywood itself. The aberrant sexuality of the stars was, however, a deep, dark secret known only to a few, never to the adoring masses who lined up to buy the tickets.

There was only one solution when gay actors wanted to become true stars—they had to marry. There was even a name for it—a "Hollywood marriage"—a euphemism that meant that the husband was gay and that the wife might be gay as well. In private many gay actors would be quite vocal about how much they hated the need for deception, but they inevitably shut up in public. Others behaved outrageously, then denied that they were anything less than 100% hetero. Many were so deeply closeted that they refused to have anything to do with anything even remotely gay. For them in particular Cal would have been a horror. Had he somehow cracked the code and gotten work in Hollywood, these men would have refused to have anything to do with a picture in which he acted. In the glamorous world of the silver screen, appearances were everything, and no one was willing to step out from behind the protective veil of heterosexuality. Anyone who is aware of the recent controversies regarding gays on television will be aware that nothing much has changed in the more than 25 years since Cal made his unsuccessful bid to cross the line.

However, there actually appeared to be serious possibilities for Cal, especially at first. He met director John Schlesinger and actor/director Raymond St. Jacques. Both men were interested in Cal—for various reasons—and both encouraged his thespian talents. By Cal's own reckoning he met a lot of film people in the wake of his *Boys* success and discovered that they were very curious about him. "I met a lot of people who wanted to find out what I was like. We'd talk for a while, and they'd say, 'You know, you're very nice. I didn't think you'd be this nice. I thought you'd be sort of, I don't know, a creep or whatever.' People had some conception that I would be sort of a cunt or something, that I would be very offensive, a hustler type. And I thought, 'Well, why shouldn't I be nice. I'm a nice guy.'"

The point is that they probably did expect him to be some "hustler" type—crude, boisterous, and offensive. That he would somehow be totally inappropriate to the hallowed realms of Hollywood. But he wasn't. And it gave all of them pause. "And it gave all of them an excuse to experience Cal up close," Jake Getty confided.

"Once when Cal was out in L.A., he called me up one night, practically frantic with excitement. 'You'd never guess what I've been doing out here,' he began, which made us both laugh. 'I saw so-and-so, and I had a date with such-and-such, and did you know that *he* was gay?' Honest to God, he was having the time of his life. Cal was funny about celebrities, you know. It didn't so much matter who they were as *what* they were. I once told him that I was convinced that he'd get a hard-on at the Forest Lawn cemetery. He just got this twinkle in his eye and winked at me."

In addition to his being considered for a film of Mary Renault's novel *The King Must Die*, Cal also said that "this Greek gentleman who owns the rights to the story was very impressed with me and really wanted to help my career and put me in this film. I mean, the part is not set, what I'm going to be doing, but I have been promised a part in that film. It's in the works." He was also approached by a man whom he coyly identified as an "unnamed filmmaker" who had, according to Cal, exquisite taste, great ideas, tons of financial backing, and whose every project turned to gold. "He's coming out with a feature and…he really wants me to do it."

And there was Raymond St. Jacques who told Cal that he thought Cal was "gonna make it big in the film industry, and I would like to help you in any way I can. I haven't signed a contract yet, but Raymond has asked me to do his new film…Raymond told me 'When I saw *Boys in the Sand* I thought to myself, "If that kid can be that relaxed doing sex in front of a camera, there's got to be something there in being able to act."'"

In addition, a director-choreographer, "whose name I really don't want to mention at this point," was reportedly working with Cal on a nightclub act that was called *Casey at the Baths* and was slated for an opening at the Continental Baths. Shades of Bette Midler.

One of Cal's biggest dreams was to do the movie version of Patricia Nell Warren's best-selling novel *The Front Runner*. There was talk of Paul Newman playing the coach, and Cal was actually approached by the producers at one point to sound him out for playing the part of Billy Sive—the runner of the title. The prospect was bandied about for years, but nothing ever came of it.

And then there was the unnamed director—perhaps Michael

Bennett of *Chorus Line* fame—who "came up with a fantastic idea for a musical that he's writing for me—it's incredible, just brilliant, completely original. He had become very kind of infatuated with me. He just felt that something was going to happen to me, and he wanted to help me make it work. So I have been sort of collaborating with him, giving him a lot of ideas for it, but my job is to really get my voice together and learn to tap dance. And it's my own undoing 'cause I created this incredible tap number for the show, so I've got to get it together."

In addition to all the theatrical possibilities, Cal was supposedly collaborating with photographer Roy Blakey on a book that would have interspersed fan letters to Cal with Blakey's photographs of Cal. "Again, it's that sort of cult thing, of buying a book with pictures of Casey Donovan. But a lot of people have made money on me, and I'm going to start making money on what's happened."

*   *   *

One of the really great things that had actually materialized for Cal in 1973 was landing a series of bit parts in the Ellis Rabb production of Shakespeare's play, *The Merchant of Venice*, at Lincoln Center. The play starred Rosemary Harris and Christopher Walken, featured a very '70s homosexual relationship between two of the main male characters, and provided Cal with yet another chance to strut his stuff in public. He had, according to his count, "about five different shticks," the most memorable "in this incredible masque, with huge heads and headdresses and costumes and a boy on stilts wearing a dress. It was just incredible, really a nightmare, and I played Jesus Christ. I had my crown of thorns and my G-string and my 8-foot cross, and that was it. So it was quite a moment." Quite a moment, indeed, as Cal appeared on the stage in a chain-link G-string, no less, his buffed body at its most delectable.

Family and friends were in the audience cheering him on. This was a part of his career that he could openly share with his family, and he made it a point to invite them, then provide good complimentary tickets and trips backstage after the performance. Helen Van Fleet and daughter Alice made the trip into the city on a regular basis. "We saw all the plays Cal did in New York," Alice said. "All of them." His mom came, and so did his brother, Duane. "Oh, yeah. We went into New York and saw some of his plays and movies," Duane said. "Movies" it should be clearly understood did not include the hard-core features. It was the one aspect of his life that Cal kept as far from his generally accepting—if sometimes bemused—family as possible.

*   *   *

Cal did seem to be "getting it together," as he had suggested he should, but there were already signs that things were beginning to fall apart. There had been that trouble at the Wilhelmina Agency. "I really thought I was gonna get the ax from my agency last year. I've had a couple of instances where I've lost modeling jobs because people know who I am, and they're uptight about using me because they're afraid that somebody in East Podunk is gonna know who I am." Maybe the folks in East Podunk knew, maybe they didn't. The important thing was that the modeling agency knew and the executives who controlled the ad content knew. Rumors got around. He lost the Arrow Shirt ads, then the Sunday supplement of the *New York Times* declined his services. A proposed travel poster was killed—they were advertising an upscale vacation, not a holiday in Sodom, they said. Ultimately Cal lost his lucrative Valentino connection. Finally, he was no longer a viable property among the modeling agencies.

In some ways Cal just didn't seem to get it. As Jake Getty recalled, he had difficulty separating the legitimate theater from the world of porn. "Cal threw a cast party for the Rabb production of *Merchant of Venice* where he actually screened *Boys in the Sand.* He had brought in a projector and a screen and set it up in the living room of the apartment. It was really bizarre. Some people sat and watched it. Others left the room. I'm sure that in Cal's mind he did it to let them know that he was a star in his own right, not just some extra doing a walk-on in their play. He wasn't the least bit shy about it. He obviously viewed it as a special little treat for his coworkers. It was quite clear to me that they didn't have a clue what to make of it. They were, for the most part, dumbfounded. Cal was blissfully oblivious to it all.

"He really did see himself as the king of gay porn, as the man who was going to bridge the gap between porn and mainstream. He really didn't see—and I honor him for it—the difference between the two mediums. To him it was all an expression of theater. To give him some credit, there was a great deal of legitimate theater with nudity and sex, implied sex in any case. Cal felt that there was no difference, that it was just a matter of how you perceived it. For him it was all a matter of the expression of emotion. He saw no difference between the nudity in *Hair* and the nudity and sex in *Boys in the Sand.*"

Cal, although he was concerned about his declining marketability, did his best to be philosophical about his work in pornography. "I don't have any regrets. I've done it, I have to live with it and cope with it. I can't turn back and say I wasn't in it. There it is, for all the world to see. I'd never deny that I've done it. I mean, I can't. Why should I?"

Why, indeed? Cal was ready to move forward, to fulfill the promise that some saw in him. There had been an article in *Variety* that had singled Cal out as the bridge from hard-core to legitimate features. Cal really believed that his career had been legitimized and that nothing stood between him and the great world of fame and stardom. "If someone comes along and legitimizes my career, there's no use going backward. And I just feel that doing porno is going backward, it's not going to advance me. I mean, My agent just came back from California, and evidently I have a big, big fan following in California, and people do talk about me. I'm sort of an interesting commodity, but a lot of people are afraid to take a chance with me because I've done the porno films. That's why I don't want to do any more. Because I'm really afraid now of jeopardizing, now that I do have a legitimate film career going, and I don't want to jeopardize any good modeling jobs."

Cal was, for a time, perfectly willing to consign Casey Donovan to the ash heap. "It's a very funny thing being recognized and being known by some people as Calvin Culver and being known by other people as Casey Donovan. A friend of mine said the other day, 'Jesus Christ, you talk about Casey Donovan like he's a third person.' And I really do, because I just have to separate him. I feel he's an entirely different person, someone else.

"Now I'm at the point of my career where that's really difficult, because I'm absolutely schizophrenic. I have to play one against the other. I haven't exactly killed Casey Donovan. I thought at one time I was going to take out an obit in *Variety*, and I was going to put 'In Memoriam Casey Donovan,' and I was going to officially kill Casey Donovan. Then I decided I better not because I might need him one day when I need some bread, so I decided he's just away." It was to prove a wise decision as the years ahead of him took shape.

*   *   *

Wakefield Poole was very blunt in his assessment of the situation. "The truth was that he was a homo porno star, and once he did the films, his career was down the toilet. He could never have had a career other than porn after he had done those films. The same thing happened to me. I had several irons in the fire, but after *Boys in the Sand* came out, and then *Bijou* and *Moving*, all with my name on them, everything went up in smoke. Bottom line, the legit film line couldn't be crossed. They would exploit you, but they didn't dare let you do a legitimate movie. The ugly truth was that there was no crossing over. None at all."

*   *   *

One unpleasant brush with reality occurred in April of 1973 when Cal lost out on his chance to costar in Frederick Comb's play *The Children's Mass*. Cal's participation had been heavily promoted in *After Dark*, his magazine of choice, but to no avail. For some reason after five days of rehearsal Sal Mineo, the man who had brought Don Johnson and gay sex to the stage in *Fortune and Men's Eyes* released Cal from his contract. Combs had starred in both the stage and film versions of Crowley's *Boys in the Band* and was attempting to make his mark as a playwright. Cal, of course, was anxious to move into legitimate theater. What happened?

Different people had different stories to tell. Jake Getty was brutally candid. "He just wasn't a good actor. He got cast in a production of *The Children's Mass,* which was being done off Broadway. It actually had some literary merit, which was more than could be said for many of the gay-themed plays on the boards during that era. I remember sitting around in Cal's kitchen one night with Sal Mineo and Tom Tryon doing a reading of the play. Unfortunately, Cal just had no knack for getting the lines out. He was stiff and wooden. It was really painful to listen to because he just didn't realize how bad he was. I tried to help; Tom tried to help. Sal had really wanted him in the play. It was no good. He was let go during the first week of rehearsals. It was quite traumatic for him because he really wanted to make it in the legitimate theater."

Cal himself talked quite openly about the play, but he had a slightly different take on the situation. "I was released from the show 'cause I was just not right for the part. A lot of people are going to be very disappointed, because of course I was in the big ad in *After Dark*. They realized when they let me go that they were losing a great box-office potential, because you know my name has a certain draw and was going to sell tickets.

"Anyway, it's very chic this season to have your contract terminated. Everyone I talked to, agents and people who read the play and whatever, they all said they were very glad I wasn't doing it after all. It's probably the best thing that happened to me, because evidently it's just not working. If it wasn't meant to be, it wasn't meant to be."

In the event Cal was basically vindicated by the critics. Although praising a couple of the actors and a scene or two of the play, *After Dark*'s reviewer Robb Baker found that "the show pretty much falls apart; a sketchy plot bogged down with muddled religiosity, one-dimensional characterizations, and even two young children on the stage…I was also irritated by the ploy of having what was basically a gay theme filtered through the viewpoint of a playwright-character who happens to be 'respectfully' straight. Didn't that kind of normalcy-by-association 'liberalism' go out with 1950's attitudes towards Negroes-and-other-nice-quiet-minority-groups?" The show may have been a flop, but the brutal truth was that Cal had been judged inadequate to appear in it.

*   *   *

In the larger world around Cal, other gays were being subjected to more literal beatings. Increased visibility had created a backlash across the nation, bringing with it an upsurge in anti-gay violence, arson, and increased police harassment.

Offsetting these difficulties, however, were ordinances and resolutions passed in several major cities that banned discrimination against homosexuals in housing and employment. Perhaps the single-most-important step forward on the path of gay liberation was the decision by the American Psychiatric Association's board of trustees that homosexuality was no longer to be considered as an illness. This did not stop the bigots, or the police harassment, but it did legitimize the struggle for equal rights.

*   *   *

Cal really wasn't feeling the ill effects of his pornographic exposure or his perceived lack of talent quite yet. He was maintaining—his natural ebullience helping him over the rough spots. He was also enjoying the adulation of the men who congregated night after night at the stage door to get a look at the hunk who was playing the part of the near-naked Christ in *The Merchant of Venice.*

Eric Stone, blue eyes sparkling in his tan, unlined face, was one of the bold ones who stepped forward, captured Cal's attention, and bagged him. "I saw *Merchant,* and I let him distract me from the substance of the show. He was amazingly hot. He had the most gorgeous thighs I had ever seen on any man.

"Well, after it was over, I went up to an usher and told him I wanted to go backstage and get an autograph from Rosemary Harris who had portrayed Portia in the play. He directed me through a door, and I went back into the realm of lights and ropes and scenery and sweating extras that had brought the show to life.

"I finally saw him, talking to one of the other cast members whom I recognized as that guy who played the cowboy in *Boys in the Band*—(that guy was Robert Tourneaux who had gone from featured player to extra in short order. Playing that gay-identified role was a curse for him and effectively kept him out of the movies.) I got Cal's attention and asked him out for a drink. He smiled and accepted.

"We had our drink, and during the conversation, it was implied that there would be a charge for his services. I was ready to pay, so it wasn't a problem. We took a taxi to my place and did the deed. He was more than worth the price tag. I was a very satisfied customer and took advantage of his services many times over the years. I still miss him."

*　　*　　*

In addition to meeting gentlemen for professional purposes, Cal was very much a part of the party circuit that his current notoriety as porn icon/actor had opened for him. Jake Getty remembers him as "periodically checking out the party circuit that was so prevalent in New York at that time. Cal was not a die-hard party hound. On the contrary, he was mostly a loner who preferred staying home and eating popcorn popped in his own special pan while watching television." Cal did, however, get off on all the celebrities and the feeling of being on the inside track—being ushered to the front of the line at a crowded discotheque and not being made to wait with the common folks.

And there were plenty of celebrities whom he was able to rub elbows with in the democratic decade of the '70s. *After Dark*'s editor William Como had instituted an award to honor achievement in the New York entertainment scene. The '73 Ruby Awards honored Bette Midler as the entertainer of the year. Cal was there along with a stellar cast of partygoers—Bob Fosse, Sal Mineo, Mick Jagger, Lainie Kazan, Robert Joffrey, Carrie Fisher, Ethel Merman, Bernadette Peters, Patti

LaBelle, Ben Vereen and Louise Nevelson among dozens of others. With his sense of style and his natural grace, Cal was able to move comfortably among this high-powered crew, always at ease, always cool and gracious—every bit the star himself.

*   *   *

As 1973 came to a close, Cal got a call from director Radley Metzger. Metzger had a new film in the works, and he had a part for Cal. The film was *The Opening of Misty Beethoven*, one of Metzger's hard-core efforts, and the role was a small one. "I would have used him more, but there wasn't much more for him to do in the context of this film." The film recounts the sexual awakening of an uptight whore who is turned, Pygmalion-like, into a courtesan of great sensitivity.

Cal is a part of her training. He plays a gay art dealer in Zurich whom Misty is called upon to seduce. She gets her training for the role by way of a lesbian encounter, then pulls the same moves on Cal's fey art dealer. Cal is all mincing gestures and eye shadow, but his body looks good, as does the hard-on upon which Misty impales herself in their scene together. Cal is essentially nothing more than a prop here, a stiff prick for Misty to work herself to climax with. Cal is called upon to do little, but he acquits himself admirably, even producing a respectable money-shot at the end of the scene. This film was the end of the line cinematically for Cal—and perhaps he realized it. He did, in any case, bill himself as Casey Donovan, although that may have been merely a reflexive bow to the film's pornographic content. In any event it didn't matter—from this point on his only film engagements were gay and increasingly extreme hard-core.

CHAPTER 7

Tubstrip and Tryon

In the early months of 1974, Cal took time out for a provocative photo shoot for *Viva*, a more-or-less mainstream magazine for sexually liberated women published by porn mogul Bob Guccione. In it Cal once again bared all, this time for a publication with worldwide distribution. Zee Gajda's photography captures Cal at his tightly muscled best in lush flesh tones.

In the accompanying text Cal once again stresses his resolve to leave the world of Casey Donovan behind. "That part of my career is behind me now. It helped me bridge the gap into legitimate theater and movies." He also says that he is basically bisexual—a necessity for a magazine aimed at straight women—and goes on to describe the types he prefers, male and female. "If my mood is for a man…usually I go to the baths, where you have the most freedom and anonymity to get into almost any kind of gay or S&M scene…My kind of man is a dark, muscular Italian or Mediterranean type, the construction-worker type—almost the exact opposite of what I prefer in a woman, which is a…ballerina's body."

Cal's only regret about the shoot was the fact that his mother happened upon a copy of the magazine, supplied by a "helpful" neighbor. "It was her first real exposure to the undeniable identification of me as a porn star. Mom had actually heard of *Boys in the Sand* because it was mentioned in the text of a fashion spread in *After Dark* and because I had never mentioned it to her, she quizzed me. I gave her a bare bones explanation. My folks weren't enchanted. After that 'Viva' spread hit the neighborhood—well, she and my father began thinking about selling their motel and moving out of state at about that point in time. They just had no way of explaining it to the neighbors. My mom's dream is still that I'll make a G-rated movie she can show to the grandchildren."

*   *   *

Cal was about to get a good deal more exposure, this time in a gay play called *Tubstrip*. Cal was recruited by friend and mentor Jerry Douglas, who had both written the play—under the name A.J. Kronengold—and was directing it—under the name of Doug Richards. The play had had a brief run off-off Broadway in New York City, distinguished mainly by the fact that the ceiling of the Mercer Arts Theater where it was playing collapsed on the production. New Yorkers had given the play a tepid reception. Jake Getty described it as "a fluff piece—story and all. It was little more than a group of very attractive men involved in a paper-thin story with lots of gratuitous nudity. I understand that it was quite popular on the West Coast," he concluded. Perhaps the play was not sophisticated enough for the New York audience, but there was considerable interest— and available production monies—in Southern California. Cal, still stung by his recent release from the cast of *The Children's Mass*, agreed to lend his bad-boy cachet to this production. He packed his bags and headed off to sunny Los Angeles.

The cast included Gerald Grant, Cal's costar from Metzger's *Score*, as the sadistic leather man, reprising the role he had created in New York City. Also in the cast was Jim Cassidy, one of the studs in the West Coast porn machine's rapidly expanding stable of stars. Cassidy, even buffer and blonder than Cal, was something of a legend in the urban wilds of Los Angeles where his pornographic prowess had often been captured on film. He was given costar billing with Cal, although his onstage charisma couldn't hold a candle to the inimitable Mr. Culver.

The play opened in mid June and was instantly a popular success. *The Advocate*'s J. Moriarty reviewed it and found it "erotic, bold, wild, and very often genuinely funny." The reviewer went on to give the play a barely passing grade for originality and a failing one for its few feeble attempts at serious drama but left readers with an overall impression that it was sexy enough and displayed enough taut, bare male flesh to make the price of a ticket well worth it. "Onstage…what the audience is seeing is really what they're getting—plenty! The sexual electricity that *Tubstrip* generates could knock out the energy crisis…It makes absolutely no concessions to the straight or uptight gay sensibility." Gratuitous nudity has always, it would seem, been a surefire marketing technique. One can only assume that New Yorkers had been exposed to so much of it since the liberated '70s began that they were getting jaded by it.

Gerald Grant garnered most of the accolades for his acting ability, whereas Moriarty quibbled that "the much-heralded Calvin Culver (Casey Donovan) does okay as the pouty towel boy, but oddly enough he never once (at least at the preview) flashed a frontal view." Still, it was Cal the audiences had paid to see, and he stuck gamely with the play even as the Los Angeles run was extended into early October. He had his star quality to fall back on, and he really needed only to smile and look gorgeous, which he managed quite handily.

Years later, in a memorial piece on Cal, Jay McKenna recalled the excitement Cal's arrival in Los Angeles generated. "In 1974, Cal came to L.A. from New York to star in the West Coast stage production of *Tubstrip*...The buzz on the grapevine that Cal Culver was in town and appearing live was palpable...The party life, as always, was irrepressible...Cal was still the ultimate symbol of the young gay man, and every party invitation bore the postscript: 'Cal Culver may make an appearance.'"

Michael Kearns played onstage with him and spent quite a bit of time watching him, evaluating what he had that kept audiences coming back for more. "He had a quality that demanded that you pay attention to him. He wasn't a big guy—only about 5 feet 9 inches tall—but his body was beautifully proportioned. And he had that famously big dick. As far as his work in *Tubstrip* went, he was always 'present' on the stage—not just marking time. He looked great, and he was connected to the other players. I have to say that he always did his best and gave the play every bit of his energy. He wasn't an exciting actor. Pretty much everything he did was by rote. Really skilled actors keep finding new aspects to a role at every performance. Cal wasn't able to do that. If you threw in a new bit or a different posture or inflection, it really threw him. I got the feeling he was the type of actor who carved his characterization in stone and repeated it move for move every night. He wasn't incapable, but he wasn't versatile. He acted by the numbers. Of course, so did a lot of Hollywood actors—but they hadn't done the porn.

"You know," Kearns continued, "that he had been earmarked as a likely crossover into legitimate films. During the decade of the '70s, right up until '82 and the beginning of the AIDS crisis, he was considered for lots of stuff. After AIDS, that door slammed shut and was locked up tight. He used to talk about all the roles he was being considered for, but I think the truth was that Cal was more comfortable being a courtesan than an actor. His sense of self-worth didn't propel him in that direction.

"He really loved sex. Lots of sex. All the time. He was a fascinating guy. And he had a terrific impact on the gay community. He did a great amount to dispel the shame that gays had always been forced to feel about their sexuality and their bodies. For him it was all about not being ashamed. He really did make it OK to be gay and to have hot, wild, wonderful sex. He said, 'This is me; sex isn't a bad thing. You can be the all-American boy and still have gay sex.' I really loved him for his honesty and his courage."

*   *   *

The nightly doses of applause and adulation quickly healed Cal's injured feelings over the debacle with *The Children's Mass.* Once it became apparent that the Los Angeles run of *Tubstrip* was going to be a relatively long one, Cal settled in. He had top billing in the play—especially after Jim Cassidy left a month into the run—and he let himself become the star he'd always dreamed of being. He made his star's dressing room his own, installing a telephone, bringing in a couch, and hanging photos on the walls. As Jerry Douglas remembered them, they were "mostly photos of himself, particularly with other celebrities." He rented a car, so that he wouldn't be confined during the days when his time was his own. He also made time to meet with the fans who gathered at the stage door every night after the performance.

"In particular," Douglas continued, "there was one crippled youth who attended the show three or four times a week, each time purchasing a full-price ticket at the box office. He was at the stage door every night. We called him Eve behind his back (after the stagestruck character in the Bette Davis classic *All About Eve*—"but Cal was unfailingly gracious to the guy, who was blindly in love with the golden boy."

"Eve" would have been a natural for Cal to channel his sympathies and his sexual energy toward. Throughout his life Cal championed the underdog, particularly the physical underdog. "He was one of the most generous men I've ever known," Ted Wilkins said. "He would often tell the most amazing stories about the people he had visited. Terribly deformed or ugly people, people with all sorts of physical disabilities. When I asked him about it, he told me that they were wonderful people who needed someone to talk to, to relate to. Sometimes they also needed something sexual. Cal could always see beyond the ugliness to the lonely person inside."

"Eve" wasn't the only one to whom Cal was unfailingly gracious. "He was hustling," Kearns asserted. "He was turning tricks every day in that dressing room. He didn't haul in that damned couch to take naps. It got to be something of a joke because every time we moved on to a new city there'd be a new couch. Cal didn't make any bones about it. He certainly wasn't ashamed of it. He loved the sex, and the extra money didn't hurt either."

*Randy Loggins was one of the stage-door Johnnies who lucked out with Cal. "It was definitely the hottest show in town that summer," the tall, still handsome sexagenarian recalled. "Word of mouth was out that there was plenty of bare flesh. I thought the ticket prices were a little high, but what the hell? I got together with some buddies, and we went one Saturday night.

"Well, we weren't disappointed. There were plenty of good-looking guys up on that stage, but Casey was by far the hottest. I had seen him in *Boys in the Sand*, so I knew what he had and what he could do with it. Believe me, he turned me on big time.

"So after the show, my buddies and I figured it would be a goof to go backstage and get an up-close look at him. We slipped out into the alley first and smoked a joint, so we were flying by the time we got in to see him. Well, he was even better up close.

And he was nice. I guess I figured he'd be some stuck-on-himself queen, but he wasn't. He smiled and shook my hand and made conversation.

"I really wanted him, and I guess he could tell because every time I looked over at him, he was looking at me. Not to brag or anything, but I got the feeling he liked what he was seeing too. When my buddies and I got ready to leave, he leaned over and whispered to me that I should drop by the next day in the early afternoon. Right there at the theater. You better believe I made a note of the time and let him know I'd be there.

"The next day I was feeling a little silly when I drove over to the theater. Me a middle-aged man with my own business and all. I almost kept on driving right past the place, but something told me I should park the car and see what happened. I went back to the dressing rooms and knocked. He answered right away, draped in that same sexy towel he'd worn for the show. He saw me and this huge grin spread across his handsome face.

"He shut that door behind me and locked it, and we went at it, no holds barred, not a word spoken, just all raw chemistry. He was good. I was good. Hell, together we were great. We came once, then looked at each other and grinned. We started up again and didn't quit until there was nothing left to give. I don't know anything about him hustling. We were fucking, and there were no charges involved."

The majority of Cal's encounters that summer were of the pay-to-play variety, however. Jack Rockford was a handsome young model/escort who attended many of Hollywood's very private gay parties in the '70s. "It was all incredibly closeted—until you got behind those locked and guarded gates and were surrounded by the privacy of those high walls. Then it was unbelievable.

"There were actors, writers, directors, cameramen, agents—the whole gamut of Hollywood talent required to make a movie. Everything but the leading ladies—the female ones, that is. And, of course, there were always plenty of gorgeous guys clustered by the pool just hanging around, waiting for something to happen.

"Cal Culver was very recognizable. His picture was in the magazines and gay newspapers advertising his play and the X-rated movies he'd done. He was older than most of the other guys-for-hire, but he looked terrific. He also had real style. Most of the guys just stood around and preened and flexed their pecs, waiting for somebody to make contact with them. Culver was different. He mingled with those powerful movie people, talking to them, treating them like he was every bit as good as they were, which he was, of course. All of us were; we just didn't realize it.

"It was interesting, watching him work the crowd. For the most part he ignored the other young acting hopefuls—as often as not, they were looking to exchange a piece of ass for a shot at a good part rather than searching for a lay for themselves anyway—and went after the older guys. He'd be with the producers and directors, guys who could've been useful to him, I guess. Anyway, he'd turn on the charm, and then a little later you'd see him wandering up to the main house, side by side with one of them, chatting like he was closing some major deal."

Not all the functions Jack attended were as sedate as that. "There were some orgies when the chemistry was right and the booze and drugs had been flowing freely enough. The hustlers would get the word, and they'd start messing around, coming on to the guests, and getting them all worked up.

"People could be pretty uptight at first, but then after a few started to strip, things would really get going. Maybe it would start out as skinny-dipping, any excuse to shed the clothes, but it generally ended up as a sexual free-for-all." Cal would usually be right in the middle of it, stark naked, his often-photographed member at the ready, inspiring the troops.

"No matter what it was, he was into it. And he didn't stand around waiting to be serviced. He got in there and got down.

And he didn't zero in on the hottest little stud there, either. He'd be just as likely to make out with some unattractive older guy as anything. And he'd do anything—suck, fuck, you name it. He genuinely loved it all. You could tell that just by looking at him. The guy was damned good at what he did."

*   *   *

"In spite of being quoted in the June issue of *Viva* as saying 'that part of my career is behind me now'…the hot rumor in Hollywood is that Cal Culver will indeed make another 'Casey Donovan' type gay film," gay gossip columnist Harold Fairbanks trumpeted in the pages of *The Advocate*. "Cal will be in Hollywood for the summer in the stage hit, *Tubstrip,* at the Hollywood Center Theater, so his days are free to do other work, if he desires. Cal acknowledged that he has been approached to do a film while he's here, but so far, it's only in the talking stage."

In another column Fairbanks pushed another angle. "*Tubstrip* topper, Cal Culver, will *Break a Leg* for producer Lowell Chain. The movie, described as a '40s theatrical comedy-melodrama, goes into production at year's end."

As Cal settled into his *Tubstrip* run, the rumors were flying regarding upcoming film projects. The legitimate films were mere will-o'-the-wisps—the porn work materialized. Wakefield Poole was on the West Coast, and he was putting together a new concept. Three male couples were involved—the first and last involved in fantasy sex, the middle in a straightforward coupling.

Cal was in the first segment, "House for Sale," with Val Martin. Cal is inspecting a large, empty estate where he fantasizes seeing Martin in a greenhouse, on a tennis court and—shades of *Boys*—beside a swimming pool. Cal looks wonderful, as does Martin, but the latter can't seem to find an erection in his bag of thespian responses. Cal sucks him and otherwise does everything in his power to arouse the man, but to no avail. Martin appears to possess a sadistic side—punishment perhaps for Cal when Martin can't achieve an erection? Notably, Cal is given what amounts to his on-screen introduction to fisting in this film. The technique was employed in *Boys*, but so briefly that it was nearly invisible. Still, the segment, although surrounded by superior cinematography and solid production values, fails to deliver any real satisfaction. Cal's money shot is perfunctory; Martin's nonexistent.

That didn't stop Cal from screening it for his fellow *Tubstrip* cast members one night after his segment had been completed. "I was shocked," costar Michael Kearns said. "He got the whole cast together to watch this film he had made. He acted like it was *Gone with the Wind*. He really behaved like a star—not temperamental but like a real star. He didn't feel a bit of shame about what he did on the screen. Even when he was getting fisted, there was a certain elegance about him. He had incredible aplomb."

*   *   *

Cal hadn't yet given up on his plans to cross over, and he kept trying to negotiate the tricky waters of the film business. None of the contacts he made ever bore fruit. The problem was that people would tell him anything he wanted to hear just so they could get into his pants. Jake Getty saw it happen again and again over the years. "All it took was for someone to praise Cal, to tell him that he was going to be the next Tab Hunter or Robert Redford. He loved the praise. It was what he wanted to hear, and he believed it. It made Cal easy to manipulate. A business lunch, a half hour of bullshit talk, and down went the pants. Once he'd been had, the film man's mission was accomplished, and Cal would have to wait till the next one came along. He never made the connection and never found the man who was willing to put his money on the line for Cal and give him the chance to do his thing in Hollywood.

*   *   *

In the autumn of 1974, while *Tubstrip* was still running, Cal and Tom Tryon got together at a party at Richard Deacon's Los Angeles home. They had kept in touch since Cal had left New York City, and the chemistry between them was stronger than ever. The Tryon relationship was proving to have legs. What had, by most accounts, begun as a paying relationship back in New York when they got together at Cal's house party in January of '73 had developed beyond client/whore and friendship into something more serious. Was it love? Maybe. Was it intense? No doubt.

"It was all Sturm and Drang,'" in Ted Wilkins's view. "The two men fed on one another; their strengths and insecurities seemed to dovetail. Cal was probably not exactly an image of the type Tom had in mind as a cohort, but Cal was a wonderful, dedicated lover to him. I suspect that Tom might have used Cal from time to time as a lure to attract sex partners. On the other hand, Tom was in a position to be quite useful to Cal because of his contacts in the film industry."

Rob Richards observed the glamorous pair as well. "Cal and Tom were genuinely a couple. They were meant for one another in many ways. Tom definitely appealed to Cal's sense of glamour. He was a movie star, and he had connections. Of course, Cal had connections as well. When they got together, Cal was the boy getting all the attention, and Tom was a washed-up 'B' actor. Then Tom regained his success with his books and was propelled to stardom again."

But there was a darker side to the relationship, a hidden rot that threatened to spoil all the glamour for Cal. Wilkins put it quite bluntly. "Tom was a raging alcoholic, and I suspect that he used drugs as well. Cal didn't approve of either, which was all to his credit. He hated it when Tom drank. He didn't even want to be around him. Cal would occasionally drink a glass of wine, but he always claimed that even such a minor indulgence made him sick. I suspect it was the thought of what it did to Tom that made him sick."

Tryon was extremely closeted. As his career began to revive under the guise of best-selling author, he couldn't afford exposure. "Tom was very worried about discovery," Wilkins said. "He was very much into being a pain-in-the-ass writer. He was very moody, and I always thought that he was unstable."

This fear of discovery did have its humorous side. A woman friend of Wilkins let it be known that she was a huge fan of Tryon's and asked if she could meet him. Ted arranged a luncheon in a chic New York City eatery. "My friend and I were seated at a good table when Tom came in. He was literally swathed in furs. It was the biggest fur coat I had ever seen. He swooped through the restaurant and settled down in a welter of animal skins. No one in the place could have been unaware of the fact that the queen was lunching there that day."

Richards saw Tryon's instability and moodiness run amok. "All the paranoia caused by living in the closet made the drinking worse, and the drinking triggered the violence. Tom beat Cal. There would be horrible fights, and Cal would come to my place, all bruised and distraught. He'd go back to his own apartment—he kept his own place during the whole time he was involved with Tryon. They never really lived together, you know. Then a few days later, Tom would return, all smiles and apologies and promises. Cal would go back because of the glamour and because he really believed that Tom wouldn't do it again." It was a classic pattern of domestic abuse. But, of course, it wasn't all the time. And Tom was handsome and cultured and well-connected and famous. And he made it clear that he wanted Cal to stay. And he helped Cal. And he needed Cal's help in very important projects that were coming up.

* * *

Given his druthers, Cal would have left *Tubstrip* after the Los Angeles run and gone off to enjoy some dark version of domestic bliss with Tryon. He was growing weary of the constraints of performing nightly. "If they do a film of *Tubstrip*, it ought to be an animated cartoon," he groused to an interviewer who caught him during the San Francisco run. He also told the interviewer that he wanted out before the end of the local engagement and definitely wanted to bail before the show returned to New York City for a rerun—"for personal, off-the-record reasons"—reasons having to do with Tryon's feelings about Cal's all-too-public persona. But he felt obligated to continue. He realized that all the other people associated with the production were counting on his name to bring in an audience. He was the one element in the show that couldn't be replaced without endangering its viability. He was for a while, at least, indispensable.

And so he packed up at the end of the Los Angeles run and headed up the coast to San Francisco. Cal was especially delighted because Tryon joined him. When the cast arrived in San Francisco, Cal was beside himself with excitement at this new twist his life had taken. Michael Kearns met Cal at the hotel and rode up in the elevator with him. "We went from the first floor to the ninth. Cal was going on at about 90 miles an hour, talking about 'Tom this' and 'Tom that.' When the elevator stopped, Cal swooped out and made his way down the hall. I turned to one of the other guys on the elevator and asked him, 'Tom who?' Cal just assumed that everyone knew all the details of his life because it was *his* life.

BOY IN THE SAND

"Tryon was really a number. I mean, he was incredibly handsome. He kept a very low profile, never going to parties or anything like that. Cal became a stay-at-home as well. They were very much a couple.

"Tryon stayed with Cal throughout the San Francisco run of *Tubstrip*. He would sit in the back of the theater every night and just watch Cal. After the play was over, Tryon would come backstage and give Cal notes regarding his performance." After all, Tryon had been a relatively successful actor in his own right. Cal was a very receptive subject for his suggestions, attempting to do what Tryon wanted, anxious to gain his approval.

Gaining his approval did not, it would seem, extend to the point of becoming monogamous, at least not at first. Kearns was around Cal day in and day out and knew what was happening. "Cal was hustling through it all. The word was that he had first met Tryon as a paying trick, so the man was definitely aware of what Cal did for extra cash." Chances are, Tryon liked having a whore for a boyfriend. There was something very erotically charged about having a lover that other men were willing to pay for, buying pieces of what Tryon himself could now have for free any time he wanted it.

Besides, Tryon had little room to criticize Cal on the faithfulness front. He had left a lover of his own back in Los Angeles, a man he had no intention of breaking up with. Clive Clerk was an actor, a handsome man who would soon go on to play the role of 'assistant director' on Broadway in Michael Bennett and James Kirkwood's landmark musical *A Chorus Line*. The relationship definitely wasn't a ménage à trois; it was something extra on the side for Tryon, although Clerk was evidently willing to tolerate it. How ungrudging this toleration was is a matter for some debate. "Clive had an attitude," one acquaintance admitted after assurances of anonymity had been obtained. "Actually, he was kind of a prissy little prick." If so he probably had his reasons.

Tryon was certainly not the most undemanding of lovers. If he treated Clerk like he later treated Cal, Clerk may have been happy enough to have him out of the house. In any case Clerk kept the Los Angeles house up and running while Tryon was off screwing the famous porn star. Theirs was, apparently, a prototype of the open relationship of the '70s.

*   *   *

Cal was lucky to have the sexy distraction provided by Tryon. Not only was he bored with his role in *Tubstrip*, but the critics were also beginning to snipe at him. The play was still packing them in, but it was getting mixed-to-bad reviews, and the golden boy was taking a particular drubbing. He had never really had serious training as an actor and had begun to realize his limitations. He even admitted to one interviewer that his career was mostly a fluke, made possible, in large part, by his exposure in *After Dark*. There was also the unwelcome attention he got from San Francisco gossip columnist Herb Caen when he donned a tuxedo and did a big print ad for the prestigious I. Magnim department store. Caen brought up Cal's porn career in his column, which left nervous advertising executives at I. Magnim worried and ended all of Cal's hopes for further employment as a legitimate model in the city.

Tryon, although still enamored, wasn't too happy with Cal's notoriety himself. He saw himself as a quiet, dignified man with a huge reputation to worry about—a reputation that in the '70s could have been irreparably damaged by public exposure of his sexual preferences. As the cast packed up and moved the show back to New York City, Tryon went along as well, counseling Cal to give it all up and become a private citizen once again. From what we know of Tryon, this counseling was very likely given while he was in his cups, backed up by his big, powerful fists.

*   *   *

Cal resisted at first. He loved the notoriety his career had brought him. During an interview in San Francisco, Dennis Forbes got it exactly right: "Cool Culver digs being hot Donovan, gets off on taking friends to see himself on screen as Casey, doing what he does best, hand dialogue." He loved walking down the streets in almost any major city and having people do double takes. Although his pond was quite small and quite specialized, he was a very big frog in it, and he loved the accolades his assets brought him. He also liked the money he could exchange for a quick feel of those assets and was loath to give it all up. Still, he was paired up with a very hot, very famous, very well-connected guy, a guy who took him places and introduced him to people. Even if he happened to be the third wheel in a relationship, he was the one Tryon was sniffing around the country after, so who knew what might ultimately happen?

So Cal played *Tubstrip* out to the end, turning tricks in the afternoons in his dressing room at New York's Mayfair Theater where he was billed above the title, doing the show in the evening, then going off to Tom's Central Park West apartment most evenings, doing there what he did best of all.

The release of Poole's *Moving* stirred up just a bit more notoriety for Cal, highlighting him yet again as a devoted sex pig in a pornographic setting. He was his usual gorgeous self, but the fisting scene was beyond the bounds of what was considered—in public at least—polite gay sex, especially in the circles in which Tryon ran. He was, after all, a member of a social set of gays who were very successful, not to mention relatively discreet about their private lives.

In private Tryon very much liked the sense of sexual adventure Cal brought to his life. What more likely to pique the libido of a mature, strictly closeted man whose young manhood was squandered during the repressive '40s and '50s than a sexually liberated man such as Cal Culver? The golden boy of porn had libidinal skills enough to make a strong man weep—or scream for joy. Tryon was a willing participant in any exotic bedroom frolic Cal cared to devise. It was only in the much more public world beyond the bedroom door that he began to feel increasingly uncomfortable.

*   *   *

Fortunately for Tryon, he had something in mind devised to keep Cal busy—and under wraps. Tryon had had a book about Hollywood on the back burner for years. He had submitted a portion to his publisher a few years earlier and was told to wait until he had been away from Hollywood for long enough to gain a perspective on it. Now that *Lady* was on the shelves in the bookstores, it was time for Tryon to start something new. He decided to revive the Hollywood concept.

It was tough going at first. "I spent Memorial Day 1975 in the depths of depression," Tryon commented. "At two in the morning, my phone rang. It was Michael Bennett. *A Chorus Line* had opened, and he talked to me for about an hour. I think he was kind of stoned, and I was very sleepy, and I don't remember what he said, but he pepped me up to the point that the next day I sat down at the typewriter, put a page in, and wrote. It started coming, and before I knew it I'd pretty well finished a first draft of the first story in *Crowned Heads*."

Tryon ran with the idea to Robert Gottlieb, the editor in chief of Alfred A. Knopf, who loved it. There was only one catch, however. He wanted the remainder of the book finished in less than three months. Tryon balked, but Gottlieb held firm. The writer finally agreed and rushed back home in something akin to a panic. How the hell was he going to prepare so much manuscript in such a short time? Enter Cal, the pedagogue and private secretary, specs perched on his nose, typing fingers limber and ready.

Cal was an educated man, well-read, trained as a teacher. He was there with Tryon during the whole of that summer, retyping manuscript, making corrections in spelling, suggestions in continuity. Tryon worked 14-hour days, and Cal was there beside him, offering technical assistance when needed, comfort of another kind when the day's work was done.

As a result of all their hard work, the manuscript was completed in just five weeks. Although critical reception was mixed, the financial outlook was aces all the way. *Crowned Heads*, the collective title for Tryon's four novellas, had earned $4.5 million before publication and was purchased by Universal Studios for $1 million. The original novella, *Fedora*, that Tryon had taken to Gottlieb for his opinion was filmed by director Billy Wilder, but received only moderate critical success. There was talk of *A Chorus Line*'s Michael Bennett undertaking to direct another segment, but the project never came to fruition.

One can only assume that Tryon was grateful to Cal for his help, although he did not dedicate the book to his friend. Tryon did, however, provide Cal with access to the famous, glamorous people he so much admired. One of the celebrity whirls Cal was dropped into was that surrounding *A Chorus Line*, which was a phenomenally successful musical. Tryon was a friend of choreographer Michael Bennett and writer James Kirkwood, two of the men who were most instrumental in creating the show.

Arthur Beckenstein was Kirkwood's life partner and occasionally socialized with Cal. "Cal was very handsome, very attractive. He always dressed impeccably and was nothing at all like the porn image that he projected on the screen. One night I remember sitting next to him in a bar in the theater district before a play. He was all dressed up and wearing horn-rimmed glasses and I was looking over at him, thinking how he was more like Clark Kent than a porn star. He and Tom made a very attractive couple."

Cal loved it. He loved the glamour and the excitement of theatrical evenings, chatting and dining with famous men and their lovers, the high-society feel of it all. Tryon, on the other hand, did not. There was some discomfort with having both his gentlemen friends on the same coast. Clive Clerk had come to New York City and was performing in *A Chorus Line*. Liberated as their relationship may have been, Tryon's friends intuited that the affair with Cal was being carried on mostly behind Clerk's back.

In addition to matters of domestic comfort, there was the problem of being identified publicly as a gay man. Friends and associates in the entertainment industry knew all about his preferences—his extensive reading public did not. They knew him as a military veteran and a divorced man—he was a two-year survivor of one of those "Hollywood marriages" arranged by the studios to protect their gay leading men. He and Cal tried to be discreet, but it wasn't easy when walking around with the most recognizable porn star in the country, if not the world.

One afternoon during the intermission of a matinee of the musical *Annie*, Tryon was approached by a vitriolic columnist who hissed in his ear: "Gee, Tommie, that's the cutest trick I've seen you with in a long time." Tryon stiffened, paled visibly, turned on his heel, and stalked away. He and Cal did not return to their box after the intermission.

"They were basically very private—especially Tom," Jake Getty said. "They were just an ordinary couple—at least they appeared to be. They entertained at home when they were together. Tryon was keeping up his house out in Los Angeles, flying back and forth, juggling the various aspects of his life. Cal had his own apartment and his own friends as well. It was a very open relationship. All Tryon wanted was for Cal to be totally discreet about his life. It wasn't an easy task for Cal because he loved the limelight."

Roy Blakey had opportunity to observe the couple as well. "They made a gorgeous pair. I always rented a house on Fire Island for the summers with a couple of friends, and Cal often came out to stay with us. Tom came with him once or twice. He was unfailingly gracious. I went to a party he gave for Cal's birthday at his place in the San Remo on Upper Central Park West. The apartment was exquisite." It had, as a matter of fact, been decorated by Clive Clerk and when Tryon later gave it up was occupied by designer Calvin Klein. "I remember being struck by the beauty and opulence with which he had surrounded himself. He had a wonderful lifestyle. I was struck by how spectacularly successful he was. He maintained this life by writing books and selling them, rather than being a lawyer or a broker. Cal clearly felt right at home."

Cal's good friend and mentor, Wakefield Poole, also had opportunity to observe, or in his case, to not observe them. "When I lived in San Francisco, Cal brought Tom to my home there. They planned to stay the evening and ended up staying for two full days and nights. Cal wanted him to see *Boys in the Sand*. Cal evidently didn't have a copy at that point in time—this was before videos—and Tom wasn't the type of guy to venture into a porn theater. So I agreed to show it for them. I made dinner for them, started the film, then disappeared. Cal came into my room later and said they wanted to see more. They hung out in that bedroom and watched movies for two whole days." Apparently Tryon couldn't get enough of watching Cal's performance, in bed and on-screen. "Afterward they disappeared. Maybe they just wore each other out."

They continued in this fashion for almost five years, jetting from coast to coast, maintaining lives together and apart. When the break finally came, it was caused by the homophobia of Hollywood, not by any censure from the New York City scene. "In New York, Tryon could deal with his life with Cal," Jake Getty asserted. "In New York nobody asked or cared if a person was gay. In New York you could go to the Tony's with a lover. You could never do that at the Oscars in Hollywood. It was the Hollywood press corps that blew their friendship apart. Gays repress other gays in Hollywood. They are terrified that the trail will lead back to them, and they can't allow that."

In the end the break was abrupt—and permanent. Tom had been secretly planning a vacation with Cal. He wanted the two of them to go to Edward Albee's beach house in East Hampton. Everything seemed to be going smoothly, but there were spies about. On the third day of their stay, Albee showed Tryon a copy of the *Hollywood Reporter* with Rona Barrett's gossip column circled in red. The snippet of gossip was petty, pointless, and terrifying in its accuracy. "What male porn star is honeymooning on Long Island with an actor turned writer?" it asked.

It was more than the closeted Tryon could take. He panicked. He packed up his suitcase, booked a flight out, and was back in Los Angeles within 24 hours. Rob Richards had seen it coming. "Tryon had it all and wasn't willing to lose it. Cal was a great guy, but Cal was a whore and a porn star. Tryon couldn't deal with the risk of that kind of self-identification."

Tryon turned his back on the situation as though it had never even happened. Tom never saw Cal again. They kept in contact for a while, but they didn't see each other. "He was hurt by it," Jake Getty said. "He understood the immediacy of Tom's reaction to that bitch's blurb in her pathetic gossip column. He understood the need for damage control. What he didn't understand was the total cutoff in relations that it led to. He always believed you could work things out. His trust was shattered. He was genuinely hurt at the end. He was just this nice, defenseless guy. He had no street smarts, no fighter instincts. He had really believed that he could have it all, that everything could be fixed and made right. He was wrong."

Cal went back to the San Remo, gathered up the things he had been keeping there, and left. It was the end of the fantasy. He had discovered that he couldn't step out of his past and move on to new things as the partner of a glamorous, mainstream author. He was branded, set apart, banished. He later told Rob Richards during an interview that he had finally realized that he was being used. "During my second relationship [with Tryon] I began to feel I was being taken advantage of—that I was being taken for granted and not getting enough emotional feedback. Today, I'm not so sure I could have a lover again."

Cal was too optimistic, too ebullient, and too resilient not to make a comeback. He had been hurt, but he had not been destroyed. He had no savings, no career, no prospects. Still, he had his face and his body and an almost simpleminded faith that things would somehow work out. He walked out of Tryon's apartment for the last time and made his way across town to his own more humble dwelling. It was time to burrow in and come up with something new. It was time to bring Casey Donovan out of retirement.

CHAPTER 8

Alone Again

When Cal parted ways with Tom Tryon in the summer of 1977 and made his way back into New York City's gay scene, things were hopping. Gay bars were proliferating, becoming increasingly extreme in the tastes to which they catered. Cal, although not an avid bar person, was always a man who wanted to know what was going on. Besides, he had been effectively out of circulation for a while, and he wanted to get a firsthand look at what was happening.

*   *   *

A great deal had been happening indeed. Since the sexual revolution of the '70s had begun, there had been an exponential increase in the number of gay bars in the Village. They played host to the young, the beautiful, the rich, and the famous, jamming them all together seven nights a week. Drugs were sold openly, and the air reeked of marijuana smoke. The '70s were under way. Some of these new bars were exciting, although most were just pale copies of a particularly successful predecessor. One of the wildest of the former type was The Anvil, a notorious establishment located in the meatpacking district of the West Village at the corner of 14th Street and 11th Avenue. After other bars closed at 4 A.M., hundreds of gay men would descend on the place, swarming around an upstairs bar studded with go-go dancers. Downstairs, men checked their shirts, watched porno movies, and slipped into a pitch-black back room to have that paradigm of gay life during the '70s—anonymous sex.

"I saw him there several times," said *Carl Porter, now a buttoned-down broker who was an inveterate bar hopper in those days. "It was no big deal really. Any night of the week, there'd be hundreds of guys there, some of them so famous you couldn't believe your eyes, some of them so sleazy you'd instinctively grab for your wallet. They all came to The Anvil. He wasn't there as a sight-seer either. Those were easy to pick out, standing around, hugging themselves, looking like scared rabbits. Sometimes the rabbits would get spooked and run out." Carl chuckled softly. "Sometimes they'd end up in the back room."

Carl agreed that Cal was no rabbit. "He was intense. He had this look on his face, this serious look that said he wanted to get laid. Lots of the guys had that look, so it wasn't hard to read. He was a great-looking guy, so lots of people noticed him. But the fact of who he was didn't get anybody too worked up. Compared to some of the people hanging out in the shadows, he was a minor celebrity.

"He pretty much did what all of us did back in those days— dance a little, cruise a little, and go back and have a little sex. I never saw him doing any drugs, but that doesn't mean he wasn't doing it. Hell, the whole world was on drugs back then—or so it seemed. My personal favorite was a Quaalude washed down with a couple of shots of scotch. When I felt like I was floating about a foot off the floor, it was time to head to the back room for a little action.

"I had a system. The back room was pitch black, but I still wanted to know what I was getting into. Maybe you could say I was selective." Carl laughs deprecatingly. "Anyway, I'd have a little cache of joints in my pocket, rolled damn near thin as toothpicks. I'd make a big deal lighting the joint, toking, then holding it up. Never took more than five seconds for a whole bunch of hands to come climbing up my arm for that doobie. The light from the match gave me a chance to see what was going on around me—such as who was blowing whom, that sort of thing. As long as I kept the joints coming, nobody bitched too much about the light.

"I followed him into the back room one night, did my routine with the match, got a bead on him. He was kneeling on the floor, giving head to about five guys. I slipped over there and wormed my way into the lineup. I popped the buttons on my fly and just let it hang out. We were all standing real close, hip to hip, and hands were everywhere. Somebody grabbed my piece and started frigging it, and I reached out and grabbed a hard-on that was all slippery with spit. I started working it, then the hand on my piece went away, and I was engulfed by this hot whirlwind with a tongue in the middle of it. I mean, that guy could suck. He did me for about a minute, then moved on, leaving me panting. The guy to my right snorted, and I knew he was getting it then.

"At one point in the proceedings, I lit up another joint to pass around. I was getting blown at the time and I looked down while the match was still flickering. I caught his eye for just a second. Man, was he intense. It was like sucking that lineup of pricks was the most important thing in the universe. Who am I to say? Maybe it was."

Perhaps the wildest, most intense place in the city was The Mineshaft at 835 Washington Street in the meatpacking district. It had opened in October of '76 and quickly became legendary. It had been a bar catering to laborers—truckers and meat packers in bloody aprons—who stood around and drank beer after their shifts ended. It was transformed into a place of dark desire and forbidden passions—a place that for most people was strictly beyond the bounds.

Everything about it was hyper—the setting, the sex, the music. It seemed, according to some patrons, to induce a dream state. Or perhaps if it hadn't been for all the appropriate drugs, a nightmare state. Every fetish was readily available—piss, S/M, fisting, bondage, humiliation—and there was always someone who wanted to participate.

Celebrities hung out here as well. The German film director Rainer Werner Fassbinder found the atmosphere of the place quite appealing. Scenes of every type were acted out, every fantasy, no matter how bizarre, was possible. Fisting scenes were common—with naked men splayed out, crucifixion style, on a scaffold. Another man would stand below, slowly inserting his arm into the bound man, sometimes up to the elbow. There were wild rumors that Cal had appeared more than once on the scaffold. Cal—or one of hundreds of the city's gays with a similar physique and a leather hood—undoubtedly was there. For every masked supplicant who appeared, a dozen rumors arose that he was this famous actor or that well-known model or a particularly debauched socialite. Given Cal's affinity for this particular variation on the theme of sex, it is possible that he was up on the scaffold at some point, although there is no solid evidence to prove it.

In white porcelain bathtubs in a room in the basement, other scenes of degradation were played out as men crouched in the tubs, begging to be pissed on. Chemical stews of all kinds were available from on-site drug pushers to enhance the experience. The bar offered a weird obverse view of the end result of decades of repression that gays had endured. It was total freedom, veering into dementia.

*   *   *

Perhaps the most sociable of the gathering places for gays as they celebrated the new climate of liberation were the discos. Entrepreneurs turned abandoned spaces into meccas where gays danced, drank, and drugged their way to happiness. By 1975 there were hundreds of discos across the country—dispensing dry ice, flashing lights, and a pounding beat. Increasingly sophisticated drug combinations were thrown into the mix, spawning a subculture of music and sex.

The final, most extreme flowering of this mania for discos took place in an abandoned television studio that had originally been built as an opera house. When Studio 54 opened its doors in 1977, it was in a terribly unfashionable section of Manhattan, on the fringe of the theater district. Although only Thursdays and Sundays were officially "gay nights," the boys were there every night, and the clientele was always very mixed.

The club was huge, capable of holding 2,000 people. The lighting was eye-poppingly complex—reportedly programmed with more than 400 separate sequences—there was a "man-in-the-moon" figure with a cocaine spoon who descended from the ceiling periodically, and the decor was changed regularly. And, of course, there were the people. Everyone who was anyone hung out there: Calvin Klein, Andy Warhol, Bianca Jagger, Halston, Michael Jackson, O.J. Simpson, Mikhail Baryshnikov. Even the infamous Roy Cohn, who had persecuted gays while on Senator Joe McCarthy's staff during the homosexual persecutions of the '50s, was a regular. He brought in tricks and important clients alike to show off his power and influence. Actor John Burke was there one night dining with Cohn. "Tom Tryon was there that night—along with owners Rubell and Schrager and designer Halston—that crowd. I would also see Cal there from time to time but never with Tryon." This would have been when the two were no longer a couple, and Tryon was doing his best to avoid Cal.

The place was a veritable den of drugs and sex. There were the public areas where the masses partied, and then there were the VIP areas, reserved for the most glamorous of all—Warhol, Calvin Klein, Halston, and Liza Minnelli among them. Once a person had penetrated the inner sanctum, sex, drugs—anything you wanted—was available.

Cal, although by no means an inveterate disco hound—"neither of us was into the big dance craze," Jake Getty recalled—he would sometimes drop in just to see and be seen. He still had the connections and the panache to get in without waiting in the ever-present line that snaked down around the block. Sometimes he would drop in after a gallery opening, a play, or a concert and table-hop for an hour, then disappear into the night, making his way home to change so that he could continue his evening in the park or at one of the city's bathing establishments.

*   *   *

Cal actually preferred the baths. There was something more focused about them, more honest. Here, there was nothing to distract from the main attraction—sex, sex, and more sex. Clothes, inhibitions, pretense, and all social distinctions were checked at the door when identity was exchanged for a white towel and a key. It was the perfect democracy of the flesh.

The Everard, originally a church, was converted into a bath-house in 1888 by James Everard, a prominent financier, brewer, and politician. It was in the heart of the notorious Tenderloin entertainment district in lower Manhattan, surrounded by famous theaters, restaurants, and whorehouses. In its early years it was known for its wealthy and middle-class clientele. Gays had been frequenting the place since World War I. By the early '70s, the Everard baths was notorious as a gay cruising venue—the boys christened the place "Everhard"—and remained so until it was destroyed by fire in May 1977 when nine patrons lost their lives. The place was revered by many as a camp, with its fake Roman front that some thought resembled a marble mausoleum. That, however, did not deter Cal and hundreds of other gay men from flocking there.

Retired photographer *Richard Nichols remembered him vividly. "I was 'resting,' if you will, between encounters. I had a room and was sitting on the bed with the door open. Well, I looked out into the hall and noticed this number who had taken up a position just across the hall. His face was in shadow, but his rather perfect body was on conspicuous display. In retrospect that was a good thing because if I had known who he was, I wouldn't have been able to perform. I would have been too intimidated.

"While I was sitting there staring at him, he pushed himself away from the wall, walked into my cubicle, knelt down at the side of the bed, and proceeded to give me the most fabulous blow job I had ever experienced. When he was done I looked down at him, and he looked up. I was completely shocked. I was speechless at first. Then when I finally managed to gather my wits about me, I said: 'Excuse me, but weren't you Casey Donovan?' Well, he thought that was very funny. He burst out laughing, and so did I. He got up off the floor and sat beside me on the bed, and we talked. He told me that he loved having sex, especially with older men. He was quite gracious and witty and charming. No wonder people were willing to pay big money to have him. And just think, I got lucky. I had him for the cost of admission to the Everard."

There were many bathhouses in New York City at that time, and Cal was definitely an aficionado. There was the Saint Mark's with its chrome snack bar, its chic black-tiled showers, and the portholes in the steam rooms. There was also the Continental

Baths where performers on the way up—and on the way down—
performed for towel-clad patrons. In addition there was Man's
Country in the Village where a mock-up of an 18-wheeler dominated the third floor. Cal visited them all, striving to scratch the
itch that drove him throughout his life.

*   *   *

Cal's other preferred venue for meeting tricks was the street.
The streets of New York City in the '70s were a great gay cruising ground, especially in the environs of Greenwich Village.
Streets were crowded with handsome, available men of all ages
and types. In the afternoons a man could wander along Christopher Street, maybe even as far as the piers, and find some action.
There were always good-looking guys hanging out, ready to talk,
share a joint, then go back to their apartment—or yours,
whichever was more convenient—and have sex.

"A lot of us saw him out and about," *Sam Kaiser recalled.
"Even if you hadn't seen any of the movies or the pictures in magazines, there was some friend who'd poke you in the ribs and say,
'Hey, man, that's Casey Donovan. He's the one who made those
incredibly hot fuck films.' It was cool, you know, not that much
of a big deal. Hell, everybody was fucking like rabbits, so the fact
he had done it on film wasn't that special. Of course, he had done
a hell of a job at it.

"So this isn't even my story. It's my buddy Gary's story, only he
isn't around to tell it. But I remember it, so here goes. Gary was
out on his day off, running errands, keeping his eye on the talent
as he went. Believe me, Gary was a real looker—body by
Michelangelo—so the local talent was eyeing him right back.
He'd taken care of the mundane stuff—the dry cleaning, the shoe
repair, picking up some underwear while it was on sale—and he
was thinking about going back home. But first he wanted to go

into this record store that he really liked to look for a recording.

"In he went, right over to the musicals section. Gary was a nut for musicals. You know, one of those guys who knew all the words to every show that had played on Broadway for the past ten years and who would camp out for a weekend to get a ticket to an opening. So I guess Gary was looking through one of the bins when he bumped into this guy who was also looking for a recording.

"After the 'excuse me' and all that, they went back to their searching, and it turned out that they were both looking for the same recording. The only problem was, there was only one copy left. Well, Gary had recognized the guy as Casey, and he insisted that he take the recording. After a few rounds of 'you first, no, you first' Gary gave the recording to Casey. Then when he was leaving the store, Casey came up to Gary and asked him if he'd like to go to the theater with him. He assured Gary that he could get tickets for that show, which as Gary told it were impossible to get. Gary gave the guy his number, figuring that would be the end of that. But damned if Casey didn't call with the tickets. Good ones, too, according to Gary. So my buddy got it all—the porn star and the musical." There were hundreds of other guys on the streets in those sexual glory days of the '70s, and Cal managed to reel them in by the score. He had the look, the charisma, the libido—he wanted them all it seemed, and he got them all.

There were also many big parties, and Cal was always on the guest list for the big parties. He didn't look forward to them avidly or plan for them weeks in advance as many in the New York City gay set did in those days, but if the names were interesting enough, or if a friend wanted to go with him, he'd go.

At one of these parties, Federico Fellini, the famous Italian director, was guest of honor. Cal took his buddy Jake. "It was extremely bizarre. We got there, and the place was littered with dozens of pretty-boy types. Everyone was standing around waiting for something. It was like being on a set before the director calls for action. Then I saw Fellini. He was examining the boys. It quickly became clear that nobody was allowed to start partying until the man had made his choice of companions for the evening. Once that ritual was complete, people relaxed. From then on all was right with the world."

*   *   *

But not all was right. There was a huge cloud looming, casting a shadow of epidemic proportions over the partying throng. Syphilis and gonorrhea were spreading throughout the United States at an alarming rate, reaching epidemic levels in the overall population. Worse, the gay community was experiencing what health experts termed a "pandemic," a subject the gay public simply didn't want to talk about.

The statistics were horrifying: half of the nation's male syphilis victims were gay, giving gay men five times as many chances of having syphilis as men in the general population. The statistics for gonorrhea were equally disturbing: gay men were four times as likely to have gonorrhea as their straight counterparts."

Because of deeply ingrained homophobia, there was very little information available about gay venereal disease. It was viewed as a moral problem not a health problem. In Portland, Oregon, for one chilling example, a medical association survey revealed that more than 80 percent of physicians who responded said that they would refuse to treat gay patients. In 1975 the federal government spent only about one-half of 1% of its venereal disease budget on gay men despite the government's knowing that gays accounted for a significant proportion of the venereal disease problem.

Many gays weren't even aware of the fact that gonorrhea could affect the throat and the anus. Sexually active gay men needed regular throat and anal cultures, but they weren't getting them. The straight clinics weren't at all understanding of, or receptive to, the gay clientele, so the gay community finally began opening clinics for their own people. The results were encouraging, but still many people didn't bother to go in for checkups. It was a problem that would become devastating in the years to come.

Cal, given his post at the center of the sexual maelstrom of the '70s and '80s, was almost certainly exposed. He was a fastidious man—a man who was almost neurotic about cleanliness. If he had ever been afflicted with venereal disease, he would have made a quick, discreet trip to his physician for the appropriate course of medication. For all the up-front attitudes about sex that were prevalent at the time, venereal disease wasn't often discussed openly. It was, at worst, a minor inconvenience easily cured by a quick trip to the clinic. Besides, many swore that a skinful of penicillin on Friday meant that you were invincible and could play all weekend with impunity.

*　　　*　　　*

Right around this same time, in 1977, the religious right began to stir. It started when a gay rights ordinance was proposed in Dade Country, Florida. Gay and lesbian Americans were beginning to come out of the closet in large numbers, demanding equal rights. The courts of the land still didn't get it, but cities like Miami were sympathetic to the rights of their citizenry, even those who happened to be gay.

Christian fundamentalists viewed gay lib as a call to battle. All they needed was a mouthpiece. Enter Anita Bryant, former Miss America, spokeswoman for the Florida orange industry, star manque. Bryant, hounded by her own demons, headed a coalition that was determined to defeat the Dade County gay rights ordinance, considering it a "threat to our children." The subsequent campaign against "predatory" gay men and lesbians worked. The ordinance was repealed, making it clear that gay men and lesbians would still have an uphill fight to gain their civil rights.

*   *   *

There was a darker side to liberation—a side that was becoming more prevalent. It was worrying to many but embraced like a holy cause by others. One of the most potent images of this state of grace was the back room. Arnie Kantrowitz wrote hauntingly—disturbingly—of the subject in an issue of *The Advocate* in 1978. "Back rooms may lie somewhere between the borders of extravagance and excess; they may be an extreme of sexuality; but they are nonetheless a truth, a necessary data for those of us who love to explore more than the socially approved aspects of our human nature…Here there is the relief of shamelessness…Promiscuity is part of the unique heritage of gay men, and because there is potential good in it, we should fight to preserve it along with the survival of our identity as a community." These words, and the attitudes they represented would come back to haunt gays with a vengeance.

*   *   *

This attitude toward promiscuity was, in part at least, the way in which Cal chose to define himself for the remainder of his life. He perversely became something of a poster boy for this type of excess, even though it did not by any means represent the sum total of the man he was. It was another part of his victimization, the victimization of gay people in general by the straight world. The furtive habits were too deeply ingrained to disappear instantly, even for a man as open about his sexuality as Cal Culver. Although he maintained a weird, schizophrenic innocence up to the end of his life, the path he chose was the one of greatest excess.

Jake Getty was in a position to watch this period of experimentation. "When we first met, Cal was pretty much a vanilla type of guy. I remember that we were at a party, and we met some people who were into S/M. They talked about what they did, and Cal just couldn't understand it. He was really shocked. He thought it was kind of silly, actually."

He got over that feeling in later years. As early as 1973 in the film *The Back Row*, he was trying on leather harnesses and hats, riding dildos and exploring the accoutrements of S/M. A few years later he ran into a man in Los Angeles who initiated him fully into the mysteries of serious S/M. The man was referred to only as Officer Master, and he and Cal got together to "play" a number of times over the years. Cal laid out the relationship in "Men and Films," a 1983 video interview originally intended for a gay cable television show.

"Officer Master stands for a very hot pal of mine. He has about 37 sexual slaves that he plays with. I was always his number one. I never had a number, because I was his S/S—his special slave. When I went to L.A. in 1980 to celebrate paying off one of the mortgages on my house in Key West, I decided I wanted to be his slave full time for three days. I gave him this tattoo as a present." Here Cal bared his flank, exposing a small, discreetly tattooed O/M to the camera. "This man is the most professional sexual person I have ever met. The most imaginative fantasy man. I can tell you that he's taken a lot of people, including me, to a lot of interesting heights. He's very special. He's the hottest daddy in L.A."

During the filming of *Boys in the Sand II* in 1983, Cal filled Rob Richards in more fully regarding the juicy details behind his connection to Officer Master. "Cal was staying in a house by himself, not with the rest of the cast. He asked me to stay with him. There was an early call one morning. There was a shot in the bay that had to be nailed down before there was any boat traffic around. We got up for a 5 A.M. call and were rushing around, trying to get ready. He was in the shower, and I was shaving. When he stepped out and began to dry off, I noticed this tattoo, this tiny O/M on his right flank. I asked him about it, and he told me that 'it was the mark of a master.'

"He had that look on his face like he wanted to say more, so I quizzed him. He told me that the mark was required for anyone who dealt with this particular master. He then told me that the identical mark appeared on the flank of an actor who had starred in one of the mostly wildly successful films of 1977. The man's career bottomed out in the early '80s but took off like a rocket about four years ago. Now he's on the top of the heap again. Cal loved the idea that he had the same S/M master as this guy. If he were alive today, he'd be ecstatic about the proxy celebrity of it all."

*   *   *

Cal seemed to think that he had to try everything and everyone at least once. Perhaps it was a preparation for a life of serious hustling, which was the career that seemed more and more likely to be his lot in life. Acting wasn't in the cards, not in legitimate films at any rate, and teaching was so far behind him it seemed like another lifetime. If he planned to hustle, then he would study it and apply himself to being the best hustler possible.

He had a fling with the legendary porn star John Holmes, what must have amounted to a sort of "clash of the titans." He also slept with a few women. Jake Getty remembered that there was one blond woman. "She was something of a chunky girl. Cal was actually kind of proud of having managed it, I think. It was mainly done as an experiment. He was giving everybody a chance. He wanted to experience it all."

He took a shot at drugs, but it was an unmitigated disaster. Getty was there again. "Cal was definitely not a druggie. He knew this man named Dennis. He was quite a handsome fellow. Anyway, Dennis had a date with Cal and gave him some LSD. They went out but were back within the hour. Cal wasn't handling the drugs, and Dennis couldn't deal with it. I was there with a friend, and we spent hours talking him through it. He never did it again."

When Cal would go out to parties or bars, people would come up to him and give him packages of drugs as gifts—cocaine, acid, marijuana, pills—the whole pharmacopoeia of 1970s recreational medications. Cal would unfailingly accept the gifts, thank the giver, and then promptly give the stuff away. He hardly drank; he didn't smoke cigarettes. Aside from the use of poppers occasionally during sex, Cal Culver was a regular Boy Scout. It was generally assumed that he did drugs because of what he was, not who he was.

Rumors, especially regarding cocaine and Quaaludes, continued to dog him, although friends and costars never saw evidence of it. Michael Kearns knew that "there were rumors around the fisting stuff, although I personally think that he was too vain to risk doing drugs and ruining himself." Erotic costar Derrick Stanton concurred: " When I worked a shot with him, some of the crew talked of wild parties that he threw at his home in Florida and that he had a bit of a cocaine problem. Well, to my surprise when Casey appeared on the set of *L.A. Tool and Die* he was very much a gentleman and looked the picture of health." Cal made a strong case for staying drug-free during an early '80s interview. "I don't do drugs, although I experimented a little at the time. I don't smoke or drink alcohol. I'm trying to keep it together. I know about 40 people who have died in the past two years. Without drugging and drinking, I'm keeping healthy."

*   *   *

The later '70s saw the publication of a number of porn star biographies. Jack Wrangler cranked one out—*What's a Nice Boy Like You Doing*; Michael Kearns threw his manuscript into the ring—*The Happy Hustler*; and a fellow named Marc Stevens penned an epic with a not-so-cryptic title—*10 1/2*. So it isn't surprising that Cal thought he should try his hand at a bit of autobiographical tell-all.

"I'm planning to do my own book as a serious self-analysis," Cal told Rob Richards during an interview. "It's going to be by both Casey Donovan and Cal Culver. I want to do it as an interview between my two personas—getting into both my minds so to speak—to explore both the wholesome, corn-fed boy and that other person who does all that wild fuck stuff on film."

Cal contacted Bill Gross, then the editorial director of Pocket Books, late in 1976. They had a couple of meetings, and Cal allegedly wrote a couple of sample chapters that covered his teenage years, although they have since disappeared. Then he suddenly abandoned the project. Gross got the strong feeling that he was being encouraged not to write. "His friends didn't seem to want him to tell the tale. Tom Tryon, in particular, didn't want to have their relationship laid out for public scrutiny. Given the abruptness with which the project was abandoned, I just always assumed Cal mentioned to people that he was writing this book to make some money and that they responded with gifts."

Cal had no business sense and had never been good with money. When he and Tryon broke up, he hadn't been working regularly in theater, films, or even hustling for a couple of years. His piggy bank would have been quite empty. There would have been no possibility of going to Wilhelmina or any other legitimate modeling agency to look for work—he was poison in the industry as a result of his overexposure in porn films. He worked for a while as a waiter at the Sea Shack restaurant in Cherry Grove on Fire Island, but tips wouldn't have supplied the finances to support Cal's lifestyle.

Given Cal's personality and temperament, it is quite likely that he would have mentioned his plans as a matter of course. He was always talking about what he planned to do—to his friends, to interviewers, to the columnists who still followed his career. It is also quite likely that he would have accepted any gifts that were offered to him. If Tryon offered him any money, Cal most probably richly deserved it. What is highly unlikely is that he would have set out to blackmail anyone. That would have required a degree of calculation and cynicism that simply wasn't a part of the man's personality. It would, finally, have been destructive of the only career that remained open to him. Successful whores must, above all, be discreet. And Cal would prove to be one of the best ever.

CHAPTER 9

Hustler, Porn Star, Lonely Hearts, Tour Guide

On December 22, 1977, a new issue of *The Advocate* hit the stands, launching Cal on yet another phase of his career as the answer to every gay man's dream. Although Cal had hustled off and on ever since he was dismissed from his teaching position at the Ethical Culture School, he had never made it his central focus. It was more of a game to him, a bit of a sexual thrill and a surefire way to provide additional spending money. Now, however, with nothing lucrative looming on his employment horizon, he had to find a viable way to earn a living.

"I was all at sea," he confided to Rob Richards during a 1981 interview. "I had no income and no idea of what my next move should be. One day, when I had lots of time on my hands, a friend told me about a hot ad he'd read in *The Advocate*. I read it, thought about it and decided to call." The call opened his eyes to a new way of cashing in on his fame as the golden boy of porn. "My whole existence is based to this day on that one movie. I've done 13 other films, some obscene, some never seen, but everything since is predicated on *Boys in the Sand*, including my hustling."

Once he had set his mind to it, Cal decided to do some research. His call to *The Advocate*'s ad put him in touch with a very compelling young man. "I'd never paid for sex before, and I thought I should see what it felt like being on the other side. I'd been *collecting* for years. The boy turned out to be as hot as his ad." As the pair talked after their session, the young hustler encouraged Cal to give the life a try. "He convinced me to have a go at hustling. It had always been a fantasy of mine to run an ad in *The Advocate* anyway…I sent my ad in despite my fear of police entrapment, etc., at the end of November, not knowing when the issue would hit the stands."

When it hit, it hit big—making it clear that Casey Donovan may have been away, but he had not been forgotten. "Suddenly on December 22 my phone kept ringing off the hook. It was sensational. I was *everybody's* Christmas present. I only wish I had done it years earlier when *Boys* first went into release—that would have been a very good year. It got me that house in Key West—clients from *The Advocate* helped me to put that project together, because they believed in me. Some hookers buy drugs; I bought a house!"

Hustling, as Cal quickly discovered, wasn't all silk sheets, languid poses, and easy money. It was hard work. And if it were to work for him, it had to be steady work. "I have a quota to meet every week. I have to make a certain amount to meet my obligations. If I have a bad week, I just go crazy! As you well know, any kind of freelance work is nerve-racking, but it's a special hassle knowing you have to have sex because you need the money. I've gone through periods of great emotional trauma these past couple of years trying to meet responsibilities and emotionally I'm exhausted. Praise God, I'm holding up physically."

When asked what he did when he just couldn't face the prospect of another penis in his life, Cal's response was quite simple and to the point—he unplugged the phone. "I like my clients too much to shortchange them just because I have a mortgage payment due. If I go to them and can't produce a hard-on, they're going to be pissed off and rightly so."

And Cal did genuinely like his clients, enough so that a number of men who began as paying clients ended up as friends and confidants. To Cal it all seemed logical. "My sex life is my social life is my business life is my sex life," he once replied to the question of how he could do what he did. And no man was beyond the bounds of possibility—at least once. "I'm often asked how I can have sex with so many kinds of people, some of them seemingly turn-offs. I can always get past their bodies, because I'm interested in who they are, what they are, what they think…of themselves…of me. My attitude is to give, if not the best, at least the nicest sexual experience they've ever had."

And by all accounts he did just that. Jerry Douglas once asked him how he managed to gear up for clients who didn't turn him on at all. He told Douglas that no matter how unattractive a client might be, he could always find at least one thing about the man to focus on. "If I like his eyes, for example, I can deal with the rest of it." He told Douglas that he had never had a client so gross that he couldn't get an erection, but he did admit that there had been one man who was so offensive that he couldn't bring himself to return for a repeat performance.

There were also clients who were so bizarre that Cal took them out of his Rolodex, but they nonetheless often made for amusing tales. Cal, although generally the soul of discretion, would occasionally regale friends with some of his more off-the-wall antics. Jake Getty would occasionally join Cal for breakfast, and they would laugh together over the vagaries of human sexuality. "One guy wanted Cal in boots, a jock strap, and a blindfold," Getty told me. "He told Cal, 'When I tell you to start jumping, you jump up and down.' Cal put on the blindfold and started jumping. Right away he heard this 'crunch, crunch' sound. A few minutes later, the guy yelled for him to stop. Cal heard him scrambling around, then the chair he'd been sitting in creaked. 'Start jumping!' the guy yelled. Cal began jumping again, only this time he peeked. He was jumping up and down on those little turtles, the kind you get at Woolworth's, and his trick was watching him kill the turtles while he jerked off. Cal finished the gig, but he never went back."

Some clients were just too fabulous to keep completely quiet about. Rob Richards, who began by interviewing Cal for an article and ended by becoming a friend and confidant during the latter part of Cal's life vividly recalled one such instance. "Cal was a consummate professional—in all aspects of his life. Once in a while we'd be out together at lunch or at a movie, and Cal would check the time, then make his excuses. That usually meant that he had an appointment with a client. He was rather blasé about most of them, but once in a while he'd meet a man he just couldn't keep to himself."

Gianni Versace was such a man. "Versace was just coming into his own as a fashion designer when Cal met him, and Cal was ecstatic to be Versace's choice in the sack. He loved the celebrity cachet of going to bed with a man the media was fawning over and whose fashions were draping the frames of the rich and famous. He was also impishly pleased to describe Versace's charms—his big, uncut charms, as Cal was quick to assure me. He was quite funny about it all. He adored the limelight even when it was only reflected."

There were other times when Cal used his stable of johns to provide him with luxury items that struck his fancy. Once after Cal had moved into a new apartment, he was showing it to Getty. "He told me that he had seen some magnificent potted ficus trees that he wanted to put in the living room. When he told me that they would cost $1,500, I told him that he was nuts. I knew that he didn't have that kind of money. Cal never had that kind of money. He just smiled at me, picked up the phone, and made a call. A few minutes later, he was on his way out to spend the evening with one of his gentlemen. The next day the trees were delivered."

Although sex on demand might have been something of a trial for Cal from time to time, sex was, if not his favorite thing, at least a contender for first place. He was by all accounts insatiable, given to squeezing tricks in between hustling appointments. Roy Blakey recalled such an incident. "He had to go from Cherry Grove to the other end of the island to meet a client. He was walking along when he saw an attractive man. They cruised, Cal followed him into the trees, and they made it with each other. Then Cal said goodbye and went off to work. The man just couldn't get enough. What more perfect business for him than the sex trade?"

What, indeed? And the sex trade did have its perks, especially for a man with Cal's stellar qualities. Cal Culver was strictly carriage trade throughout his hustling career. During his heyday—which lasted into his 40s—he charged $500 a night, $1,000 for a weekend. He was flown around the country—and the world—at his clients' expense and was often treated to extended sexual vacations. As Cal told Rob Richards in 1981, "I've had some lucky treats lately. A couple of months ago I had a job that took me first class to London for five days, on safari to Tanzania and Kenya for 17 days, topped off with nine fascinating days in Egypt. It was fucking fabulous, and I got paid by the day!" On yet another occasion Cal was flown to France to attend official ceremonies to celebrate opening of the restored gardens at Monet's country home in Giverny.

His friends included not only the rich and famous but also the politically influential. "Cal would go to Washington, D.C., every once in a while," recalled *Dick Morgan, a New York lawyer who began as a client of Cal's and ended up as a friend. "He had a client who was an elected government official—Republican, I think—who used to call on Cal for a little tension release once in a while. They'd go to the man's office and do it on the couch there. Once they were going to do it on the floor of the House of Representatives, but Cal's client got spooked by some cleaners, and they went back to his office. According to Cal, and I had no reason to disbelieve him, he had a number of clients in Washington."

*Carlton Randolph, scion of a very old, very distinguished Southern family, met Cal while vacationing in New York and later invited him to his home in Savannah, Georgia. "I would never have gone with a common street hustler, and before I met Cal, I certainly wouldn't have brought any of the men I tricked with into my home. I was living with my mother at the time, and she was a very proper Southern lady. There was nothing that got beyond her, so I never had what could rightly be called a sex life as a young man—at least not when I was at home. I traveled as often as possible, but my life was still very difficult.

"I had been with Cal on several occasions and he had always been more than just somebody to have sex with. He was a good listener and a great conversationalist. After we got to know one another, we would go to dinner and the theater before going back to my hotel. It was like a date, not some sordid transaction of sex in exchange for cash.

"Well, once when I was in a particularly rebellious mood, I invited Cal to Savannah to stay in my home with my mother. I think I was trying to assert my own identity or something along those lines. Well, he came, he met my mother—and they got along like a house afire. Cal had her totally charmed from the moment he entered the house. He would be the perfect gentleman with her all day long, and when we'd finally manage to get some time alone, he would be sexually ravenous. It was almost frightening—not that I ever complained, of course. He and my mother exchanged Christmas cards until he died."

*   *   *

There was more to what Cal was doing than just sex. He seriously considered himself to be an uncredentialed sex therapist, doing his best to make men more comfortable with their sexuality. "There have been many instances where I've been able to help clients. So many people are so fucked up sexually—just so many," he told Rob Richards. "One strange thing about hustling is that the sex is usually the shortest part of the hour. Much of the time is spent in simple conversation. Lots of men work in businesses that allow them no gay outlets, and they just want an hour to be gay, to let go, to get into what gay men get into. Also, a great many men just need desperately to be held—to feel someone's arms around them—to make them feel wanted and important. Sometimes I hold someone, and his entire body just quivers. It's so sweet, so gratifying to fill that need. I hope I can continue doing what I do. I feel I'm contributing an important commodity. I've helped a lot of people...I feel like 'Doctor Donovan' more often than I feel like 'Casey the Hooker'...It's really sad when people aren't sensually developed."

Carl Smith was one of those people. Twenty-four at the time, enrolled at Columbia University, and just starting an internship at a prestigious New York City law firm, Carl was a bit young to be paying a hustler, but he had a problem. "I had been brought up in a religious fundamentalist household. My parents' take on religion was strictly fire and brimstone, so I grew up thinking that sex was somehow dirty. The very idea of gay sex was anathema to them, so when I discovered that I was gay, I was horrified."

The sense of horror wasn't strong enough to keep Carl from having sex, but it did tie him up in knots psychologically. "I was so guilt ridden that I became impotent when I was with another man. Even when I was alone and masturbated, I felt so guilty afterward that I was nauseated. I had gay friends who went out and had fun and got laid, but I got to the point where I just couldn't. My life was hell."

Desperation led Carl to call the number listed in Casey Donovan's ad in *The Advocate*'s pink pages. "It took me two weeks to get up the courage to make the call. I carried the ad around in my wallet, pulling it out from time to time, listing all the reasons that I should or shouldn't make the call. I was making myself crazy when my buddy Joe picked up the phone one day and stood over me while I dialed. I left a message—I'm surprised he even replied because I sounded like a stuttering idiot."

But he did reply, arranging to come to Carl's apartment the following afternoon. "As the appointed time approached, I began to panic. By the time he got there I was a wreck. I almost didn't answer the door. When I opened it he was there. I mean, it was Casey Donovan. I guess I had figured it was some kind of scam and that it would be someone who maybe looked a little like him. I don't know. And he smiled at me and introduced himself and shook my hand.

"He wasn't anything like I expected him to be. I don't know; I guess I thought he'd sort of walk off the screen and into my apartment, his cock leading the way. But he wasn't like that at all. He was well-dressed and he acted like we were friends, not like I was going to pay him for sex. I think he sensed my nervousness and he just started talking. He picked up a book I'd left on the coffee table and told me he had read another by the same author. Before long I had almost forgotten the reason he was really there, except that I was getting genuinely horny.

"He reached out and touched my arm and said something

about my having a nice build. I tensed up, the old terror coming back. He got this real concerned look on his face and asked
me if anything was wrong. Well, I just looked at him and blurt-
ed it out. He listened to me, then took my hand, and pulled me
to my feet. He undressed me, all the time talking about how
hot he thought I was, and I could tell from his eyes that he really meant it, and I started to believe him. When I was naked
he started kissing me and touching me all over, getting me hotter than hell.

"One thing led to another, and then he was on his knees
blowing me. After I came I started to feel bad, as if I'd done
something wrong, and I started to shake. He got up and
hugged me and held me and kept telling me that everything
was all right and that I was a hot guy and that he really got off
on me. By the time he got me all calmed down, he had been
there for more than two hours, but he didn't charge me any
extra. I called for Casey's services several more times during the
course of the next few months, and he was always a prince of a
guy. By the time he was through with me, my problems with
impotence were history."

*   *   *

Always a welter of contradictions, this socialite cum sexual
whirling dervish cum culture hound was seen by close friends as
primarily a quiet guy. "I remember one night when we were sitting in the living room at my place," Jake Getty recalled. "A
friend came over, looked at Cal and did a double take. 'What are
you doing sitting around here on a Saturday night?' he asked, really scandalized by the idea. 'Haven't you heard, darling?' Cal
replied in his best stage voice. 'It's lonely at the top.'"

Lonely? Perhaps, but it was the way Cal wanted it. Friends
rarely visited Cal at his place—he preferred to come to them.

Ted Wilkins remembered him as "a very private person. He never minded being alone." He cherished his private time, more and more as he grew older. "I think I may want to live in a house in the country when I'm 60—alone," he told Rob Richards. "He reveled in his solitude," Getty confirmed.

For a libertine, he had some odd little quirks. "He was incredibly modest," Ted Wilkins said. "I mean really modest. Cal always had a room reserved for him at the beach house Walter and I own on Fire Island. The place is completely private, and the two of us wandered around naked all the time. Cal, on the other hand, wouldn't even pop from his bedroom to the bathroom without putting something on first. He had a very strong sense of propriety. It was a tribute to the way he was raised I'm sure. I never heard him swear either. Never."

Cal had an excellent sense of humor, poking fun at human foibles, not least of all his own. "I was sitting at home talking with a couple of friends one Saturday afternoon," Jake Getty told me, "when I received this frantic call from Cal. There had been a catastrophe, he told me. I told him to come on over, not knowing whether to call the police or the fire department.

"When he arrived he was wearing a cap pulled down to his ears—not his standard look at all. He stalked into the kitchen and sat down at the table. We gathered around waiting to hear what tragedy had occurred. Finally, dramatically, he removed the cap. Cal's famous blond hair was green. He wasn't a natural blond, you know. He had gone to the hairdresser to have it frosted, and something had gone wrong with the chemical balance. It looked like he'd had a pea soup rinse. 'Well,' he said, looking from face to face, 'I guess you know what this means, don't you?' Nobody ventured a guess. 'There will be no sex taking place in this town tonight. Not with my hair looking like this.'"

*   *   *

KENN DUNCAN

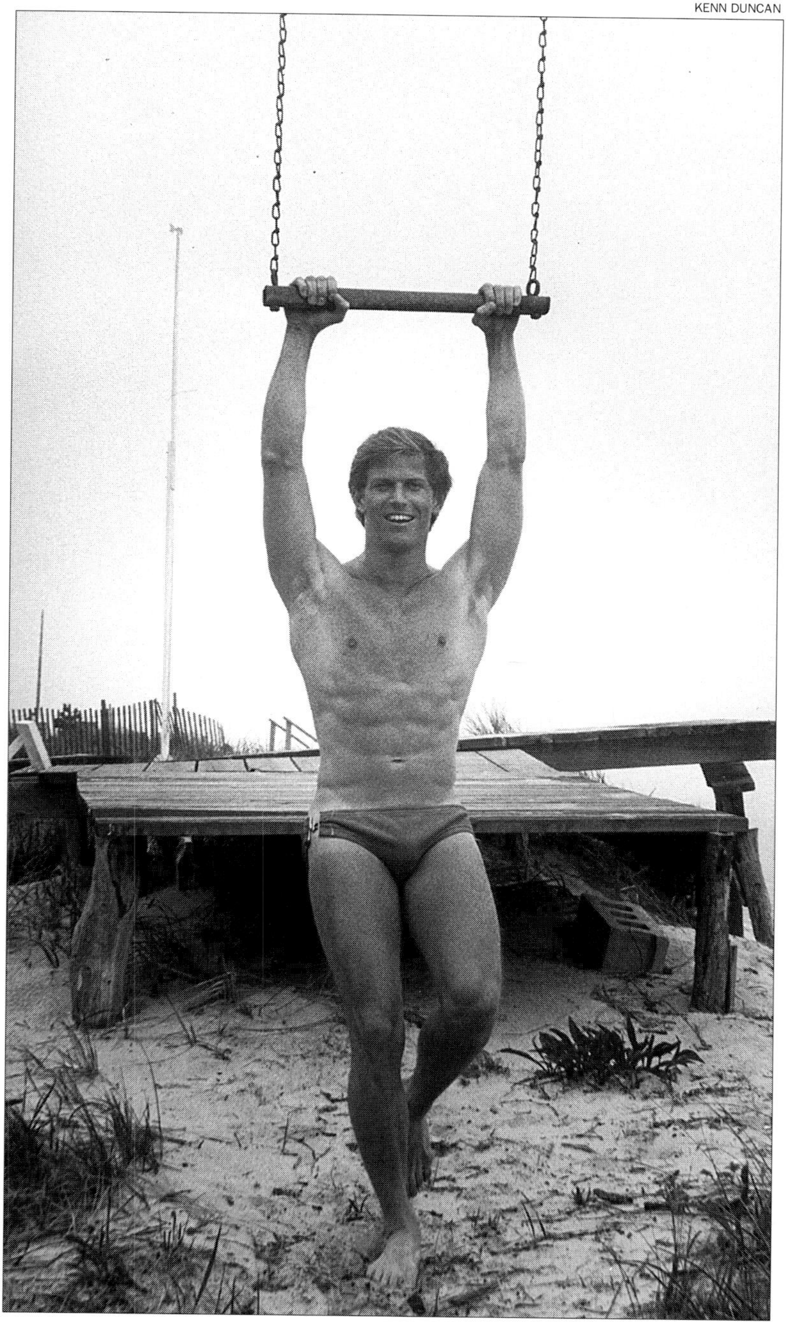

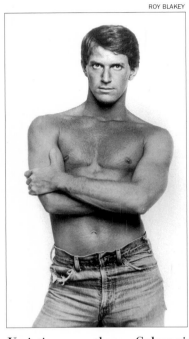 

Variations on a theme: Culver viewed through the lenses of Roy Blakey, Jack Mitchell, and Wakefield Poole. *Previous page:* Cal and his abs, as captured for *After Dark* by photographer Kenn Duncan.

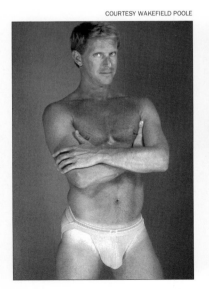 

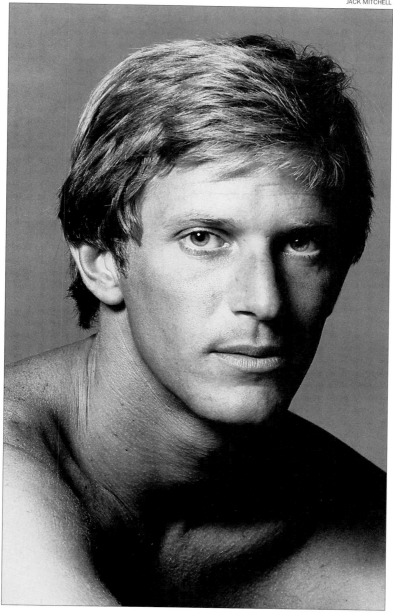

An image of Culver that was featured on the December 1972 cover of *After Dark*.

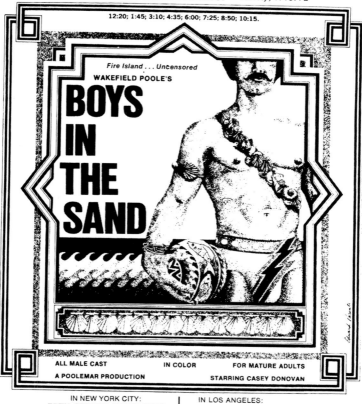
Opposite page: This series of video captures from *Boys in the Sand* shows Culver emerging from the sea and then with costars Peter Fisk, Daniel DiCiccicio, and Tommy Moore. The screen captures do not do justice to the original film. *Above:* The original ad for *Boys in the Sand*.

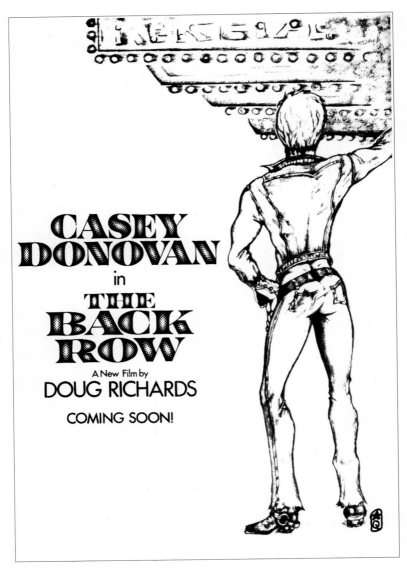

The original ad for Culver's film *The Back Row*.

Culver, handcuffed to a tree—the rape scene from *L.A. Tool and Die.*

Culver, alone on Fire Island.

Now that Cal was back on the scene, single, footloose, and hustling professionally, he decided to return to X-rated films. It had been four years since he worked with Wakefield Poole on *Moving*, and by 1978 he was more than ready to put it all out there again for his public. There had been rumors that he was making plans for a comeback as early as April of 1976, when *The Advocate's* gossip page let it be known that Cal, in his Casey guise, was in California to shoot an all-male erotic film that he was planning to produce, write, direct, and perform in. "The working title for the epic: *Masked Marvels*. The new film will be silent and episodic, in both color and black and white, and will deal with 'fantasy sex for the everyday man.' If he gets it off as planned, Donovan's finished product will offer porn flick audiences 'a touch of class with a pinch of kink.' A late summer release is hoped for."

Nothing came of this particular project—a problem with many proposed projects throughout Cal's career, both mainstream and porn—probably because his final break with Tryon had not yet occurred. What Cal did do in the spring of 1976 was to begin marketing Roy Blakey's famous image of himself. In the photograph a pensive Cal, stripped to the waist, arms crossed, stares directly through the camera's lens into the eyes of the beholder. The body is trim but hardly spectacular. It is the eyes that grab you, make you look back, make you believe that whatever it is you desire, he desires it too and, most importantly, can deliver. At a cost of $5.00 plus 50 cents shipping and handling, it was a bargain—especially when you considered that the price included Casey's signature, and, if you wished, a personalized inscription.

*　　*　　*

In July of 1978 Falcon Studios provided the vehicle for Cal's comeback. Falcon, now one of the premier producers of gay erotica, began in the early '70s as an eight millimeter mail-order company, selling its films as 15-minute loops. The company was planning to launch a new line of film—the Falcon Pack, and Cal's film was to be the first of the series.

The Other Side of Aspen was Falcon Studio's first big hit, and the credit is mostly due to Cal and his extraordinary sexual performance with costars Al Parker, Dick Fiske, and Jeff Turk. "The person who really anchored that shoot was Casey Donovan," Dick Clayton of Falcon Studios said in a 1989 interview with *Manshots* magazine. "When he got a look at the cast, he told me he just couldn't wait to fuck with all of them." Cal is obviously ravenous for all the men in the film, at one point taking them all on in a gang-bang session, bent spread-eagled over a coffee table.

Then in a particularly intense segment Cal is fisted by the legendary Al Parker. The chemistry of the pairing is electrifying. Cal knew who Al Parker was—he told an interviewer that Parker was one of his "porno dream men." However, they had not met prior to the filming, which for Cal was a plus. He liked not knowing the men he was going to have sex with on film. "I think it's easier, because then you can perform on a strictly chemical level…I like the spontaneity of anonymous encounters…Al and I never met until the afternoon we flew from San Francisco to Lake Tahoe. A couple of hours later we did our first scene together, and he wound up fist fucking me. *Quite an experience!*"

It was quite an experience for the viewers as well. Cal was catapulted back into the sexual limelight. The film became an instant classic, proving to the world—if the world needed proof—that Casey Donovan, at the ripe old age of 35, was still hot enough to melt paint. When *The Other Side of Aspen* was released, it put Casey Donovan's name back before the public and before long *Boys in the Sand, Casey,* and *The Back Row* were making the rounds again as well. Cal's hustling business took off, keeping his phone line busy and allowing him to exploit his sensual nature to the fullest.

*   *   *

In contrast to Cal, some gays were beginning to believe that gay men were altogether too sensually developed. So much so that other aspects of their lives were in danger of being overwhelmed. The alarm was first sounded by Larry Kramer in his controversial novel *Faggots*. "Why do faggots have to fuck so fucking much?" His narrator asked the question of a world that, for the most part in those years before the acronym AIDS had been coined, didn't want to think about it. They just did it. It was natural—the result of liberation from the strictures of the closet in which gays had been forced to live prior to Stonewall. Besides, who the hell was Larry Kramer, anyway?

Prior to the onset of AIDS, promiscuity had been seen as one of the benchmarks of gay liberation. Gays no longer had to hide, and they certainly didn't have to emulate their heterosexual peers. Unlimited access to sex was one of the best parts of being gay. It set gay people apart like membership in a risque, secret club. Now, unfairly as most thought, the idea of unlimited, unbridled, uncommitted sex was being attacked.

Novelist John Rechy—*Numbers, Rushes, The Sexual Outlaw*— added his voice to the discussion, deploring the growing alcoholism among younger gay men, the popularity and institutionalization of sadomasochism, the reliance on drugs for physical rushes, and the frantic clamoring for sexual experiences that he considered limiting rather than liberating. "To me what's happening on the homosexual front is a great confusion between liberation and destruction. I think we're destroying ourselves and calling it liberation…There is a point where…the 'sexual outlaw' in me begins to wonder and question the direction in which our sexuality is now going…I know that I have had as full a range of experiences as other people. Yet now as I look in alleys or orgy rooms, I see increasingly haunted faces."

*　　*　　*

Fucking too much wasn't an issue for Cal. He had more practical things to consider. He wanted to find a place to invest some of the cash that he had earned from hustling. Cal decided to buy a home. The house that Cal purchased in late 1978 was located at 617 Whitehead Street in Key West. The two-story house was instantly dubbed Casa Donovan by Cal as he set about creating his own little bit of paradise in what was then rapidly becoming a gay mecca on the southernmost speck of land in the United States.

In its heyday, Key West was the most popular destination for gay tourists in the country. Men from around the world were drawn by its charming architecture, sunny clime, and aura of total hedonism. The party in Key West never ended, and the parade of handsome men was inexhaustible. It was the winter getaway of choice for all of the sun-starved gays on the East Coast and beyond.

It should have been the perfect investment for Cal. All those visiting men needed a place to stay, and many enterprising gays were buying up the beautiful old homes in the historic district, refurbishing them as guest houses, and making a killing. The supply of guest rooms could barely keep up with the demand, and it was nearly impossible to find a decent place to stay during the high season. It was a seller's market, and the very idea of failing to make a go of it as an innkeeper was almost laughable.

Yet Casa Donovan was never a money-making proposition. Try as he might, Cal was always teetering on the edge. "It was a dreadful little house," Hanns Ebensten, the gay travel agent who became Cal's friend and employer recalled. "He poured tons of money into it, but no matter what he did, it never turned out right." Rather than making money from all the paying guests, Cal was forced to hustle to make the mortgage payments. Bottom line: Cal was a bad businessman, and the whole proposition failed miserably.

Jake Getty clearly saw what was going on. "Short and simple, he blew the guest house. He was always trying to connect it to the porno persona. I mean, it had to be Casa Donovan, not just a guest house that he happened to own and operate. Gay guest houses were doing very well in Key West at the time. He should have separated himself from the porn legend and done it as a business venture, but he couldn't do it. Cal really believed in the Casey Donovan legend and thought it was what would carry him through. I guess he had to. He had sacrificed everything to it."

By all accounts Casa Donovan just wasn't a very nice place, and it couldn't keep up with the competition. The successful guest houses in Key West had pools and gardens and terraces and breakfast pavilions. Cal's place had none of these amenities. It wasn't a complex of charming houses; it wasn't a Victorian mansion; it wasn't a verdant urban jungle with cottages tucked deep within the foliage—it was a run-down boardinghouse that had nothing going for it beyond the fact that its handsome blond proprietor was a famous porn star. "He just couldn't see what the problem was," Ted Wilkins said. "He didn't realize that the guest house wasn't what he wanted it to be. He just refused to acknowledge the truth of the situation, which was that he had chosen badly."

For the first couple of years, Cal tried to tough it out. He worked on the guest house in conjunction with his friend Garron Douglas, dividing his time between his hustling and the day-to-day details of running a guest house. After all, Cal had innkeeping in his blood. His parents had successfully managed the trailer park and motel for years, but it took concerted effort and hard work. It wasn't fun—and it certainly wasn't the least bit glamorous.

*Larry Gaines stayed there when he visited the Keys from his home in Boston in the autumn of 1980. "It was a haphazard operation," he recalled. "I remember taking a taxi from the airport. There were nice houses along Whitehead street, but 617 wasn't one of them. I got a key and went up to my room. The bed had been made, but the wastebaskets hadn't been emptied, and there were no towels in the bathroom. I went down to the front desk for towels—a project that became a daily chore while I was there.

"I distinctly remember the guys who were working there, and it was clear that they had no idea of how a bed and breakfast should be run. The guy behind the desk had it pretty together, but the rest of the staff was a joke. They seemed to think that the guest house was a steam bath. It was no wonder the beds didn't always get made.

"I kept putting up with it all, thinking that I was going to see Casey Donovan and that something was going to happen. I guess I'd watched one too many porn films or something. He wasn't there, and the guy behind the desk kept saying he'd be there any day, but I couldn't pin him down to anything specific. By the end of my stay, I was pissed off. I felt like I'd been cheated. When I went home, I bad-mouthed the place to my friends."

Cal had a definite idea of what he wanted Casa Donovan to be. "I'm running it like an old-fashioned fraternity house, but everyone's out of the closet." Way out of the closet, if the rumors that were current at the time can be believed. There were whispered tales of wild parties, all-night orgies, cocaine, and any other drug in the pharmacopoeia—all available as a part of the standard vacation package at Casa Donovan.

*Norm Le Grange wasn't a guest at Cal's house, but he was invited to a party there by a paying guest. "When we got there— and this was really late, after the bars were closing down—you could hear the music a block away. We went in, and the place was literally crawling with men, most of them naked, the modest ones in jock straps. There was beer packed in tubs of ice, and everyone there was either high or getting there.

"The guy I came in with took me upstairs. Every door along the hall was wide open, and something was going on in every room. I hadn't been out all that long, and I thought it was all pretty scandalous. I distinctly remember one room where this gorgeous guy was sprawled out naked on the bed. There were guys all around him doing lines of cocaine that one of them was putting on the guy's chest and belly. When they had all done a line, they packed some up a soda straw, and then this one guy got down between the legs of the guy sprawled on the bed and blew the cocaine up his ass through the straw. After that they all piled onto the bed and started going at it.

"The guy who'd brought me took me into his room. We had to step over people to get in, but nobody seemed to care. He took my clothes from me and hung them up in his closet, then we wandered around the place just taking it all in. I remember at one point the guy nudged me and pointed out Casey. He was coming up the stairs, smiling at people and talking to them like he was the host and was throwing a party. In a way I guess he was. He was wearing swim trunks, and he was tanned and really good-looking, but I didn't see him having sex with anyone. He looked a little distracted—like maybe he was wondering what the hell was going on in his place. If it had been my place, I would've been freaking out. I mean, nobody was deliberately trashing the place, but Vaseline handprints and the occasional glob of come on the wall will take a toll eventually."

*   *   *

The mundane concerns that went along with the day-to-day operation of a guest house soon began to take their toll on Cal as well. Orchestrating raucous orgies or hosting his "moonbow" tours—little jaunts around Key West, led by Cal-as-Casey when the moon was full—could be fun. Having a group of admirers padding along behind him as he pointed out the former homes of Hemingway, Audubon, and other celebrity inhabitants appealed to Cal's natural instincts as a tour guide. Less appealing were the chores associated with keeping a nine-room guest house up and running. Making beds and scrubbing toilets was hardly Cal's speed, although he could do it like a champ. All that time working alongside his mother, making the beds in the guest cabins summer after summer back in East Bloomfield was a skill that had stuck with him. Still, it was hardly the way he wanted to spend the rest of his life. Organizing others to look after those chores didn't prove to be his forte either. He kept hiring guys for their looks and for the way they filled out a pair of tight pants rather than for any hospitality industry skills they might have possessed. As a result, his staff was usually better at getting made in the beds rather than making them afterward.

As the debts continued to mount, Cal turned over the daily management of Casa Donovan to others and concentrated more on his hustling. Hustling was one thing he was good at, and he needed the money it brought to keep from losing the house. Casa Donovan was his only link to the puritanical, work-bounded world of his youth.

It is interesting that Cal chose the same means of livelihood that had supported his parents throughout most of their lives. It seems to have been a rather transparent attempt to gain their approval by finally doing something mainstream and normal—at least as seen from a safe distance—that they could understand. As much as he refuted it at every turn, there was always an inbred puritanical streak that he could never entirely escape. In response to a question about how he managed his unorthodox life and remained well-adjusted, Cal replied that much of it was because of "the Puritan Ethic that was instilled in me very early on—my mother's still there shaking her finger over my shoulder. A good deal of my trying to…be successful has been done as a tribute to my parents."

*   *   *

While Cal was struggling to make a go of his guest house, the gay movement was forging into the '80s full steam ahead. Gay culture was in the vanguard of theater, dance, music, and poetry. Harvey Fierstein's *Torch Song Trilogy* went to Broadway, won a Tony award, and became the year's hit show. *The Front Runner*, Cal's long-standing dream of mainstream success, languished in the wings, but Harry Hamlin and Michael Ontkean made history with *Making Love,* and Julie Andrews and Robert Preston starred in the hysterically funny comedy *Victor/Victoria.* Even television got into the act with public television's immensely popular *Brideshead Revisited,* which made Jeremy Irons an instant star and glamorized gay romance along the way. Gay scholarship was flourishing as well, as represented by John Boswell's monumental work, *Christianity, Social Tolerance, and Homosexuality.* Gays everywhere were taking up the core question of how to balance their unique take on life with the mainstream of America.

The gay lifestyle was predicated on health—glowing, sleekly muscled health as pictured in Charles Hix's *Looking Good,* which had its place on nearly every gay man's coffee table. This take on life was represented most openly by the first Gay Games in 1982—the homosexual answer to the Olympics. And the country seemed to be following our lead—mayoral candidates in Los Angeles, Houston, and Atlanta were openly wooing gay voters.

But as the decade got under way, the first signs of something sinister began to appear on the horizon, a dark catastrophe that would soon threaten all the gains gays and lesbians had made in the past decade. It began with what some were referring to as "gay cancer"—an extremely rare form of malignancy called Kaposi's sarcoma. It usually affected only elderly men in Mediterranean areas and was so rare that most physicians had never heard of it. Soon, clusters of cases began to appear in New York, Los Angeles, and San Francisco. Shortly after, five gay men in Los Angeles were diagnosed with *Pneumocystis carinii* pneumonia. By 1982, ten to 20 cases of the unnamed disease behind these symptoms were being certified every week by the Centers for Disease Control. At first there was a pervasive denial by gays—most major gay publications saw talk of the new disease as hysterical blather, an attempt by doomsayers to derail hard-won gay freedoms. Gays, for the most part, stood firm in their efforts to defend "sexual freedom" and "recreational sex" in the wake of the first cases of the AIDS epidemic.

The big question at the time was whether the urban gay lifestyle, centered around drugs and sex, was responsible for making gay men sick. The battle lines were drawn quickly. On one side stood the largely heterosexual medical community and the conservative social establishment, people who were quick to attribute the epidemic to debased, immoral sexual practices. On the other side were the urban gay males who were determined to hold on to a way of life that allowed easy access to drugs and anonymous sex. Any gay male who didn't side with the latter group was considered a traitor, a gay homophobe.

The debate in the gay community was fierce and acrimonious. Larry Kramer came down on the side of caution, urging moderation, and telling gays that "the men who have been stricken don't appear to have done anything that many New York gay men have not done at one time or another...It's easy to become frightened that one of the many things we've done or taken over the past years may be all that it takes for a cancer to grow from a tiny something-or-other that got in there who knows when from doing who knows what." He was excoriated by his critics for taking an antigay, antisex stance.

On the other side of the issue, novelist Edmund White, author of the gay travelogue *States of Desire* and coauthor of *The*

Joy of Gay Sex, believed that "some moralists are using the appearance of Kaposi's sarcoma as a pretext for preaching against gay promiscuity under the guise of giving sound medical advice. In fact, no one knows the causes of any kind of cancer, much less a kind to have emerged so recently among young and middle-aged, gay male Americans...Given how conformist gay life has become, one could just as easily single out any other feature of a clone's existence as being carcinogenic—wearing button-fly jeans, perhaps, or weightlifting, or excessive disco dancing." The controversy surrounding promiscuous and anonymous public sex—safe or otherwise—is still unresolved.

Cal was fully aware of the growing epidemic—living in New York City, Los Angeles, and San Francisco made ignoring it impossible—but he continued with his hedonistic ways. Given the nature of his business, and the lack of consensus on the causes of the disease, any other course would have appeared unreasonable to him. Cal, and thousands of other sexually active gay men, chose to close their eyes to the realities of what was going on until the middle of the decade when the death toll had become too horrifying to deny any longer.

*   *   *

After Cal decided to branch out in an effort to escape from the constraints of innkeeping, he was able to find a number of opportunities to keep him busy and in funds. The hustling was going well—pulling down the cash, keeping Cal as busy as he wanted to be. He liked being flown from city to city, met at the airport, transported to fine homes and penthouse apartments. He felt, as he once told an interviewer, "like a Park Avenue call girl. In fact, I often think that if I was a woman, that's what I would have been."

Cal was still a bonafide porn star, and his name could still add cachet and market clout to a product. But what kind of product was he going to promote? He had starred in Falcon's premiere series effort but had no desire to continue forever playing the blond surfer/skier type he had created in *Boys*. At 38 years old, he was at a point when his image needed an update.

The image makers he chose were Sam and Joe Gage, talented New Yorkers whose star's looks were diametrically opposed to the California surfer image adhered to almost religiously by most other gay filmmakers. The typical Gage man is macho, wears Levi's and leather, drives a truck, and has hair on his chest. He is extremely masculine, a man's man, a stud who has no time for twinks. The typical Gage film featured orgies, plenty of verbal sex patter to enhance the visuals, and a down-and-dirty attitude toward man-to-man sex.

The golden boy of porn began shaking loose his boy-next-door image, appearing on-screen unshaven, slowly transforming himself, moving toward the sex pig persona first captured on film in *The Back Row*. In short, Cal/Casey began to make the transition from youth to mature man.

Cal's first work for the Gage brothers was in *L.A. Tool & Die* (1981), the final segment of their legendary trilogy about the sexual adventures of a truck driver, which also included *Kansas City Trucking Co.* and *El Paso Wrecking Corp*. In the film Casey is carjacked by a woman and handcuffed to a tree. He calls out for help, which arrives in the guise of a big-dicked man whose face is never seen. The man tears Casey's clothes off and fucks him, then releases him as we learn that the whole gambit was a setup devised by Casey and his boyfriend. The sex is blazing hot, and Casey delights in being used and abused in the deep, dark woods.

The faceless man who topped Cal in *L.A. Tool & Die* was veteran porn star Derrick Stanton. Although he had been in the business for a number of years himself, working with the best directors and garnering his own coterie of avid fans, Stanton was nevertheless somewhat in awe of Cal's legendary status. "In the 1970s Casey Donovan was a name I always saw listed in the male porn ads of the *L.A. Times*. As a teenager I used to fantasize what his movies would be like, what his body would look like naked, the shape and size of his dick when it got hard. These ads, I knew, were just a tease. I could never have imagined then that years later I would fuck him in the ass in a porn movie."

Although more than 15 years have passed since their encounter, the moment remains etched vividly in Stanton's mind. "The cast and crew met one day for our scene on the eighth floor of an old downtown skyscraper in L.A. The Gage crew had built an elaborate set simulating a grove of trees at night. I would wait most of the day before meeting Casey and doing our scene together. All I knew about him was that his real name was Cal Culver and that although he was already a legend in the porn industry, he was supposed to be a real nice, down-to-earth guy.

"During the course of the day, there were rumors on the set about him. Some of the crew talked of wild parties that he threw at his guest house in Key West and hinted that he had a bit of a cocaine problem. Upon hearing this I wasn't sure what to expect since I had met egotistical, drug-addicted porn stars before.

"To my surprise, when Casey appeared on the set, he was very much a gentleman and an extremely sweet and endearing person, friendly to cast and crew alike. I was nervous when I walked over to shake his hand, but he immediately put me at ease with his relaxed demeanor. There was a certain assured calm about him.

"Well, when it finally came time to do our scene together, my nervousness returned with a vengeance. I mean, this was a man I used to fantasize about as a kid. Aside from being nervous, Sam Gage, the director, insisted that we do our scene in one take, and demanded that after pumping Casey's ass, I pull out and shoot without jacking off. In most porn films the 'top' usually comes by jacking off because of the extremely artificial nature of porn films, so this was going to be tough.

"To make things even worse, the crew kept blowing these clouds of what I later found out was industrial insecticide to simulate fog. Over the course of the first few takes, everything went wrong. Either the breakaway clothing wouldn't tear away, or I was standing in the wrong position for the light to reflect off my cock, or I was gagging on that damned artificial fog. Sam Gage was a perfectionist and kept changing his mind about what he wanted. By the time we got to take a short break, I was a nervous wreck. Casey turned to me, smiled, and said, 'Relax, Derrick. The next take is gonna be the one, honey.'

"When the director called us back, I walked forward with all the butchness I could muster, tore Casey's shirt off, undid his belt, yanked his pants down, and slid my hard cock up into him. It was an incredible sensation. This wasn't work—it was ecstasy." It quickly became evident that Cal was going to fulfill the director's desire of having Stanton shoot without benefit of using his hands. "It was incredible what that man could do with his ass. I mean, no wonder he was a legend. I plowed into him and soon felt my juices rising from within. I waited until the last possible moment, then pulled out and gave the money shot to the camera. Before I could even catch my breath from this fantasy come true, it was over. Casey hugged me, kissed me, and then was gone. That scene that I did with my adolescent fantasy was the most talked about in the movie. He was really a sweet man."

A few months later the Gage brothers called on Cal again—this time to play a featured role in *Heatstroke* (1982). The film, set in a Montana town during a rodeo, tells the story of a restless ranch crew on a long-overdue free weekend as the temperature—weatherwise and otherwise—relentlessly rises. Cal/Casey—listed in the credits as having appeared by special arrangement with Casa Donovan—plays the part of a naturalist who is lost in the woods. He looks terrific, complete with a scruffy beard shadow, as he anchors two orgy sequences, putting the proof to his voice-over claim that "the best homo sex is impersonal, promiscuous, anonymous, public."

Cal's performance is a tour de force: he services all and sundry, black and white, both orally and anally, with enthusiastic elan. As the orgy progresses, Cal becomes the focus for every man's orgasm. And by the time the scene ends, he is literally drenched with jism, his lean body glistening, his eyes hooded, sated by the sheer excess of it all. His performance is a sort of how-to guide for orgy etiquette in the early, pre-AIDS 1980s.

Also in 1982 Cal began an association with Christopher Rage, a filmmaker with a very personal, very raunchy vision. Rage's films lean toward group sex, raunchy talk, lots of sweat, sex toys, and leather. Rage was reportedly a very intense man with a knack for getting his models to strip away all their inhibitions and bare the deepest, darkest lusts hidden in their minds and souls. His models represent a wide array of ethnic and racial types, tweaking the convention of the more-or-less caucasians-only school of California gay filmmaking.

Sleaze (1982), Cal's first collaboration with Rage, is not, according to its narrator, "really a story. It's more of a family album of a sex gang that meets in an abandoned building on 42nd Street in New York City." This is not your standard nuclear family by any means. The action begins when porn star Scorpio sucks off a denim-and-plaid–clad Casey, then moves on to a series of combinations of three, four, five, and more performers performing virtuoso variations in the key of lust.

Scorpio and Casey were featured in another Rage vehicle in that same year. *Best of the Superstars* (1982) was a compilation of solo scenes, duos, and three-ways. Casey and Scorpio led the way in a sweat-soaked pairing on a bed in a sun-drenched room. The viewer feels like a voyeur on a fire escape, spying on a pair of guys who are totally into each other, the moment, and the sex. They talk dirty while exploring every orifice and body surface. The atmosphere is intensified by the overwhelming sense that these two men are totally involved with each other and the pursuit of mutual pleasure.

The scene was one of Cal's favorites. He found it very hot. "With all the verbalization between us, it looks like two people having a very private sex scene with no one else around." During the interview he continued to expound a bit about film pornography as a genre. "Sex is really a very private thing between two people, and that's why making porno films and showing hardcore sexuality on the screen isn't quite normal. It is a chemistry between two people, and it is distorted when there are lights and machinery and extra people who have nothing to do with that sexuality and aren't part of the scene." This distortion was a rather fine distinction most of Cal's myriad fans probably never noticed.

*   *   *

In a further effort to augment his income, Cal agreed to a proposal by friend Jerry Douglas, now editor of *Stallion* magazine, to write a monthly column. A combination of advice to the lovelorn, sex therapy, health tips, and travel information, *Letters to Casey* continued until a few months before Cal's death in 1987. It was a natural for Cal, as he told Rob Richards in a 1984 interview. "For years, I'd been receiving fan letters with questions the writers couldn't seem to ask of anyone else—with me they felt comfortable—so when Jerry Douglas approached me to do an Ann Landers type column, it seemed a natural. I could see that I might be able to help some men become happy homosexuals—and, as it has turned out, it's been wonderful for me. It's given me the opportunity to actually sit down and write."

The column illustrates a somewhat troubling split between Cal/Casey. In midyear of 1982 Cal is warning a reader concerned about the new "gay cancer" to limit his sex partners, give up drugs, and take care of himself physically. At the same time Cal was making some of his raunchiest films, celebrating anonymous, multiple, down-and-dirty sex at its most extreme. Ironically it is quite apparent that Cal was dead serious. He has his facts straight, and he takes the righteous, conservative line, espousing rest, good nutrition, and exercise—moderation in all things. It was a regimen that Cal could prescribe but that Casey would find it impossible to adhere to.

*   *   *

One of Cal's great passions had always been travel. The problem was that traveling to exotic climes and staying in pleasant surroundings cost money. Cal had always lived simply and saved his funds to take his beloved trips, but he was now a man of property—expensive property that sucked up every spare dime. Cal's dilemma was how he could best manage to travel without depleting his funds, most of which were already earmarked for keeping *Casa Donovan* afloat? The answer, as it turned out, was surprisingly simple.

Cal had been traveling since he was a callow youth, making his first foray into Europe soon after he graduated from college. He had studied, he had seen, he had paid close attention. As his hustling career took off, he found that he was often called upon to be a paid companion for discreet gentlemen who wished to visit foreign ports with a suitable companion. If he could guide tours for one, why not try doing it for a group?

Gay travel was coming into its own in the early '80s. There were thousands of successful gays, some out and proud, others much more circumspect about it, who had the money and the time to see the world in style. What they had never had before was the chance to go with a gay tour group where they could be open, relaxed and comfortable.

Cal's debut as a celebrity tour guide was with *Star Tours Inc.*, a firm that was operating in Hollywood offering the opportunity to "tour with the stars." The jaunt to Italy in October 1981 touched down in Milan, then moved on to Venice, Florence, and Rome. Cal stares out from the print ad in the famous Roy Blakey photograph, billed as "Mister Personality Plus himself, Superstar Casey Donovan."

It was a perfect gig for Cal, permitting him to do a celebrity turn while visiting some of his favorite European locales. In Pete Sandifer's memory of the event, it was a pretty perfect trip as well. Pete had just turned 40, and the trip was a birthday present to himself. "I'd always wanted to go to Italy. I had a framed poster of the Grand Canal in Venice on the wall in my kitchen; my dishes were made in Italy; I liked Italian food; and I lusted after Italian-looking guys—I was a junkie. But I didn't want to go by myself, and the tours I'd always heard about were mostly for retirees and spinster schoolteachers. When I saw the ad for this trip in the pages of *The Advocate*, I had a feeling it might just turn out to be what I was looking for.

"I certainly wasn't in the least bit disappointed, although Casey wasn't at all what I expected. I saw the photograph, of course, and I was aware of his films, although I hadn't seen any of them. I had always been somewhat demure—all right, I mean uptight—and when my friends would ask about my upcoming trip, I hesitated to tell them many details, thinking they might assume I had signed up for something degrading. That hadn't been my purpose, although I have to admit that the photograph in the ad had swayed me ever so slightly.

"The great day arrived, and I grabbed my bags and went to the airport. I don't know what I expected—I mean, I really didn't think he'd be standing nude at the ticket counter—but I wasn't prepared for this good-looking guy in a blazer, with a bow tie and glasses. He was very handsome, but he looked like an accountant, not a porn star. I also remember that he wasn't very tall—maybe 5 feet 9 or 5 feet 10 at the most. I expected him to be taller. Anyway, I showed him my ticket, and he checked my name off on a sheet of paper on a clipboard he was carrying. Then he whipped off the glasses, flashed me a smile that made my knees turn to jelly, and shook my hand. From that moment I was captivated.

"He obviously loved what he was doing. He knew all about every place we visited—the history, the art, the architecture, everything. It was so great because he made it all come alive for me without being pedantic about it. It was like he had lived in those cities for years and knew everything there was to know about them. A couple of times we were in a cafe or a shop and somebody would recognize him. I remember this little gray-haired lady who looked up from behind her counter, all business. Then she saw him and she just beamed. She started chattering in Italian and came out and shook his hand. You could tell that he just loved it. I remember thinking how wonderful it must be knowing people in countries halfway around the world. He was beaming, and she was chattering. It was a wonderful moment."

There were other wonderful moments in store for Pete—moments not mentioned in any of the information he had been sent before embarking on his Italian vacation. "While we were in Rome, I was down in the lobby of our little hotel writing postcards. Most of the guys were up in their rooms or wandering the streets near the hotel. I saw Casey come down—I had seen him the night before as well—and wander out into the night. I promised myself that if he did the same thing on the third night, I was going to ask if I could walk along with him.

"Well, the next night he came down to the lobby, left his key at the desk, and stepped out into the street. I hurried after him. He saw me and said hello. I took a deep breath and asked if I could accompany him on his walk. There was a moment's hesitation, then he looked at me, smiled, and nodded. I fell in beside him and we set off through the narrow streets of Rome's historic district.

"As we skirted the Roman Forum, the Coliseum gradually came into view. It was gorgeous, lit up against the night sky. He walked right by the main gates, following a shadowy stream of slender men who suddenly seemed to disappear off the sidewalk into thin air. Well, we got to a point in the fencing that was loose, and we slipped into the midst of one of the great monuments of all time.

"I was terrified. It was pitch black, the only sounds the faint echoing of leather soles grinding against the sand-covered stones in the dark passages we were traversing. As my eyes began to adjust to the light, I saw that we were not alone. There were men on all sides, leaning up against the walls of the passageway, the embers of their cigarettes glowing like the eyes of demons. God, my heart was pounding. I had never done anything like this—not even remotely. Casey, on the other hand, was totally at ease. He put his hand against the small of my back and propelled me along. That touch made me feel calm, like as long as he was there things would be just fine.

"Suddenly we stepped out into the open again, and I realized that we were standing in the middle of the Coliseum. I mean the real, honest-to-God Roman Coliseum. I had been reading about this and looking at pictures of it for almost my whole life, and here we were, after closing time, right in the middle of it. And we weren't alone. There were dozens of men standing all around, leaning back against the ancient stones, looking cool and calm.

"I remember Casey asking me if I'd be all right on my own. My first thought was, 'No, absolutely not.' But I must have said yes because he smiled and nodded and then slipped off into the shadows, leaving me all alone. I stood there listening to my heart pound. Then this man, this gorgeous Italian man, walked over to me and smiled. What happened next is strictly none of your business, but it provided the absolute high point of my holiday. Afterward, I stood there, watching and listening to the shadowy goings-on all around me. Before too long Casey reappeared smiling like the cat who swallowed the canary and walked back to the hotel with me. I never mentioned the incident to another soul on the tour, figuring that it was just our little secret. If he did the same thing for anyone else, I never heard a word about it."

*   *   *

It was another tour company, however, that provided long-term employment and a real chance to see the world. He had first been on one of the Ebensten Agency's gay tours when he went to Haiti in 1978, a feat he managed without stirring any associations in Hanns Ebensten between Cal Culver and his infamous alter ego. In 1982 he was drawn back by a discreetly worded ad touting an upcoming all-gay trip to China. He signed on as a paying member of the tour, cementing what was to become a long association with Ebensten and his agency. Ebensten's initial reaction to Cal was mixed at best. "To be quite frank I found it very distressing that a porn star was on the trip with me, but I soon discovered that I was traveling not with Casey Donovan but with Calvin Culver. The man I knew was a real gentleman, a highly educated teacher who had been a kind of private secretary to novelist Tom Tryon. He was an enormously well-read, considerate man with impeccable manners who always dressed very conservatively. Prior to our journey he had immersed himself in Chinese history and was knowledgeable about all aspects of our itinerary.

"I must confess that I absolutely despised China. Especially in the early '80s, there was no respect for their monumental past, and we were hemmed in by the guides and prevented from mingling with the real life of the cities and villages. Calvin, however, was enchanted by every aspect of the country, and his sense of humor and flair considerably lightened my mood during what otherwise would have been an unrelenting ordeal.

"I remember two instances of his special style quite vividly. The first occurred when a young Chinese woman guide, having heard that we had a movie star with us, asked him to describe a film in which he had appeared. I and the rest of the tour members were holding our collective breath as he calmly recounted the tale of a group of people from New York who went to an island resort for the summer and dealt with the complications of their relationships there. The film, of course, was *Boys in the Sand.*

"The other occurred when we were visiting the Summer Palace near Beijing. We were being herded through along with the droves of other tourists. Well, in one of the halls, there was a throne where female visitors could pose and be photographed, for a fee, wearing a court robe dating from the reign of the last Chinese empress dowager. Cal got a glimpse of the robes and simply had to have his picture taken. I saw that the whole crew was ready to cut loose, and I offered to pay for group photographs. My group accepted the offer with alacrity and began to pull the heavily embroidered, bejeweled gowns from the hangers and try them on, then discard them, searching for one even brighter and gaudier. They chose the most enormous hats and diadems with bells and feathers and pom-poms and cut-glass ornaments like chandeliers. The women attendants were frantic. 'Is dresses for ladies,' they shrieked. 'We know, we know,' my crew replied, not slowing down for even a moment. Tourist traffic was brought to a halt as everyone tried to see what the crazy American men were up to. It was a priceless moment."

Cal went on several of Ebensten's other tours—both mixed

and exclusively gay—including trips to the Grand Canyon for a rafting expedition, a safari to Tanzania, a climb up Mount Kilimanjaro, and a tour of Peru's famous Inca sites, including Machu Picchu. "After he'd been on several trips, he found out that I was looking for tour leaders, and he asked to be considered for a job. I said yes. It was very daring of me. Not only was he a porn star, but he was also a prostitute, advertising his services for a $100 a throw, $500 a night. Did I really want a man like that working for me?"

Of course he did. Ebensten's gay tours were very button-down, very proper. What better way to titillate a group of discreet, homosexual gentlemen than by a whispered rumor that there might be someone scandalous aboard. Cal was using his real name as a tour guide, so how would prospective customers make the connection to the infamous, notorious, undeniably sexy Casey Donovan? A word was dropped here, a rumor there, the word of a satisfied customer was heard in another quarter. It was a very clever marketing ploy, and it kept the tours booked. For every person who demurred, there were two more waiting in line to take his place. Cal was a great find, and Ebensten quickly realized it. "Because he knew many members of the international bon ton, he was able to enhance the pleasure of those who toured with him by chance encounters. During a tour to the Carnival in Venice, when he led the group into Harry's Bar, a distinguished Italian prince arose from his banquette and called out, "Calvino, mio caro! What a surprise!" and promptly invited him and his tour members to afternoon tea next day in his palazzo." If you're going to hire a prostitute, by all means hire a classy one with a stable of titled tricks.

Ebensten used Cal on tours for the general, heterosexual public at first, and he was enormously successful. Cal was always the perfect gentleman. He could speak intelligently on any subject. He charmed all people of both sexes; he was meticulous about paperwork and finances; and he learned quickly. "He…had the patience of an angel…and he could be depended upon to turn potentially troublesome situations into interesting travel experiences…He was, in short, the perfect tour guide."

After Cal had proved himself, Ebensten took the plunge and sent him on his rapidly expanding roster of gay tours as well. "It was understood that there would be nothing improper going on. Quite a number of men were scandalized when they heard that Cal was to be guiding their tour, and one even called to complain that he was a prostitute who had a big dick." Ebensten's eyes narrowed as though the complainant was still on the phone. "I told him that I didn't know Casey Donovan. I know Calvin Culver. As for his big dick, that will remain concealed beneath the fly of his Brooks Brothers suit, and you won't see it. And that's the way it was."

Well, almost. Boys—even wealthy, closeted ones—will be boys, given the chance. During a 1984 journey to the Inca ruins at Machu Picchu, the tour stopped off in Lima, Peru. "Lima is probably one of the poorest cities in South America," Cal wrote in one of his travel pieces for *Stallion* magazine. "Lima was not, however, without sexual adventure and interesting liaisons. Several members of our group met young men in or near our hotel and were escorted to local gay bars in Miraflores or were in turn introduced to other friends for 'English lessons.' Never one to leave a baths in any foreign city unturned, I found the 'Fuji' and met a wonderful thirty four year old Peruvian who works for a stock broker…He certainly was the creme de la creme of those on their lunch hours that afternoon, but there was something for everyone at the 'Fuji.'"

Cal's activities, according to some, weren't confined to visiting steam baths in foreign lands. "Call me 'Anonymous in Cleveland' and leave it at that," one former tour patron demanded. "First let me say that the tours were well-managed, well-operated, and gave terrific value for the money. They were also quite staid and buttoned-down. Now just ask yourself this question— if you were a wealthy, discreet man, staying in a cozy hotel and had probably the most famous porn star in the world sleeping next door, what would you do? I answered that question to my satisfaction, and I wasn't the only one. We were quiet and discreet, and nobody knew, so what was the harm? Cal was a gentleman, and he never gave any indication of what went on by a word or a glance. He was also the most accomplished sexual athlete I ever encountered in my life. The experience was well worth the outlay."

Cal would go on to work his discreet magic for the Ebensten Agency's travelers from December 1983 until just a few weeks before his death. The job provided an outlet for one of the grand passions of his life and also offered some of the respectability he was beginning to crave. It also held forth the possibility of employment suited to a man of a "certain age" who was beginning to feel the need for a change of pace.

CHAPTER 10

Revivals, Sequels, and the Final Exit

In the spring of 1983 while he was still testing the waters with Hanns Ebensten, Cal took a big chance on reviving his stage career. He had always, at some level, considered himself to be an actor first and foremost, and he still wanted to prove himself to the world at large. His chance came about when producer/director Michael Bavar decided to revive Terrence McNally's play *The Ritz* as a vehicle for Warhol superstar Holly Woodlawn. In the autumn of 1982 Cal was brought in as coproducer and costar, set to play the role of Brick, the detective with the high-pitched voice. Bavar reputedly sank $100,000 into the enterprise, and Cal spent months rounding up cash himself, much of it from clients. "It's not easy getting your hands on cash these days," he told pal Rob Richards prior to the opening. "We're not completely financed. I'm still searching desperately for a hot $10,000 fuck, but we're forging ahead." This was to be his return, his vindication, his chance to establish a power base in New York City to produce other plays. "Having been an avid theatergoer for the past 16 years," he told journalist John Hofsess, "I've developed some pointed criticisms about what's wrong with Broadway, and putting on *The Ritz* gives me an opportunity to test some of my theories."

Brave words for what turned out to be an unmitigated disaster, both critically and financially. There were many problems, beginning with the concept. McNally had written the play in 1975 as a showcase for Rita Moreno. Moreno played the role of Googie Gomez, a singer at a gay steam baths who was constantly mistaken for a drag queen. Moreno was inspired in the role, onstage and in the Richard Lester film of the play. Using Holly Woodlawn, a drag queen, to play a woman mistaken for a drag queen seemed to the critics to take away a layer of irony or, perhaps, to add one too many.

Photographer Roy Blakey did the publicity stills for the play and had a feeling that all was not going to go well with the production. "They came to my studio to do the pictures, and it was definitely a comedy routine. I had just finished doing some portfolio shots for a very large black female vocal artist when Holly and Cal burst in. Cal was his usual professional self, quietly stripping and wrapping a towel around his narrow hips, his lean body appearing quite fit and youthful. Holly Woodlawn seemed a bit disoriented. She kept popping into the dressing room of the vocalist I had just finished with, asking to borrow makeup, a scarf, a hair brush. It seems humorous now, but I remember that I was very annoyed at the time. It was totally unprofessional, as was, or so I heard, the production."

By the second week of April 1983, it was clear that something strange was going on with Woodlawn. Rumors were rife, and the director began looking for a possible replacement. In a recent interview Woodlawn owned up to the preopening disorientation. "During rehearsals I was drinking alcohol, but the producer sat me down and told me to lay off. I did as I was told because I knew that he would replace me, and I wanted to be in that show. I was not on drugs or booze while performing in that show."

During rehearsal the show appeared to be going well. Preview audiences were enthusiastic, and everyone's hopes were high. Opening night was slated to be wildly glamorous—Prince and Princess Egon von Furstenberg sent out lavish invitations inviting cast and audience to a "black tie or towel" celebration after the show—and the house was packed with friends who wanted nothing more than to cheer and have fun. The lights went down, the curtain went up—and *The Ritz* bombed.

The critics were merciless. "During the second act of Terrence McNally's *The Ritz*, the patrons of a gay men's bathhouse hold an amateur-night contest," critic Lee Alan Morrow reported in *Back Stage*, a theater magazine. "Frankly, it was impossible to differentiate what were supposed to be the intentionally bad performances from those that constituted someone's true efforts...Michael Bavar, the director, treated the McNally script like a buffoon, grinding out cheap little jokes. The comedy...was completely swamped by poor casting, poor staging, and nary an ounce of original interpretive thought. Rather than reviving *The Ritz*, Bavar and his colleagues buried it."

In *The New York Post*, reviewer Clive Barnes threw more dirt on the coffin: "There are some revivals that make you seriously, but dangerously, wonder whatever it was you saw in the original.... This new Xenon production looks undernourished, undercast, and underfulfilled.... [It] is much more gay than the original, but much less cheerful."

John Burke played a small role in the production and was also horrified by what was going on. "*The Ritz* was directed atrociously. Michael Bavar was completely ridiculous as a director. The man didn't have a clue as to what he was doing. McNally had agreed to let Bavar revive the play at Xenon, a disco in what was formerly the old Park-Miller Theater." It was the very theater, as a matter of fact, where Wakefield Poole got his inspiration to create *Boys in the Sand*—a little bit of history that Cal hoped might just repeat itself. "Just before we opened, McNally came in and saw the play, and he was completely mortified. It was disastrous. He tried to doctor the production, but it was too late to do anything to help out." In fact, his insistence on restoring a number of dialogue cuts at the last minute confused the performers and added to the chaos.

"Cal was the sweetest guy in the world," Burke continued, "but he wasn't a strong actor. He couldn't rise above the production the way a real artist often can. He let the director lead him over the cliff like a lamb going to the slaughter. He just didn't have the acting dynamic to resist bad direction. He was a star, not a real actor. I gave him lines occasionally, and he really was adorable in the role." This was an evaluation of Cal's performance that Woodlawn seconded, almost verbatim. "He even managed to keep the falsetto voice going, which wasn't easy. If there had been a strong director, I think it could have worked."

The play opened the evening of May 1, 1983—and closed less than two hours later on the same night. "It was horrible," Burke said. "There was a big audience on opening night, and they were doing a first act scene. There were some similar scenes in the first and second acts, and somehow the actors jumped from act one to act two. McNally was in the audience, and he was in a fury. I kept expecting him to jump up and stop the proceedings, but he didn't. The actors onstage just kept going, running through scene after scene. It was obvious that Cal knew what was going on, but he didn't know what to do about it. They all plugged on to the bitter end, finishing about 45 minutes and one intermission ahead of schedule. Bavar just sat there through the whole thing like a lump. He should have stood up and stopped them, apologized to the audience for opening-night nerves, then had another run at it. He was a total waste."

"Everyone panicked too soon," Woodlawn said. "The opening night was a horror, but if given a chance, things would have settled in and worked out. I had laryngitis on opening night and had to be miked. Half the audience couldn't hear me. Still, things like that happen in live theater. We just needed more time to make it work."

"Bavar should never have been allowed inside a theater," actor Don Potter told me. "He didn't have a clue about what he was doing. Cal was the one who called McNally and asked for his help. Cal knew we were in trouble but wasn't quite sure how to fix it."

Potter had auditioned for the show at Cal's urging. "I had been in rehearsal for a show called *Moose Murders*," he said wryly. "It was another huge flop—opened and closed in one night. I was free, obviously, so when Cal asked, I auditioned. I played the role of the 'chubby chaser.'

"Well, when this show had a one night run as well, I started to feel jinxed, but I had nothing to complain about compared to poor Cal. He was into it for money on the production end. I remember one night during rehearsal I asked him out for dinner. He agreed to come but told me that he had to leave by about 10 o'clock. 'I have to hustle my ass,' he said. I looked at him, and he shrugged, and I realized he meant that literally. He was off to turn a trick to raise money for the show."

*   *   *

It was all over almost as soon as it had begun, leaving Cal with an irrecoverable financial loss and, much worse, his cherished dream of making a triumphal return to the stage totally dashed. Other hopes were dashed as well. He had been looking forward to using his share of the expected profits from this revival of *The Ritz* to finance a film that he had written, celebrating the joys of turning 40. "I wanted to make a statement about aging in the gay community. I wanted to demonstrate to people that one can be hotter, older, and wiser—and have a hot time sexually no matter what age you are." He had also hoped to be able to invest some cash in renovations at his Key West money pit, the Casa Donovan. He had also expressed a desire to retire from porn and from hustling and concentrate on some other way to earn a living, "something more suitable to middle age." The crushing failure of *The Ritz* left all of these desires and plans unfulfilled.

*　　*　　*

Cal never appeared on a stage in New York City again, but he was too irrepressible to stay away from theater forever. When he scooted down to Key West to lick his wounds, he couldn't avoid seeing the Red Barn Theater on Duval Street in the heart of town. It was a community theater, and leading men were always in short supply. Cal's charm and looks helped him find a friendly niche and gave him the opportunity to stretch his thespian wings in a more friendly, less critical atmosphere.

Actress Carole MacCartee remembers Cal vividly. "We were in *The Prime of Miss Jean Brodie* together. In the play Jean talks about going to Italy. Well, Cal went to Italy and sent me back a postcard signed with the name of his character in the play. He always seemed to go out of his way to do special things for people.

"He wasn't as loose and natural onstage as he could have been, but a really good actor could bring him out and get a good performance out of him. He was in *Boys in the Band* with an actor named Charles. Charles was a friend of Cal's, and they had a scene together in the play. When Cal started to get really stilted in his delivery, Charles would put his hand on Cal's leg and slide it slowly up toward his groin. He could get Cal rattled by doing something sexual and physical to him. It would make him change his delivery, bring it more into the moment. It was fun to watch.

"I remember that he was also in Hoffman's play *As Is*. It was one of the first AIDS plays to have a real impact. These plays weren't all done in succession, though. Cal wasn't here consistently. He was always traveling. He'd be here, then he'd be off. Then a couple of months later, he'd reappear, back from some exotic clime or another. He was bright and beautiful and extremely kind."

*   *   *

Despite the debacle in New York City with *The Ritz*, Cal remained sunny and optimistic. He hadn't come this far by listening to the naysayers, heeding the sniping of homophobes, or—some would say—paying any heed to reality. The year 1983 was an important year for Cal. It was the year he would turn 40, a much-feared milestone for many gay men that he was actually looking forward to. He gave a number of interviews in '83 and '84, all of which, in one way or another, expressed his take on this inescapable fact of life.

"When I was modeling I learned that you can work as long as you keep yourself looking good," he told Rob Richards in September of 1984. "I always felt that my biggest successes would occur after forty—later in life…I made a little vow with myself when I made *Boys in the Sand*. When it became a big success, and I was on the cover of *After Dark* and was suddenly in a prominent position as a gay person in the U.S. and was out of the closet and very open, I decided that I wanted to keep it together so that I could be a Fabulous Forty, then a Nifty Fifty. Sexy Sixty after that! Then on to the Senile Seventies!"

In a video interview he elaborated on his feelings. "I've always liked older men and wanted to be an older man myself. Early on I decided I wanted to keep it together. I'm glad that I've kept this promise to myself. I know about forty people who have died in the past two years. I don't drug or drink and I'm working to keep myself healthy…I'm still working as a hustler through the pink pages of *The Advocate*. I think it's fabulous that people are still paying for it. Why the hell not?

"I've never been overly aggressive about going to the gym. I mean, when do those gym guys find time to read a book or go to a museum or use their minds? But, I'm planning an aerobics exercise video so that I can help guys keep it together. Never give up, I say. Keep it together…I like being older. I mean, I've lived and done so much. I've been able to transcend problems and situations lately that would have ruined me if they'd happened when I was younger. Six months ago I was going crazy in Key West. I didn't know what to do—sell my guest house or keep it. I was broke and desperate. Now I've got four or five movies coming up, I'm going to be directing a film, I'm traveling to South America later this year, and I have a fantasy trip planned for the Grand Canyon. I tell you, I'm looking forward to fifty. I want to be a hot daddy."

Once he had realized that he wasn't going to be able to retire from porn and move on to whatever he may have imagined for himself, he pulled a typical Cal—he took the bucket of lemons and began making lemonade for himself and all of his friends. And he made it clear that he had always wanted, more than anything else, to be a maker of lemonade.

"There must be some perverse joy I get out of being a porno star," he mused in the *Men in Film* interview in the summer of 1983 just after his *Ritz* fiasco. "I was thinking the other day about how many millions of gays there are in the U.S. but only hundreds have fucked on film. I guess I get off on that."

Cal always claimed that his years in porn had been for the best. "Because I let them be good for me, I never tried to deny them. I did *Boys*, and then one film after another came along, and I have no idea what possessed me to keep on doing them, except that I got off on it, and that I'd become a recognizable commodity. Also I enjoyed the idea that I was doing something that very few people had ever done…My life was made much more exciting by having done those films. People—very interesting people—wanted to meet me. Fabulous people wanted to do things for me…I did plays, I was on magazine covers, in national fashion ads…I think porno worked in my life because I was so honest about it. I treated it all very lightly. After all, my whole life has been a joke. A gag! Just think of how ridiculous it is that I got involved in this.… You have to have a sense of humor and treat the whole thing as a goof. Every day was like a party and I went along for the fun."

Cal discovered that resilience and a sense of humor were indispensable parts of surviving the things that happened to him. "Big film projects were talked about—like the film version of Mary Renault's *The King Must Die*. But nothing came of it. Perhaps I was naive but it was a rude awakening for me to find out that Hollywood is one of the most closeted and hypocritical cultural centers in the world. I learned that an openly gay actor like myself was not welcome to gay directors and producers who believe it is essential to keep their sexuality a secret. Once an actor has made a porn movie, it is very difficult to 'cross over'. And it all has nothing to do with how much talent one has. It is all about how an actor is perceived and prejudged. In a limited sphere, my films made me famous, but in another sense, they were a handicap.

"I tried to maintain separate names and identities at first: 'Casey Donovan' did the gay stuff, 'Cal Culver' did the other stuff, the legitimate plays and the modeling. It got increasingly confusing if not schizophrenic. Besides, the secret could not be perpetuated endlessly. Nowadays it doesn't matter who knows who I am or what name they call me as long as they call me.

"Once I realized that my appearance in gay films was held against me in some quarters, I decided to put sex to even greater use—not less—in augmenting my income. We live in a society with deeply rooted feelings of guilt and shame about sex of any kind. If somebody makes a porn film, they are automatically beyond the pale. If somebody hustles, there must be something wrong with him. Maybe for some, not for me. I'm the living proof that it doesn't have to be that way. I'm still pretty much 'the boy next door' that I always was. I don't smoke, I don't drink, I don't use drugs of any kind. A long time ago, even before I began to see the destructive effects of certain aspects of the gay lifestyle, I resolved to live in such a way that I would enjoy getting older.

"I think my greatest accomplishment so far is something that doesn't show up in lights or get reviewed—and that's simply the sexual sanity that I have tried to contribute to over the past twenty years. I have never done anything to make a sick society any sicker. I've tried to be honest, kind, and understanding with as many different people as possible, and I think that's much more important than just being gay. My goal is to live each day to the fullest."

*   *   *

The particular brand of sexual sanity that Cal was championing was coming increasingly under fire, challenged by the specter of AIDS. While in doubt, Cal did what many gay men were doing—nothing. He continued his hustling and his moviemaking just as he had before the outbreak of the AIDS epidemic. In fairness to him it must be noted that he was by no means alone in this decision. Until the middle of the decade, no firm consensus had been reached on the means of transmission of the disease. Cal was quite aware of AIDS—as early as July of 1982, he addressed the question in his *Letters to Casey* column in *Stallion* magazine, counseling fewer sexual partners, drug and alcohol avoidance, and aggressive health maintenance. Years later when a test was developed, he counseled those who wrote to him to take it—yet he steadfastly refused to take the test himself. He told Jerry Douglas privately that he hadn't been tested and had no intention of doing so. He believed that he was positive and didn't need to take the test and be depressed with confirmation of something he already instinctively knew to be the case.

*   *   *

For once, all of the movies Cal spoke about having on tap materialized. Although his idea of a film titled *Forty* never came to pass, he made a number of films in his last years that were a paean to the older man. In *Hot Shots* (1983), Cal plays a chauffeur who imagines sex scenes while getting ready for work in the morning. The scenes contrast younger and older men, demonstrating that the older guys like Cal and costar Rick Madison are easily able to hold their own against the younger generation.

Cal was also busy in 1984. He did *Split Image* for his old friend Wakefield Poole and *Non-Stop* for director Steve Scott. In the former film he portrays a "daddy," literally and figuratively, joining "son" Steve Kay in a three-way with one of the younger man's tricks. In the latter he plays with boys his own age, engaging in yet another three-way scene with Steve Collins and Steve Anthony. In both these films Cal appears hale and fit, wearing his age well, still able to do the deed with style, vigor, and conviction.

In the late summer of '84, Cal's pornographic film career came full circle when he and Wakefield Poole at last got around to making the long-proposed sequel to the epochal film that started it all, *Boys in the Sand*. Cal, Poole, and the cast packed up and made the familiar trek out to Fire Island for the shoot. The first footage, including atmospheric shots of Cal walking along the boardwalk and young Pat Allen reprising Cal's immortal emergence from the waves, was lensed on August 20, 1984. That same day, Rob Richards was there to interview Cal.

In response to Richards's question regarding how he felt about watching Pat Allen, his youthful costar, re-create the opening sequence of the original *Boys*, Cal was completely upbeat. "I loved it!" he said enthusiastically. "I've waited a long, long time to experience this déjà vu. For years Wakefield Poole and I have talked about doing this sequel—although I never anticipated that he'd repeat that sequence so exactly...I had no vision of losing my crown as the 'king of gay porn.' It was wonderful watching young Pat do the scene—seeing him looking so much like me out there in the water."

Further along in the interview, Cal makes an interesting observation about his life in porn. "You have to have a sense of humor...and learn to ride on the assets of a porn film career...once you've done this, you've done it and you have to move ahead. There's no going back—it's out there! It's been done and film lives on!" He also advocated balance: "The only gay venue I've worked in has been films...I have worked in plays that had gay content, and I have appeared in theaters where my films were showing, but only to greet customers after the movie...I've never worked in bars or gay burlesque—but a lot of kids stay too immersed in this gay, gay, gay lifestyle...I've also never been caught up in the disco scene, and I don't like seeing the people I'm fond of stoned and fucked up...I don't think it's healthy—you have to become more well-rounded to survive, more of a citizen of the world."

Citizen Cal left Fire Island with extremely high hopes that this sequel was going to propel him once again onto magazine covers and A-lists across the country. Jerry Douglas saw him a few days after the shoot and noticed that "he was more ebullient than ever, and I could clearly see that he was trying to keep in check his fantasies of becoming the man of the moment all over again." Unfortunately it was not to be. While Poole was editing the film that autumn, the producer died of a heart attack, and ownership of the film stock was thrown into litigation for two years. By the time it was finally released late in 1986, the buzz had dissipated and Cal found that he had been deprived of the accompanying burst of celebrity. *Boys in the Sand II*, although superior to the original conceptually and technically, never equaled its predecessor's impact or its financial success. By then, with the advent of VCR technology and the subsequent volume of video porn churned out to feed the home-viewing market, the field was so crowded that *Boys II* had to stand in a long line just to get a viewing. The world, as it turned out, was not waiting quite so avidly for the *Boys* sequel as Cal might have wished.

In the fall of '84, Cal was approached by Philip Blackwell and Laurence Sevelick. The pair were the producers of *City Men,* a new show based on Claire Booth Luce's deliciously bitchy play *The Women*—immortalized on film in 1939 by George Cukor—which was scheduled to open in December of 1984. Cal's friend John Burke was also set for a featured role in the production. "Cal was to play the Norma Shearer role, and I was going to do the Joan Crawford part, you know, Crystal Allen. It was a good script. Unfortunately Cal got sick and couldn't carry it off. He just didn't have the strength to concentrate and learn his lines."

Burke was one of the few who saw Cal at less than his best at this time. Cal was in deep denial—never mentioning to anyone that there was a problem with his health. When people asked, he was invariably "fine." When he wasn't "fine," he holed up in his apartment until the face he presented to the world was the one his fans expected to see.

Fortunately Cal still had long periods of relatively good health and sufficient strength to lead tours for Hanns Ebensten, guiding his charges through Italy, the Grand Canyon, the Australian outback and across the vast expanses of Canada. Despite all of his best efforts, Cal finally lost Casa Donovan in 1985, which was more of a blessing than otherwise. At last he was free of the burden of trying to make a go of the ill-fated guest house.

Also in 1985 Cal made a pair of safe-sex films, *Chance of a Lifetime* for the Gay Men's Health Crisis and *Inevitable Love*. Although the tapes manage to make safe sex entertaining and relatively erotic, Cal's performances were less than stellar. That may have been partly because Cal really didn't believe in safe sex. Longtime costar Michael Kearns reported that Cal refused all safe-sex practices in his films and in life. "Perhaps in his delusion, he convinced himself he was immortal. Stars do not die, not from sexually transmitted disease."

*   *   *

To his credit Cal did turn more and more of his energy and attention to the AIDS crisis in the last two years of his life. In addition to his work on the two safe-sex films, Cal began to work for various AIDS charities when he was in New York City. In a short demo tape for the Outreach project of the Gay Men's Health Crisis, he spoke to Kevin Mahony about eroticizing safe sex. "Like a lot of people, I used to think that using rubbers was a bore," he confided to Mahony. "Now I know that they are not only easy to use, they can save a life. I am more and more surprised to find that rubbers are at the bedside or in the pocket of most of the men I know." Cal went on to explain all about rubbers, with visual aids enhanced by still photographs of his own famous penis. "They are getting to be a lot more fun," he concluded dubiously, looking somewhat less than comfortable in his role as the "rubber man." "Use a condom because it is good for you." It was excellent advice. Unfortunately it was advice that Cal was unwilling to take.

Cal continued to lead Ebensten-organized tours around the world, enhancing the travel experiences of many a man with his reflected glory and social savvy. Up to the very end when Cal traveled, he was recognized by old friends and clients he had encountered along the way, validating his fantasies of a life lived large.

In the late spring of 1985 Cal journeyed to Colorado—where his brother, Duane, had settled with his family—to attend his niece's high school graduation. Cal also made it a point that year to retrace his steps to Canandaigua to help his old mentor, Helen Van Fleet, celebrate her retirement. He blew into town amid the bustle and fuss that became a celebrity of his stature, visiting with his schoolmates whose lives had never been quite as dramatic or as flashy as Cal's. Everyone knew all about his career in the legitimate theater—most knew all about his raunchy twin Casey Donovan—but they all had remained fond of the genuinely likeable former cheerleader and class officer.

Cal and his favorite teacher had kept in close contact since his school days, and he insisted on playing a prominent part in the final send-off from her distinguished teaching career. Cal came not only to attend but also to perform for his old mentor. Her daughter, Alice, remembered the event fondly. "It was really wonderful. He had written a parody of the title song from the musical *Mame*, and he sang it to her. It was an account of all the things they had experienced together over the years. It meant the world to her." The performance was roundly applauded, and Mrs. Van Fleet was charmed.

"When Mom heard of his death a couple of years later, she was devastated. Mom had always accepted Cal for what he was, but she worried about him. His promiscuity bothered her. She didn't think it was right that he hadn't settled down with one special person. She feared what might happen to him. Unfortunately she was right."

*   *   *

By the middle of 1986, Cal knew something was now seriously wrong, but he still refused to face it. Friends tried to tell
him he looked unwell, but his denial was absolute. He wasn't
really all that sick, he reasoned, and there was nothing he could
do about it anyway. Besides, when he felt good, as he still often
did, he still looked terrific. People told him so, so why shouldn't
he believe it?

"He did look good," Roy Blakey insisted. "It was 1986, I
think, and I was walking in New York on Tenth Avenue. Approaching me from about a block away was this gorgeous young
man. As he got closer to me, I realized that it was Cal. He looked
absolutely untouched by all the years and experiences that had
passed since I had first met him. I remember being struck by his
seeming immunity to aging and change."

Wakefield Poole saw him on a number of occasions during his
final years. "He was always in good spirits, full of life. About a
year before he died, he called me up and asked me the strangest
question. 'Have we ever had a date?' 'No,' I replied. 'Well, if
you're not busy Friday night, would you go on a date with me?'
Of course I said yes.

"He had been given tickets to a play by the publicity manager
for the Circle in the Square theater. The man was a client and a
friend of Cal's. It was the opening night of *The Marriage of Fi-
garo*, the play, not the opera. It starred Christopher Reeve. We
went to an opening night party after, and Cal taught me how to
table hop. 'Just follow me,' he told me, and I did. We went from
table to table, chatting to people, making introductions, telling
little jokes. The man certainly knew how to work a room," Poole
mused, the admiration clear in his voice.

"After we'd touched base with all the celebrities, we loaded our
plates at the buffet and went, not to the banquet room where the
party was taking place, but out into the hallway. We sat on the
floor and ate our meal with the waiters and busboys, laughing

and talking about movies. It was our one and only date, and I had a wonderful time."

Poole continued to see Cal up until shortly before his death. "I'm convinced that his ego made him keep up appearances as long as he could. He always told me that he was fine, that he didn't understand why he wasn't positive. I saw the man five weeks before he died, and I swear he looked great—dressed up, buttoned-down, the scent of woodsy soap clinging to him. He came to me to ask to borrow some cash. The next thing I knew, he was back in Florida, and then he was dead.

"When we filmed *Boys II* in August of 1984, Cal was a poster boy for good health. He looked gorgeous—full of vigor and good humor. I can't imagine that he knew at that point. However, since the film wasn't freed up from litigation until 1986, people thought I knew he had AIDS when we were filming. It wasn't true at all, but it gave me a bad name. It was one of the reasons that I quit making films."

Cal may have been deep in denial regarding his own impending demise, but he had become morbidly fixated on death. He took to going to all of the celebrity memorial services in Manhattan, services that were occurring with increasing frequency as the AIDS epidemic claimed more victims every week. "He loved them almost more than anything except sex," Jerry Douglas said. Early on in the epidemic, memorial services were often elaborate productions where the audiences might feature more celebrities than a Broadway opening. Cal had always been drawn to the celebrity circuit, and this was merely a natural extension of that fascination.

The last time Jerry Douglas saw Cal was on a steamy day in the middle of the summer of 1987. "He had just been to the funeral of a well-known theatrical agent, and although he was as immaculately groomed as ever, and although he bubbled cheerfully about who had been at the funeral and what had been said, he looked haggard and gaunt. I asked him about his health, and he assured me, with the denial he maintained up to the moment of his death, that he was 'fine.' Cal never missed a service, so when he didn't show up for erotic film director Arthur Bressan's memorial on the sixth of August, I knew that he must be really ill."

*   *   *

The portrait of Casey Donovan/Cal Culver as Dorian Gray that Cal had joked about so long ago was horrifyingly updated in 1986 in Cal's final film for director Christopher Rage. In the movie the golden boy of porn, the man who had managed to retain his reputation as the boy next door, the elegant, buttoned-down courtesan who had made a career out of his body for nearly two decades, finally self-destructs.

"I couldn't watch it," Cal's friend Jake Getty told me. "I started it, but Cal looked so spaced out, so lost, that I had to stop." Cal and his old friend, Clay Johns—identified in the film as John Clayton—are in Rage's *Fucked Up* together—and fucked up they are. Both men are ill at this point in time, and all taboos regarding drugs—whether as a result of despair or dementia—are off. The film explores the extremes, its participants zonked out, pushing the limits of sexual experience over the edge.

"*Fucked Up* was the saddest thing I had ever seen," Rob Richards confided. "It was a horrible film. When I saw it I just couldn't believe it. Cal was so far gone, and he was being so used and abused. The whole thing was beyond abandoned. He was holding what appeared to be a big mayonnaise jar full of poppers or ethyl chloride—I'm sure there were other drugs in him at the time as well—sitting in the corner of a room. These faceless people arrive and push toys and fists up into him. He's drooling, and it is absolutely terrifying. I couldn't believe it when I saw it." It was, as a reviewer for the gay X-rated video guide *Manshots* summed it up, "a haunting study in self-destruct…a pathetic footnote to a glittering career…an unsettling record of the Golden Boy on a collision course with his own mortality."

The end was approaching, but Cal soldiered on. He was chronically short of cash, so he continued to work for Ebensten. Even as he began to decline, the pleasures of travel soothed him. And amazingly, whether through luck or sheer force of will, Cal continued to look good up until the final weeks of his life. No one on one of Cal's tours would have had any indication that he was ill. Hanns Ebensten was with him on a tour of the Amazon River basin just a few months before he died. "He insisted on swimming one afternoon at a pool in our hotel. Several members of the tour were sitting around outside and later told me that they were astounded by his taut body and youthful good looks. He was tanned and fit and glowed with good health."

Cracks were beginning to appear in the facade, however, and although he struggled heroically to hide them, more and more frequently that just was not possible. Rob Richards saw the unsettling changes in his friend one evening after the two had attended a performance at Lincoln Center. "Afterward, we went to O'Neill's Balloon, which was a restaurant in the area. We had been to the ballet and wanted to have something to eat. Cal had been fine all evening, but while we sat at the table in that restaurant, and he continued to talk, I realized that he was losing his mind.

"He started talking about seraphim, which represent the highest order of angels. He told me that the last time he had been in Italy on one of his tours, he had realized that there were seraphim following him. He said they had checked into the hotel with him. It was obviously delirium talk, like you might expect from a person with a burning fever, but he was speaking in a linear fashion. He told me that he took a bus trip to a monastery and that while he was on the bus, the seraphim began acting up and telling him what to do.

"He claimed that he had stayed in this monastery for several days with these seraphim directing him. He mentioned the names of the brothers who ran the place, but it was all totally mad, and he was obviously out of it. His eyes were glittering, and beads of sweat were quivering on his forehead. I kept saying that we should go, but he wanted to stay. He was holding my hand in a bone-crushing grip, and the table was shaking. It was frightening to me because I realized that it was one of the last times that I would see him. Finally he snapped out of it, and we were able to pay our check and go. We left, and I walked him home—and suddenly he was fine again."

This up-and-down pattern continued, but Cal was never really fine again. He made a final trip through Canada, still looking fit and hale. Brad Trenary was traveling through Canada on his way back to Seattle in July 1987. "I had been back in Montana for my folks' 50th wedding anniversary, and I stopped at a cafe in Banff for a bite to eat. It was a tourist spot, nothing fancy. I was eating my meal when I noticed three guys enter the restaurant. There were two attractive elderly gentlemen and this really good-looking guy. We all acknowledged each other with smiles and nods—standard gay behavior in a straight venue. I had been a fan of pornography for years and thought I recognized the younger guy. I sat there watching for a long time, then it occurred to me—'My god, that's Casey Donovan.' As I left I walked past him and smiled. I thought at the time that he looked older—good, but older. He was thin and seemed a bit tired. I would never have thought that he was really ill though."

Cal managed to keep up with his travels, but he was beginning to feel the strain. "He had led a tour to Egypt for me," Ebensten said. "He meant to take another. Then shortly before the trip was scheduled, he called to say that he was ill. He felt that the dust from the deserts in Egypt were affecting his lungs. 'I think,' he told me, 'that I caught something on my last trip across the Sinai desert. It was awfully dusty, and I coughed a lot.'"

"A few days after the incident in the restaurant," Rob Richards said, "Cal called me and asked me to come over to his apartment. He had never done that before. He never entertained, although it was a totally acceptable place to have friends visit. I knocked on the door, and he answered it, weak and pale, perspiring in his pajamas. He wasn't quite coherent, but he told me that he was going to go to Florida to the hospital. His folks lived in Florida.

"He told me he was cleaning his place out, getting rid of anything that might upset his family. He was obviously getting ready to leave it all. He told me that he had tossed all of his letters from Tom Tryon. Then he picked an object off a table and held it out to me. It was a miniature cow covered with real cowhide. It is quite realistic, and I still have it. Cal had bought it in Chile, and he wanted me to have it. He asked me if there was anything else I wanted from his apartment. He seemed to be tying up all the loose ends of his life at that point."

Jake Getty followed Cal's departure from New York City closely. "I ran into him on the street shortly before he left for the last time. It was a blistering hot day, and he was wearing a sweater, a tie, and a blazer. The poor guy looked terrible. He began telling me how he'd gone to the emergency room and had waited for hours but that nobody would see him. My impression was that he hadn't known what to tell them about his condition. He had denied it for so long that maybe he couldn't tell them.

"It was obvious to me that he wasn't thinking clearly. I had known that something was radically wrong for over a year. His voice was always raspy, and he had a persistent cough. I never asked him about it because we never discussed his health. After the episode in the emergency room, he called his folks, and they told him to come home. He left New York a few days later, wheeled to his seat on the plane in a wheel-chair. When he got there they practically had to carry him off the plane. He was put into the Citrus Memorial Hospital in Inverness, Florida."

Richards left Cal's place and went directly to see Jerry Doug-las. "Jerry asked me what I thought, then told me that I would never see Cal again. A few days later there was this mysterious call from the hospital in Florida, and Cal sounded very opti-mistic. I really think the call was a farewell and that he knew he was going to die, so he killed himself. I mean, he was fine, then two hours later he was gone."

Longtime friend Alice Fletcher also received a call. "He told me that he was with his folks in Florida in the hospital. I told him that I wanted to come and visit, but he told me not to. He told me that he was all right. I wish I had gone. A few days later I heard that he was dead. His mother called me and told me that when she was cleaning out his hospital room, she saw that Cal had a picture of my son on the table beside his bed. Cal had always sent my son gifts from all of his travels. He treated him like his own nephew."

Hanns Ebensten received a call on the Saturday morning be-fore Cal died. "He told me that he was feeling well but that the doctors had done an X-ray of his lungs and that they had 'found a lot of white spots, and it looked like a snowstorm.' We talked for some time, then he told me that he was very tired. 'I'll call you on Monday. Bye, love you,' he said. He fell asleep and on Sunday, August 10, 1987, he was dead."

*   *   *

Regardless of the method of his exit, when Cal's end came it was peacefully accomplished amid a flurry of phone calls to his closest friends. And he left behind many friends, clients, ac-quaintances, and fans, all of whom remembered him fondly.

Jay McKenna eulogized Cal eloquently in a column in *The Advocate*. "Cal Culver was a gay Adam, the first widely embraced gay symbol to appear during the post-Stonewall years...To young gays like myself who were struggling to come to terms with [our sexuality], Cal's spectacular emergence as Casey Donovan, unapologetic star of gay films, bordered on the heroic...He celebrated his gayness."

*   *   *

Friends in New York City arranged a memorial service for Cal at a church in Greenwich Village. "It was a nice service," Jake Getty recalled. "His old friend Helen Van Fleet spoke about him. Quite a few people spoke, actually." People spoke that day and still sing his praises a decade later when asked about him. To Rob Richards he was "classic and classy. You could take him anywhere, and he fit in beautifully." Jake Getty remembered him as "a very charming, sweet person. He would go out of his way to do nice things for you. My friend Cal Culver was a Christian gentleman. He had a terrific personality and possessed absolutely no guile." To Wakefield Poole, Cal was "genuine and real. Definitely one of a kind." Don Potter remembers him as "one of the brightest guys I ever met." John Burke called Cal "funny and fun and sparkling. He was a radiant person, so natural and genuine." Holly Woodlawn found him to be "the most gracious man I've ever encountered." Hanns Ebensten viewed him as "just a wonderful gentleman, a great pleasure to be with." To Ted Wilkins, Cal was "one of the most generous men I've ever known. All we ever did was laugh and have a good time. I was always happy with him." Roy Blakey called him "one of the sweetest people on the face of this earth. He seemed to be untouched by the porn world he was a part of. He was dazzling." Michael Kearns viewed him first and foremost as a star. "He had star quality. He wasn't a whore—he was a courtesan. I loved him as an individual and for the impact that he had on the gay community. He did a great deal to liberate us and our sexuality from shame and bring gays out of the shadows into the light of day."

*   *   *

Cal's parents had sent his ashes to New York City, and Jake Getty took them home with him after the memorial service. "He wanted his ashes to be scattered on Fire Island. Actually it was more like a distribution because he wanted a little piece of himself left at all his favorite locations. I went out with a couple of Cal's friends, and we made a day of it."

John Burke was out on Fire Island that day. "I remember it was April 4, 1988. I was working at a liquor store in The Pines called the Spirit of the Pines. I was in the front window, and Garron Douglas walked by. He came in and asked me what I was doing there so early in the season. 'Working,' I told him. I asked if he was out looking for a house, and he told me that he was there with some other friends to scatter Cal's ashes. We began reminiscing, and I ended up getting off work early and going with them.

"To start with, there had just been a few places that Cal had specifically mentioned, but as the day progressed, and we ran into more and more people, our project expanded. Everyone wanted Cal's ashes scattered in their corner it seemed. By the time we were done, we had put Cal all over that island."

Later in the day, the little coterie of friends headed into the woods to one of the spots Cal had always found to be magical during his visits to the island. "It was evening," Jake remembered. "The sun was setting and a mist was beginning to float in off the water. Suddenly as we made our way along to this grove of trees, a pair of island deer emerged on the path before us. We stopped. They stopped. We looked at each other for a long time, then they disappeared noiselessly into the woods. I'm not a spiritual person, but John and Garron both claimed that it was a spiritual moment. I was inclined to believe them."

And so Cal Culver was consigned to the earth but not to obscurity. His image lives on every time a videotape of *Boys in the Sand* or one of his other X-rated efforts is popped into a VCR. A new print of Radley Metzger's film *Score* is in release, making the rounds of the gay film festivals and at art houses. Cal's image still smiles out from the pages of photographers' career retrospectives. The name of Casey Donovan continues to resonate in the imagination of gay men. Cal Culver was the first real gay porn star. He helped gays create a new, liberated, positive image of themselves. He tested limits, pushed boundaries.

His legacy is that he captured a golden moment in gay history and fixed it in our collective consciousness. Thoughts of him take us back to a time now totally lost to us, to an age of innocence over which Cal Culver—and his irrepressible twin Casey Donovan—presided as the gay Adam.

VIDEOGRAPHY

Ginger (1970) Distributed by Monterey Home Video.
Casey (1971)*
Dragula (1971)
Boys in the Sand (1971)**
The Back Row (1972)*
Score (1972) Distributed by Magnum Entertainment.
Fun and Games (1973) Not available
Moving (1974)*
The Opening of Misty Beethoven (1974) Audubon Releasing
The Other Side of Aspen (1978) Falcon Video*
L.A. Tool and Die (1981)*
Heatstroke (1982)*
Superstars (1982)*
Sleaze (1982)*
Hotshots (1983)*
Split Image (1984)*
Non-Stop (1984)*
Boys in the Sand II (1984)*
Chance of a Lifetime (1985)
Inevitable Love (1985)*
Fucked Up (1986)

* Available through Bijou Video, 1363 N. Wells St., Chicago, IL 60610; (800) 932-7111
** Available through T.L.A. Video, 1520 Locust St., Suite 200 Philadelphia, PA 19102

BIBLIOGRAPHY

The Advocate. Various issues. 1967-1987.

After Dark. Various issues. 1971-1976

Bell, Daniel M. *Aberrant Porn-Gay Male Pornography.* Thesis (M.A.), San Francisco Sate University, 1992.

Bronski, Michael. *Culture Clash—The Making of Gay Sensibility.* South End Press, Boston. 1984.

Burger, John R. *One-Handed Histories: The Eroto-Politics of Gay Male Video Pornography* Harrington Park Press. 1994

Chapman, David. *Adonis:The Male Physique Pin-Up 1870-1940.* GMP Publishers, London. 1989.

Chauncey, George. *Gay New York. Gender, Urban Culture, and the Making of the Gay Male World 1890-1940.* HarperCollins Publishers Inc. 1994.

Douglas, Jerry. "The Legend of Casey Donovan." *Manshots.* April 1992. pp. 67-73.

Douglas, Jerry. "Gay Film Heritage: Jaguar Productions. Part I." *Manshots.* June 1996.

Douglas, Jerry. "Gay Film Heritage: Jaguar Productions. Part II." *Manshots.* August 1996.

Dyer, Richard. "Male Gay Porn: Coming to Terms" *Jump Cut,* Issue 30. pp. 27-29. 1985.

Ebensten, Hanns. *Volleyball With the Cuna Indians.* Viking, New York. 1993.

Kaiser, Charles. *The Gay Metropolis: 1940-1996.* Houghton Mifflin. 1997.

Kearns, Michael. "The Gage Boys Are Rolling Again With *L.A. Tool & Die*" *Drummer*, Issue 34. pp. 20-22.

Kendrick, Walter M. *The Secret Museum: Pornography in Modern Culture* Viking, New York. 1987.

Koch, Gertrude. "The Body's Shadow Realm: On Pornographic Cinema." *Jump Cut*, Issue 35. pp. 17-29. 1990.

Leyland, Winston, ed. *Physique—Photography by Bob Mizer*. Gay Sunshine Press. 1982.

Murray, Raymond. *Images in the Dark: An Encyclopedia of Gay and Lesbian Film and Video*. TLA Publications, Philadelphia. 1996.

Poole, Wakefield. Interview by Robert Colaciello. *Interview Magazine*. May 1972. p. 22.

Rowberry, John W. *Gay Video: A Guide to Erotica*. Gay Sunshine Press. 1988.

Turan, Kenneth, and Stephen E. Zito. *Sinema: American Pornographic Films and the People Who Make Them*. Praeger Publishers Inc., New York. 1974

Tyler, Parker. *Screening the Sexes: Homosexuality in the Movies*. Holt, Rinehart and Winston, New York. 1972.

Viva, The International Magazine for Women. June 1974. "The Naked Athlete." pp. 76-81.

Watney, Simon. *Policing Desire: Pornography, AIDS and the Media*. University of Minnesota Press, Minneapolis. 1987.

Waugh, Tom. "Homoerotic Representation in the Stag Film, 1920-1940: Imagining an Audience" *Wide Angle*, Volume 14, Number 2. pp. 4-19

Waugh, Tom. "A Heritage of Pornography" *The Body Politic*, January 1983. pp. 29-33.

Waugh, Tom. *Hard to Imagine—Gay Male Eroticism in Photography and Film From Their Beginnings to Stonewall*. Columbia University Press, New York. 1996.

Waugh, Tom. "Men's Pornography: Gay vs. Straight" *Jump Cut*, Volume 30. pp. 30-34. 1985.

Williams, Linda. *Hard Core: Power, Pleasure, and the Frenzy of the Visible*. University of California Press, Berkeley. 1989.

alyson
books

FRICTION, edited by Gerry Kroll. Friction creates provocative sparks in this first-time collection, which includes the most well-known writers of gay erotica today. Gathered within these kinky, passionate pages are the best erotic stories that have appeared in many of the nearly 60 gay men's magazines across the country.

HEAT: GAY MEN TELL THEIR REAL-LIFE SEX STORIES, edited by Jack Hart. Sexy, true stories in this unbridled gay erotic collection range from steamy seductions to military maneuvers

HORMONE PIRATES OF XENOBIA AND DREAM STUDS OF KAMA LOKA, by Ernest Posey. These two science-fiction novellas have it all: pages of alien sex, erotic intrigue, the adventures of lunarian superstuds, and the lusty explorations of a graduate student who takes part in his professor's kinky dream project.

THE LORD WON'T MIND, by Gordon Merrick. In this first volume of the classic trilogy, Charlie and Peter forge a love that will survive World War II and Charlie's marriage to a conniving heiress. Their story is continued in *One for the Gods* and *Forth Into Light*

MAKING IT BIG: SEX STARS, PORN FILMS, AND ME, by Chi Chi La Rue with John Erich.The classic American rags-to-riches story—with a twist. A young lad from Minnesota travels to California to become part of an industry he loves with all his heart: gay porn.

MY BIGGEST O, edited by Jack Hart. What was the best sex you ever had? Jack Hart asked that question of hundreds of gay men and got some fascinating answers. Here are summaries of the most intriguing of them. Together, they provide an engaging picture of the sexual tastes of gay men.

MY FIRST TIME, edited by Jack Hart. Hart has compiled a fascinating collection of true, first-person stories by men from around the country who describe their first same-sex sexual encounter.

WONDER BREAD AND ECSTASY: THE LIFE AND DEATH OF JOEY STEFANO, by Charles Isherwood. Drugs, sex, and unbridled ambition were the main ingredients in the lethal cocktail that killed gay porn's brightest star, Joey Stefano. As a child from the country's heartland, Joey's rise and tragic fall in Los Angeles's dark and dangerous world of gay porn paints a grim portrait of American life gone berserk.

These books and other Alyson titles are available at your local bookstore. If you can't find a book listed above or would like more information, please visit our home page on the World Wide Web at **www.alyson.com.**